SWORD AND SCALPEL

Frank G. Slaughter

SWORD AND SCALPEL

Doubleday & Company, Inc.

Garden City, New York

All characters portrayed in this novel are
fictitious. It is a coincidence if the name of
any real person, living or dead, is mentioned.

Contents

SWORD AND SCALPEL

The Presidio

LARRY KIRK was having trouble with his lead. For the first time in years the ace television commentator faced his typewriter with a mind empty as a cave whence even the bats had fled.

In the past hour he had tried all his pump primers; he had even resorted to automatic writing, a leftover from his last analysis. (*Face it Kirk whoever taught you to type should be drawn and quartered you cautious timeserver why not do something useful with those fat white hands besides coaxing half-truths out of these too-facile keys.*) The flash of self-contempt had been easily conquered. Ten minutes ago he had used the oldest of his self-starters—the summary, the reduction of an unanswered question to its essence.

He read that summary over now, while the wall clock in his Radio City office ticked on, reminding him that he had just thirty-five minutes to air time. It made a neat block of type in the center of an empty page:

```
Tomorrow, in San Francisco's Presidio,
Captain Paul Scott of the Army Medical
Corps, fresh from two years in a Chinese
prisoner-of-war camp, faces court-mar-
tial for treason. How it happened is a
question all too easily answered: every-
one is familiar with the techniques of
the enemy brain-washers. The burning
question is why.
```

Why, this fall of 1953, when thousands of American prisoners in North Korea had come back untouched by the Communist evil, had Captain Paul Scott yielded? Why, after what seemed only routine persuasion, had he signed another of those grotesque statements accusing the United Nations forces of germ warfare? A copy of the statement, with Scott's signature, was in the possession of the judge advocate. Why, then, did Scott refuse to plead guilty, to make a coherent statement for the press—even to produce a single witness in his behalf?

Who, what, when and *where,* reflected Larry, had always been easy to handle: life had been far less demanding when he had been only a simple newspaperman. *Why* was a harder nut to crack. Tonight (while maintaining the fair-minded pose for which his program was famous), it was essential that he give some valid cause for Scott's defection—just as it was essential that he make some estimate of the court-martial's outcome. His public would expect as much.

Larry did not doubt for a moment that this quixotic young doctor in uniform would be found guilty—or that the Army court would exact the maximum punishment. The *why* persisted, irritating as a cocklebur on the surface of his brain. Until he had banished the irritant, Larry knew that a well-disciplined talent (which usually ground out these daily TV broadcasts with ease) would continue to stumble in the dark.

He ripped the summary from his typewriter and ran in a fresh sheet. Overhead the clock ticked on in tune with his frightened heart. What would happen if he faced the network cameras tonight (and an audience estimated at forty million Americans) without a script?

For once, he told himself, you're the victim of your own pride, your insistence that you be given your head each weekday at nine. *The program that you are about to hear is unrehearsed and unedited. The opinions of international newshawk Larry Kirk are his own, exactly as they have emerged from Larry's battered old portable.* For the past year, thanks to his whopping Trendex rating, the boast of Larry's sponsors had been almost literally true. . . . Of course, there was no way of shutting off the sponsor's occasional phone call.

Earlier that evening, when Larry had talked long distance to old Herman Bowers (the president of Bowers Brewery), his backer had foamed as industriously as his product.

"What are you saying about Scott?"

"I haven't quite decided, H.B."

"Hit that Commie, Larry. Give him hell. He should go to the gas chamber."

"I can't condemn him before his trial."

"Why not? Men like Scott are America's number-one menace; exterminating them is our number-one problem. Help your listeners to see that. You always have."

"H.B., the whole country is howling for his head. Are you suggesting I make it unanimous?"

"Larry, when *you* say a man is dead he stays dead. I want you to bury this traitor."

"I'm sorry, H.B.—but I've no idea what I'll say at this moment. I will promise you to say something."

"You had better. Why else are we flying you to Frisco tomorrow?"

Larry Kirk had hung up then. He could still applaud his own courage. . . .

Glancing at the wall clock one more time, he spread his notes. There was no reason for panic. After all (as a world traveler), he had a personal image of Captain Paul Scott to offer his public. Even at their first meeting in Korea he had noticed something queer about the fellow—a quality of strain, a brooding intentness that defied such catchall labels as battle fatigue. In his way the young doctor with the haunted eyes had seemed as much an off-horse as his

battalion chaplain, the mystic the GIs called Father Tim.
. . . At the time, Larry had sensed that the two men shared
a credo they could never reveal to ordinary mortals—least
of all to a famous figure from the television world.

> Two years ago I interviewed Dr. Paul
> Scott in his surgical-aid station on the
> Korean front only a short time before his
> capture. I found him brilliant, over-
> wrought——and profoundly dubious as to
> his own future or the future of humanity.
> I also interviewed Father Timothy O'Fal-
> lon, the chaplain of the battalion——who
> said little to enlighten me on the cause
> of Scott's mental turmoil. Later, in
> Seoul, I talked to Kay Storey, the USO
> entertainer who planned to marry him.
> To her, he was also an enigma——and, in her
> own words, an enigma even to himself.
>
> Today the enigma remains. Why would a
> Johns Hopkins alumnus, a surgeon with a
> brilliant record and a clear-cut future
> before him, prefer capture by the North
> Korean forces to a dash for liberty with
> his own outfit? Why did he begin to col-
> laborate with those captors almost from
> the first moment? How, in short, could
> he commit this outrage against his con-
> science, his country, and his God?
>
> The surface facts (as Colonel Jasper
> Hardin, the battalion commander relates
> them) are simple.
>
> Captain Scott's defection began when he
> elected to remain behind in the medical
> bunker on Hill 1049, a position which
> Colonel Hardin was forced to evacuate
> under enemy pressure. The colonel ordered

Captain Scott to join the retreat: the medical officer refused to obey. Others who refused to obey the order were two medics under Scott's command—Kay Storey, the above-mentioned USO entertainer (who had been trapped there while on a front-line tour), and Chaplain O'Fallon.

Despite their attempt to fight their way to freedom, Colonel Hardin and those of his men who survived were pinned on the slopes of Hill 1049 and forced to join the march of other prisoners to the North Korean rear. Their destination was a concentration camp near Pyongyang. En route, the colonel states, he encountered Scott and his group—in the courtyard of a farm outside the town of Sinmak. Though Dr. Scott and his party had the status of prisoners, says Colonel Hardin, they were well fed and specially favored. That night Scott's group slept on dry beds in the barn. The colonel and his officers were forced to bivouac in the open in a driving rainstorm.

Larry Kirk paused long enough to note the time on the wall clock: already that malignant timepiece seemed to tick at a faster tempo. His fingers resumed their dance on the typewriter keyboard:

In the prison compound at Pyongyang, as Colonel Hardin relates it, Dr. Scott took over the camp hospital, where he ministered to guards and prisoners alike, and received the same food as the Chinese doctors, who were soon taking his orders. Later when he put down an epidemic of meningitis his favors increased. During the last months of the

war he saved the life of the camp commandant in a daring operation. Dr. Scott's
signing of a (quote) confession (un-
quote) that his country had waged bacterial warfare in Korea, said Colonel
Hardin, was the logical climax of a long
collaboration.

That, Larry reflected, was only half the wrap-up. Scott's
court-martial would be on every front page tomorrow and
stay there for its course. His broadcast needed something
beyond the surface facts—a sinister chord or two that
would make a natural carry-over to his next TV appearance, in San Francisco, after the opening of the trial.

The part that Father Timothy O'Fallon,
the battalion chaplain, played in Dr.
Scott's surrender to the evil we call
world Communism must remain a puzzling
mystery. Father Tim lies in a cemetery
outside Pyongyang: he cannot appear at
the Presidio tomorrow as a witness.

Once again, the facts are simple. When
the war ended this July, Father Tim was
ill in the prison-camp hospital: when
Colonel Hardin prepared to lead the others to their repatriation Captain Scott
insisted on remaining at the chaplain's
bedside. Weeks later, long after Father
O'Fallon's death, this lonely and con-
troversial doctor was finally sent to an
exchange point in the neutral zone.

A final element of mystery remains, the
role of the USO entertainer Kay Storey,
famous as "The Girl Next Door," a singing part that took her into Army camps
all over South Korea. As we have said,
Miss Storey was captured on Hill 1049 and
went with the others to Pyongyang; she

was a prisoner there until July when she
departed under the protection of Colonel
Hardin.

Until then it was rumored that she and
Scott would marry at the war's end:
neither will confirm that story today.
Miss Storey will soon begin work on a
motion picture, an Eric Lindman produc-
tion, high-lighting her own adventures
as a prisoner and as "The Girl Next
Door." Since she will not be called as
a witness for her alleged fiance, so far
as we could learn tonight, it would seem
that a romance, if one existed, is now a
thing of yesterday.

When the court-martial opens tomorrow
Colonel Hardin will be the chief witness
for the prosecution. Technicians, aides
and noncoms who were fellow prisoners
will also testify. Hilary Saunders, the
well-known Hollywood lawyer and a former
artillery captain in Korea, will under-
take Dr. Scott's defense. Mr. Saunders
plans to call no witnesses beside the defendant himself, since none are available.

Larry Kirk lifted his fingers from the keys. Perhaps the
package is wrapped too neatly, he thought. It's quite likely
that you've stretched your reputation for fairness to the
breaking point. Tonight you'll be telling forty million
patriots what they want to hear.

ii

A continent away, Hilary Saunders glared at the rented
television in his hotel parlor, then rose to kill the program.
It was a gesture that destroyed commentator Larry Kirk's

statesmanlike profile and Larry's resonant baritone in the same satisfying flash.

Because of the time lag between New York and San Francisco it was still daylight on Nob Hill—but Hi Saunders had been working behind drawn blinds since early afternoon, when the day had begun to boil with fog. It had always been his custom to closet himself thus the day before he took a vital case to court. The hotel desk was cluttered with the weapons of the successful trial lawyer—lawbooks and ancient briefs, a much-marked copy of the Army *Manual of Courts-Martial,* the toy donkey he kept for luck because the face reminded him of a long-dead judge who had almost, but not quite, disbarred him years ago. The air was blue with the cheap cigars Hi smoked when he was really working and had no one to impress but himself.

His suite was high in the Mark Hopkins: merely by opening the blinds of his picture window, he could have inhaled some of the finest ozone in the western world. . . . God knows the brain could stand airing, he reflected—though he made no move to relax his feline crouch above his work. It was a greater relief to glare back at the vacant eye of the TV and curse Larry Kirk as he deserved.

Not that Hi was surprised by the broadcast; like other ex-liberals he had known at Harvard, Larry had simply grown more cautious as his age, and his income, increased. Nowadays, Hi realized, his former classmate usually bayed with the wolf pack whenever a new victim appeared. Paul Scott, in short, had been tried and convicted by his fellow countrymen well in advance of his formal court-martial. As unofficial foreman of that vast jury, Larry Kirk had just summed up the reasons for the verdict.

Though he was not under formal arrest, Paul had been confined to the Presidio for his trial. Yielding to impulse, Hi picked up his phone and rang the Bachelor Officers' Quarters.

Paul was a long time coming to the phone.

"Don't tell me you were *asleep?*" the lawyer barked.

"Sorry, Hi. Tonight I thought I'd turn in early."

"Didn't I tell you to watch Kirk's broadcast?"

"I'm afraid it slipped my mind."

"I'll give you odds the judge advocate tuned in. The whole country was waiting to see which way Kirk would jump."

"You'll have to forgive me, Hi. Today I figured I'd done my good deed."

Hi Saunders scowled at the phone: he had expected this. "You've seen Kay?"

"We've just had dinner. She's promised to stay clear."

Weeks ago when Kay Storey had begged him to put her on the stand Hi had refused—because Paul had expected his refusal. There had been some point to Paul's attitude. Major James MacArdle (the able lawyer whom the judge advocate had appointed as trial counsel) would have welcomed Kay's appearance as a defense witness—and would have proceeded to tear her apart. Yet Hi had not expected Paul to take her withdrawal this calmly.

"Won't you feel a bit lonely when court opens?"

"Loneliness is a cross we must all bear, Hi; it's one of the first things Father Tim taught me."

"What does it take to get you really mad, Paul?"

"Kay deserves her career. Lindman has one ready-made for her. It would ruin her chances if she stood up for me in court. Why should she be tarred with the same brush, when it won't help win my acquittal?"

"*Someone's* got to stand up for you, Paul."

"Say what you mean, Hi. Do you think I'm guilty?"

The lawyer dodged the question neatly. "Tomorrow that seven-man court will sit with its collective mind made up. Our job is to change it. My work would be easier if I had one witness beside yourself."

"We can't call Father Tim." Paul's voice had the same

baffling note of calm. "From the start we agreed to keep
Kay out of it."

"We'd have a stronger case if your girl went to bat. Even
if she only struck out."

"Sorry, Hi—I've just sent her back to Lindman."

"What about your marriage plans?"

"We can hardly think of marriage if I draw ten years in
Leavenworth."

Paul Scott's voice had never risen above an easy mono-
tone. When he hung up the phone Hi reflected that his
friend had seemed remote as an anchorite in his cell. Remembering the Paul he had known in the lines at Korea,
he could wonder once again at the spell Father Tim had
cast—if that was what really had happened.

True, Paul's reason for keeping Kay out of the witness
box was excellent—for Kay. In Korea, as "The Girl Next
Door," she had been the USO's prime drawing card. Her
chance to star in pictures now seemed made to order—
especially with a self-confessed genius like Eric Lindman
to direct her. There was no denying the wisdom of her
withdrawal—Paul had been downright noble to suggest it.

As Paul's lawyer, Hi could wish that his client had been
a trifle less unselfish. Not that the omission was fatal, not
that there wasn't time to rectify it if things went against
them tomorrow. Hi, who knew his man all too well, had
demanded carte blanche before he had agreed to under-
take Paul's defense: he could summon Kay to the stand on
his own if her presence there seemed vital.

So far—aside from their shared ordeal at the concentration camp—Hi had not tried to plumb the relationship of
Kay Storey and his client. Unraveling the emotional life
of Paul Scott was outside his province; fighting for his
acquittal would be chore enough. The lawyer sighed and
returned to the mass of notes before him.

Cross-examinations tomorrow would be routine, he told
himself; it would be wiser to forego an opening statement

unless Jim MacArdle indulged in his usual rhetoric. Paul's
own strategy would be impossible to plan in detail until
Major MacArdle showed his hand. His reason for each act
at the prison camp had its own logic, including the farce
of the confession. It was unfortunate that these reasons
would have a hollow ring when spoken by the defendant
himself. Or that—item by item—he could do no more than
match Paul's word against the sworn indictment of Colonel Jasper Hardin, his commanding officer.

In the moment before his mind meshed with the task
before him, Hi wondered if Captain Paul Scott had foreseen the depths of his peril—if he meant to stand (or fall)
on his own testimony. Was it possible that he was courting
martyrdom, for a reason that had meaning to him alone?

iii

Ten stories above Hi Saunders' suite, at a window table
in the Top of the Mark, Kay Storey faced Eric Lindman
with a look that almost—but not quite—approached trust.

"I suppose I've lost the argument," she said.

"You can still admit it gracefully," the man in dark
glasses murmured softly.

"So you're suggesting I come back to you—just like
that?"

"Just like that," said Eric Lindman. "With Scott out of
your life—for keeps."

"Only he isn't out. He'll never be."

"At least he's being sensible—where you're concerned."

"Let's be clear on one thing, Eric. Tonight I told Paul
I'd stay away from the trial—because he *wanted* it that way.
If things go against him, I can still change my mind."

"Suppose I won't let you change it?"

Kay studied her escort under half-lowered lids. Save for
the conventional glasses and a certain imperial air there
was little of the Hollywood wonder boy in Eric Lindman.

His white dinner coat came from the best tailor on Savile Row, and his accent, like his table manners, was a thing of beauty. At first glance he could have passed for a distinguished bird of prey in any field. What's more, the concern in his tone was quite genuine.

"So my career comes first," she said.

"I said as much the day you shipped overseas. It's time you believed me."

"Suppose I'd flopped on that USO tour, Eric. Would we be sitting here tonight?"

"Of course not," said Lindman cheerfully. "The point is, you succeeded."

I *have* succeeded, the girl thought; I found myself in Korea, in a way you'll never understand. "Aren't you being kinder than I deserve?" she asked.

"I've never been kind in my life," said Eric. "You should know by now that I use people and expect to be used in return. Right now opportunity is knocking for us both—providing you watch your step."

"And stay clear of Paul Scott's court-martial?"

"Scott knows he's guilty. That's why he's kept you out of it."

"He isn't pleading guilty."

"He's guilty as charged, darling. So far, you haven't said a word to change my mind."

"I haven't tried, Eric. I promised Hi Saunders not to discuss the case."

"What defense does he have? The facts speak for themselves."

Kay listened in silence while Eric went over his version of the Paul Scott case. It was the judgment the country had long since made—from the moment the story broke with Colonel Jasper Hardin's famous (and completely damning) interview. Kay admitted that Eric was presenting it brilliantly—but then, everything that Eric Lindman did was brilliant.

An opportunist from the word go, she thought. And yet, Eric was an authentic genius, as the word is used in pictures. A creator who could smell a trend before it had taken shape and dramatize its essence with the touch of the born showman. Why else would he plan to star her in a movie called *The Girl Next Door?*

"This court-martial will be Scott's funeral, and he's stuck with it," said Eric. "The fact that your paths crossed in Korea is a coincidence we'll both ignore."

"We can't ignore Paul."

"We already have—at his own request. You aren't being disloyal, Kay—you're just being yourself. *The Girl Next Door.* Even the title was made to order."

The Girl Next Door. It was true that she stood on the threshold of a dream tonight—a dream that could easily become a shining reality tomorrow, thanks to Eric's magic. She felt the tears start behind her eyelids as she admitted how little that dream meant now. Nothing really mattered tonight but the fact that Paul Scott needed her help and had refused it.

"I'm still going to marry him," Kay said defiantly, "the minute this trial is over."

Eric shook his head. "Scott isn't buying that, darling. He told me as much this afternoon—by phone."

"You asked Paul—about us?" Kay wondered why she was not more indignant.

"Certainly. I had to know—for sure—before I put your picture in work."

"Are there *any* facts about me you don't have on file, Eric?"

"An hour ago," said the producer, "you went to the Presidio, full of self-sacrifice. But you met your match in Dr. Paul Scott. Believe me, *he* knows the score. There's no room for wives in an Army stockade."

The voice was gentle, with no hint of Eric's usual mockery. The fingers that closed on her hand were gentle too—

but there was a reminder in their pressure that Eric (no
less than Paul) had certain claims on her future. . . . Kay
took up her glass and stared down at the pattern of San
Francisco.

"You're giving a good imitation of Satan," she said. "The
Top of the Mark will do nicely for a mountain. There's
even an excuse to salve my pride. After all, why shouldn't
I come back to the studio—if the man I love won't have
me?"

"I knew you'd see the point, darling. All you needed was
time."

"Hi may still put me on the stand."

"Show your face in that courthouse, Kay, and you're a
dead pigeon in Hollywood."

"Suppose I don't care?"

"You've got to care. Day after tomorrow I'll make you
a star. And you're going to jump at the chance. It would
be un-American not to."

"Maybe I'm more than just an American. Father Tim
taught us to be citizens of the world in that prison camp."

"Darling," said Lindman, "sometimes you baffle even me.
And I know you better than most."

"You *knew* me, Eric—before I went to Korea."

"Who was this Father Tim really? Some kind of archangel in khaki?"

"He was as lonely—and as frightened—as the greenest
soldier in that camp." Kay shook her head slowly—there
was really no way to make Eric understand, but she tried,
regardless. "You see, he taught us a lesson we'll never forget—that men must help one another, even when they are
enemies."

"Is that why Scott operated on the camp commandant?"

"It was one of the reasons. I *said* I can't discuss the case,
Eric."

He shrugged. "Fair enough. Now we've agreed on that

much—when are you coming to the studio for your tests? We can't start rolling too soon. . . ."

Letting the producer's voice go on, vaguely soothed by the sincerity of his praise, Kay let her mind go back to the moment of farewell in the lounge of the Bachelor Officers' Quarters. She had stood eye-to-eye with Paul as they went through the solemn farce of good-by; she could hear his quiet pleading before she had promised to put him from her mind forever. . . . Of course she had no intention of keeping that promise. Even so, the tears had blinded her when she stumbled into a taxi and drove to this date with Eric. The selflessness that Paul had shown tonight, she thought, is not of this world.

"Are you listening, darling?"

She came back painlessly to what Eric was saying. After all, it was Hi Saunders, not his client, who would have the last word in the conduct of this trial.

"Of course I heard you, Eric. I quite agree that you can't wait to start shooting—"

If she seemed to accept the wonder boy with those ambiguous words, no real harm was done. Once more Kay Storey leaned back in her chair and let her eyes rove across San Francisco Bay: Eric's voice had enveloped her in a soothing cocoon, and she was reluctant to stir.

And yet, curiously enough, it was not the image of stardom that formed in her mind's eye. Nor was it the memory of Paul, now that her tears for his obstinacy were behind her . . . it was Father Tim she saw tonight, exactly as she remembered him from that hell-camp outside Pyongyang—and the image on the screen of memory was indeed an archangel in khaki.

iv

Colonel Jasper Hardin had been leaving the Presidio at the moment when Kay summoned a taxi at the gate. He recognized her purely by accident; as a good strategist should, he jumped into a second cab and ordered the driver to keep her in view; the fact that their destinations were the same tonight had seemed a happy stroke of fate.

Now, seated with his own companion in a wall divan at the Top of the Mark, Hardin could rejoice again at his good fortune. It was a pleasure he had not mentioned to the pretty, rather sharp-faced girl who shared his table. Nonetheless he found himself rumbling with laughter as he downed his fourth highball of the evening.

"What's so funny, Jasper?"

"Sorry, Gloria—it wouldn't interest you."

"Try me. You've been dreadfully silent tonight."

"That's because I've things to mull over. It isn't easy, being Nemesis."

"Nemesis?"

"Exactly—even when the victim deserves extermination."

"Doesn't it help to unburden yourself?"

"Naturally—in the right company. That's why I asked you out tonight." He gave his drinking companion an appraising glance, pleased to note that she had colored just a bit under his proprietary eyes. "Switch on your TV tomorrow if you want the details."

"I *hoped* you'd tell me just a little tonight," she pouted. "After all, you're the one with the inside story."

Hardin's eye roved again toward Lindman's table: he saw that the producer had just covered Kay Storey's hand a second time. He felt all the thrill of a Peeping Tom on his first mission. Lindman's after her again, he gloated. For once, the gossip columns are right.

"Can't you tell me the joke, Bunny?"

He looked sternly at Gloria. "I've asked you not to call me that, my dear. Especially in public."

"Tonight, you have your line-officer look," said Gloria. "You pulled the same face when they took that photo in

Tokyo. You know, right after you escaped from Korea——"

"I didn't *escape*, damn it. I was repatriated—after the armistice."

"Don't use such big words, Jasper. You still looked mighty pleased with yourself. I wondered why."

"Can't a man rejoice when he finds there's justice in the world?"

Kay Storey was Scott's last prop, he told himself. If she had remained loyal, it's possible the court would ponder its verdict; a man with a friend at the judge's bench is always more important than a man alone. Now, Hardin knew, he didn't have to worry any more. Lindman would never spend an evening with Kay Storey (in the most famous of Frisco night spots) if she had not already agreed to abandon Scott to his fate.

"He can't escape us now," said Hardin. "We've dead-ended him at last."

"What did Captain Scott do, Jasper? And try not to shout."

"Don't you read the papers?"

"Why should I—when you explain them so beautifully?"

That pouting smile had entranced Hardin before; tonight he had the obscure conviction that Gloria (who was not half so stupid as she pretended) was baiting him. Yet she was an audience—and, as such, deserved an answer.

"I'll tell you what I can't forgive Scott for," he said. "He made me afraid."

"I can't imagine *you* afraid of anything."

The mirror above the facing wall booth assured Hardin that Gloria's compliment was sincere. Tonight in his dress pinks he was every inch the soldier—and the row of ribbons on his breast had been earned to the last combat star.

"I know it's hard to picture," he said. "But the ordeal of battle isn't the worst thing we fellows must suffer. The fear a scoundrel like Scott inspires is far worse—"

"*Why*, Bunny?"

"Because it goes deeper. Beyond good and evil as we can grasp them. Into the night of the soul, where Communism is bred—" Hardin paused and wondered what editorial he was quoting. "So far, the firing squad is our only defense against Scott—or the court-martial, if we're not at war. Yet what can death accomplish, or a prison stockade, if the poison's done its work?"

"But what did he *do?*"

"That, my dear, is the sort of ignorance that makes the poison potent. Didn't you read how he refused to leave his bunker on Hill 1049 when I gave him a direct order? Or how I slept in the rain at Sinmak while he wallowed in a dry billet?"

"Yes, Jasper. Is that all?"

"It's only the beginning. At the concentration camp he saved a hundred Commie lives—my master sergeant kept the score. He operated on Colonal Pak—the prison commander—when the whole camp wanted Pak to die. He swore that our troops used bacteria bombs. When the repatriation order came he wouldn't budge. In God's name, girl, what does it take to rouse you?"

"Can you prove that Captain Scott was a Communist? Suppose he tells a different story at the trial?"

"He will—rely on that. I know the shyster who's defending him. It wouldn't surprise me if they were two of a kind."

"Don't they hear both sides at a court-martial?"

Gloria, thought Hardin, could be infuriating at times. As he felt his temper boil up he considered walking out on her—until he reminded himself that she had already proved an expensive luxury and he would be a fool not to enjoy his investment fully.

"Of course they'll hear both sides," he said. "Traitors get a fair trial here—that's where we differ from our enemies."

"I'm glad of that, Jasper."

"Stop acting like a fool," he snapped. "Scott's confession

is on the record—and I've witnesses to back up every point
I just made. Men who *saw* him behave like a turncoat—
and a mutineer. No matter what he's cooked up with
Saunders, it's his word against ours. The chaplain's dead.
As you can see right now, Scott's girl has walked out on
him—"

"Are you sure?"

"Would Lindman touch her with a ten-foot pole if she
hadn't?"

"Have it your way, Bunny. I was only trying to get your
story straight."

"It'll be clear enough tomorrow. The judge advocate ex-
pects a verdict in two days——" Hardin bit the prophecy
short (he had been given that estimate in secret). "I've said
too much now," he grumbled. "Let's get out of here."

"Anything you say, Bunny."

Hardin lurched just a little when he rose, but the mir-
rored walls gave back a dozen hero images, creating the
illusion that he was larger than life. He forced steadiness
into his gait and stared with a cold martial aloofness at
each face he encountered in the treacherous march to the
elevator. The slight testiness he had felt at the table melted
rapidly as he continued to pick up envious looks from other
tables. Now that he had forced Gloria to follow his timetable his sense of well-being was complete.

Ten years at Leavenworth was the minimum sentence
Scott would draw: Major MacArdle had said as much this
afternoon at the final briefing. If they played each card
well, he could be jailed for life. . . . Hardin wondered
what the Red-lover was doing at this moment. Quaking in
his boots, no doubt, and praying frantically to his strange
new gods. It was incredible that this sang-froid could last
into the eve of his humiliation.

v

After his lawyer's phone call Paul had been unable to sleep again.

Not that the call had upset him too badly; not that he was really fearful of the morrow. Captain Paul Scott had learned to put most fears behind him, along with anger and such unpredictable emotions as regret. Still, he had hoped to go to his court-martial with a clear head; after the parting with Kay Storey he felt that he had earned that much respite.

In the Korean lines it had been easy to fold his mind in black velvet whenever he could snatch a few hours' rest. In the prison compound his brain, like his muscles, had relaxed without pain as he sank into the well of oblivion. Here, in the Spartan comfort of his room at the Bachelor Officers' Quarters, he rose from his cot at last and admitted that repose had eluded him.

Wrapping himself in a bathrobe, he opened the single window his room boasted and stared across the lawns of the Presidio at the distant glimmer of the Pacific. Fog had crept in with the approach of dawn; it had blotted the lights of the Golden Gate Bridge and would soon move on to obscure the Oakland shore line. . . . Somewhere in that fog was the building that would house his trial.

Paul breathed deep of the chill air and felt a familiar tumult invade his heart. His insulation from fear was not yet perfect; anger and regret could still enter his thoughts, on crafty tiptoe. Father Tim's lessons had been well learned—but the flesh is always weaker than the spirit.

He had gone into the Korean War as one man—and had emerged as another. He was still not quite sure how the change had come about. Father Tim could have explained it, but the battalion chaplain was beyond earthly questioning. Would the padre have understood—and pardoned

—his present lonely anguish, the wild need to call Kay back, to beg her to stand beside him?

At least he had found the strength to send her away tonight; in the lounge of the BOQ he had managed to seem calm enough—to say good-by in words that had but one meaning. If Kay were beside him now, he knew he would take her in his arms and cling to her through eternity.

Yet he must learn to bear his lot—if he was destined to spend the rest of his life in a stockade on some sun-bitten prairie. Kay could never follow him to Leavenworth should the verdict go against him. But she could still have a brilliant career, with Lindman's help; she could find fulfillment without him. . . .

Or so he had reasoned when he had put her from him in the drab lounge of the BOQ. He had chosen the setting deliberately—and he had needed all his control to turn away, to focus his eyes on the painting above the mantel when Kay had left him at last. He would always remember that canvas—the Battle of Buena Vista, complete with charging cavalry, fleeing Mexicans, and Winfield Scott like a blue eagle in the rocket bursts.

A strangled sob escaped him now as he continued to stand at the fog-drenched window. At this hour (when man's will to survive is at its lowest ebb) his need for Kay Storey was tangible as hunger. It was not the last time her ghost would visit him with might-have-beens—but even now, on the eve of his trial, he knew that he could not have acted otherwise.

The ordeal at Pyongyang had made such a surrender possible: rather than involve Kay in his troubles, he was prepared to go down to defeat alone. It was a decision he could not explain (Hi Saunders had only stared at him this afternoon when he had tried to put it into words). So be it, he thought sadly. Let them brand you a Communist: you could have behaved no differently.

Father Tim could have cleared him, of course. Even Kay might have helped. As things stood, there was no voice to defend him but his own. And, though he spoke with the tongues of angels, his failure seemed foreordained.

It was three-thirty by his wrist watch, seven hours before his court-martial opened. Perhaps it would ease the pain of waiting if he collected his memories one more time —if he returned to the beginning, to the moment when his path had first crossed Kay Storey's. . . . Captain Paul Scott stood at the sill of the open window and closed his eyes in a silent prayer. The fog had filled both earth and sea when he looked out, but the image of the past was crystal clear.

Hollywood

A CALIFORNIA FOG, Dr. Paul Scott reflected, can be both friend and menace, depending on one's mood. On the waterfront at San Pedro that winter evening in 1951, he had begun by welcoming its almost feline approach across the vast, oil-slick harbor. Even now, after a year as resident surgeon at the Holt Clinic in Pasadena, he had not quite adjusted to the endless brassy sunshine: the fog, he told himself, was nature's antidote for that unrelenting flood of light. It was also a protection of sorts, a haven where a man could hide the smallness of his thoughts. And yet, as the gray blanket thickened, the very isolation had made it hard for Paul to hide that smallness from himself.

With San Pedro blotted almost completely from view and its inhabitants no more than shadows, his own world had shrunk to the space his body occupied; thanks to the toxin of rage that boiled through his blood stream, he found himself poor company in that prison. Little by little he had retreated to the infinitely smaller refuge of the soul —the fortress without walls that is man's last haven when reality seems too burdensome to endure.

Tonight the haven was cramped indeed. Never before had he surrendered so completely to the bludgeonings of fate; never had the resources within himself been so meager.

ii

That afternoon in Pasadena (when Paul had left the
Holt Clinic for the last time) righteous anger had carried
him as far west as the Hollywood Hotel, where he had de-
posited his Val-Pak. Obeying the instinct that was forcing
him toward a basic reappraisal of his future, he had driven
at once to the great staging area of San Pedro. Long before
his taxi had dropped him at his first waterfront bar he
could name his compulsion accurately. Today he was
facing his impending tour of duty in Korea head on—reminding himself (with the presence of those troop transports at the pier's end) that an unwanted war had robbed
him of the first real opportunity he had ever known.

He had worked almost a quarter century for that chance.

Even as a boy he had felt there was a special skill in his
fingers: the first dollar he had earned (in the slate pit of a
West Virginia mining town) had been set aside to help
finance a career in medicine. Years of self-denial had
brought him to a university campus; a scholarship had
seen him through pre-med, where his grades had proved
that he had chosen wisely. . . . World War II had been
only a romantic interruption. Like thousands of other
young Americans, he had ridden the white charger of ide-
alism into the ETO, served as a pharmacist's mate from
D-Day to Aachen (where he had earned a Purple Heart),
returned to his university in '46 to barrel through to a
degree.

With the GI Bill to finance him, he had entered Johns
Hopkins. . . . Until day before yesterday (he told himself
grimly) yours was a standard boy-makes-good story, complete with heiress. Is it Daphne Holt's fault, or yours, that
you failed to achieve the happy ending?

Dr. Paul Scott (who was now Lieutenant Paul Scott,
MC, USAR) continued to stare through the foggy windows
of the bar at the cluster of troopships along the quay—and

resisted the impulse to order his fifth drink in less than an hour: the fact that he was counting proved that a measure of sanity remained.

Life at Johns Hopkins, he reflected, had been a simple struggle to exist—and the reward seemed, at times, more distant than the stars. The government bounty had paid for essentials, enough for the lab fees, for an occasional flyer in research that is the medic's *sine qua non*. But there had been nights when he had served as a substitute orderly because his funds for the month were exhausted. For days on end he had eaten but a single meal, because the pennies saved brought him a step nearer the coveted M.D.

At graduation he had qualified automatically as a Johns Hopkins intern—a wonderful opportunity with practically no pay. In those final years of training a pack of cigarettes had been a luxury beyond his means, a gift of bourbon from a grateful patient a true bonanza. But his skill had kept pace with his ambition; rumors had gone abroad from the operating rooms in Baltimore, opening the way to the achievement of his dream.

Daphne Holt had brought the dream alive with a special sleight of hand that only the rich can produce.

Proving his worth had always been second nature with young Dr. Scott. Each day in medical school, in hospital work, had been a trial of strength—and he had refused to settle for second best. Daphne Holt had been something else again; not even in his wildest fantasies had he believed that she would find an orphan from a West Virginia slag heap appealing. Daphne had dominated the Johns Hopkins dances as only the daughter of a famous alumnus could: if he had cut in occasionally from the stag line, it had been only from bravado. Girls like the honey-haired Miss Holt, Paul Scott had told himself, were for well-heeled Princetonians from the Pithotomy Club who drove their own cars and swanked on their father's expense accounts at the Lord Baltimore.

His love life, so far, had been decidedly on the impromptu side. The night of a fraternity hop when Daphne
had invited him to go driving in her canary-yellow Jaguar
he had just escaped gaping. When she had kissed him,
with lingering finesse, the moment she had found a con-
venient spot to park he had been almost too flabbergasted
to respond.

The whole night had had the same Scheherazade quality. Looking back on it now, from his present plateau of
experience, Paul realized that he had been a novelty to her,
a bear from the hill country she had enjoyed taming—but
the novelty had lasted, all through his senior spring.
When the time came to join the scramble for a job Daphne
had suggested he apply for the post as resident at her father's clinic in Pasadena—an opportunity that any young
surgeon would have given his eyeteeth to win.

Once he had written to Dr. Lucius Holt, Paul had never
visioned the possibility of failure. When his name had been
posted at the head of his class on graduation day he had
taken the accolade in his stride—scholastic honors, after all,
were but one element in the dynamics of success. The same
had been true of his hospital training. Confident of his own
ability—which he had proved again and again—it had been
easy to accept Daphne's co-operation as his due. When Dr.
Holt—that paragon among California physicians—had offered him the residency he had merely shrugged a second
time and wired a calm acceptance.

Since he was now the quasi fiancé of his employer's
daughter, he had been white-haired boy at the Holt Clinic.
True, he had gagged a bit at the pastel luxury; he had
lifted a cynic's eyebrow when he scanned the financial report and learned what the wealthy will pay to keep their
livers and their libidos in order. But the surgery had absorbed him from the first day. A month after his arrival
word of his skill had spread beyond the horizons of Pasadena and the film world—and his future seemed assured.

Even his enemies (who had circulated the usual gossip) now admitted that he was the Old Man's most likely successor whenever Dr. Lucius Holt dropped the mantle from his still-vigorous shoulders.

As the summer of 1950 opened, the end of the journey had been in clear view for Dr. Paul Scott—a surgical reputation that would soon be nationwide, a position at the clinic that was unassailable. As added insurance there was a rich wife for the asking (he had never quite proposed to Daphne but he could guess her answer).

Best of all, he could honestly say that he had earned his success. As eventual chairman of the clinic he would do an outstanding job. In his hands that medical juggernaut would roll on to still greater glory—and continue to flatten most opponents en route. The rich could always afford the best in medicine, and Dr. Paul Scott was fast mastering the technique of giving the rich just what they wanted.

iii

The blow, when it came, had been stunning in its impact.

Since most of Paul's World War II duty had been in combat areas, his discharge points had piled up rapidly: after twenty-two months of service he had been granted his terminal leave. Unfortunately those twenty-two months did not keep his name from the Korean draft list. Like other veterans, he had refused to believe that he would be asked to serve when the doctor's draft was announced—but the long arm of selection (moving swiftly to answer what few Americans realized was a national emergency) had already come up with his name. Less than four months after the outbreak of war in Asia, Dr. Paul Scott (only yesterday heir apparent at the Holt Clinic) had become Lieutenant Paul Scott of the Army Medical Corps.

Dr. Holt had been furious. He had lavished much care

on Paul; he had opened every door; now he cried out that
his assistant's failure to mention his draft status had been
just short of treasonable. The scene had grown explosive
when Paul—failing to yield to the great man's scolding—
had shouted back just as loudly. Finally he had added a
few sharp criticisms of the clinic's built-in pampering.

As a result he had been suspended until his position had
clarified: he had been dropped entirely when it was evident that he would stay in the Army's clutches. Daphne—
who had been abroad at the time—had sided coolly with
her father, making it abundantly clear that Paul's status
as her chief fiancé had vanished as mysteriously as his position on the staff. Daphne was waiting for no hero to return
from a distant war without glory that no one really wanted.

This initial blow had fallen two months ago, and hectic
months they had been. Indoctrination had not been too
wearing. With his memories of World War II training still
green, Paul had mastered his new rituals with solemn efficiency: he had been careful to drop no hint of the burning
resentment against a country that had rewarded his pre-
vious service so cavalierly. As least, he told himself, he was
now a surgeon of note. As such, he would probably be
assigned to a stateside hospital service: with luck he could
keep up his connections, perhaps even salvage something
from the collapse of his career.

The crowning blow had descended in the past fortnight,
when orders had come through attaching Lieutenant Scott
to a heavy-weapons outfit about to go overseas, with the
rank of battalion surgeon. The group was already alerted.
Only yesterday it had been assigned to the transport
Millard Fillmore moored at San Pedro.

In Europe Paul had observed battalion surgeons in action; so far, the reality had been no more dismal than the
remembrance. During his brief service with his outfit he
had discharged his duties with a thoroughness that gave
no hint of the abyss of boredom beneath. But nothing had

prepared him for Lieutenant Colonel Jasper Hardin, his commanding officer. Though he had heard of such men at second hand, he had never quite believed in their existence.

To call Hardin a throwback, Paul told himself, was a gross understatement: the mold in which his C.O. was cast (though it had been useful once) had long since been relegated to the lumber room. Sun-baked posts from Cuba to Shanghai had hardened the mold; the last global war had confirmed its pattern beyond all change. If a man existed behind that glazed shell, Paul had yet to discover him. If Hardin possessed a spark of human warmth under the maze of protocol that ruled his slightest action, it was a boon he shared with no one. . . .

There was a fresh drink on the bar, though Paul had no memory of ordering it. He took it at a swallow and walked out into the fog. In another moment he was on the pier, skirting the ghostly shapes of the transports. The *Millard Fillmore* was the third vessel from the end: he paused at the gangway, with the vague notion of inspecting his quarters. Save for the light above the watch officer's desk, the ship was completely obscured: the hooded gangway lifting at a sharp angle from the pier seemed to open into a void as mysterious as the portal to another world.

It took no effort at all to ignore the guard's tentative salute and continue down the pier. All that long day the thought of boarding that transport had been more than he could endure: now that he had put himself to the test and turned aside, he wondered if he would ever go aboard. Holding the thought at arm's length, he could feel his heart beat faster with a vague fear he had yet to name.

At the *Millard Fillmore*'s bow he steadied himself with a hand on a bollard. Above him a mooring hawser snaked away into grayness; beyond, he heard the pulse of the tide, though the fog hid the water. For the first time in his twenty-eight years on earth Paul Scott could pause in his tracks and ask himself, quite seriously, what it was like to die.

Freud, he remembered, had isolated the death wish that dwells in every man; he had explained the constant battle it wages for the soul. The battle is often fought in unlikely places (as a cliff's edge, on a railway trestle, beside a rushing stream). Paul knew that men had cast their lives away at such times—as carelessly as a child might discard a toy— when every rule of nature urged them to draw back. As an intern he had gone out on such ambulance calls—most of them dead-on-arrival, mute evidence that the irrational urge to self-destruction can be stronger than the ego.

Letting his hand trail along the hawser, he took a step toward the water, and another. He, of course, would never make that final move; it was absurd to let the possibility cross his mind. Yet he continued to approach the edge of the quay; it was an exciting—because deadly—game to see how far he could go and still outface the nameless demon within him.

Fear stabbed at his vitals and the fear was real now. The discovery he had just made was a paralyzing one—the fact that he *could* face the thought of self-extinction and know he might be powerless to conquer it. He took yet another step toward the oil-slick water. Somewhere, he told himself frantically, you've a reserve of strength to draw on—but did it exist at the moment? Or had it been devoured long since by the poison of hate?

Another step brought him to the very edge of the pier— and here he paused at last, with one foot on the stringpiece, to measure the distance to the water below. At that moment a voice spoke his name in the fog.

"Going my way, Dr. Scott?"

iv

It was a familiar voice, though Paul could not place it at once; for all its gentle timbre it had cut through the skein of his madness like a surgeon's scalpel. He stood on the stringpiece a moment more, pretending to inspect the bow moorings of the transport. Then he turned to lift a hand in greeting as the battalion chaplain emerged from the murk.

"Good evening, Padre." He spoke coldly; Father Timothy O'Fallon had never been among his intimates. "What brings you into the fog?"

"God, I hope."

"Yours, or mine?" He had long since informed the chaplain that he was not a practicing Christian—so the response had come naturally enough. In another moment, Paul promised himself, he would recover his sang-froid.

"We all worship the same God, Doctor," said the priest. "Even though we give Him different titles."

"I'm afraid I've none at all, Father."

"But you have—you've just said as much. Give yourself time; you'll learn His name."

The priest joined him on the stringpiece; once again Paul noticed how puny he seemed, a mere wisp of khaki in the mist.

"Did you follow me here, Padre?" he asked, a little contemptuously.

"Yes, Dr. Scott."

"To discuss theology in the fog?"

"No, Doctor—to ask if you were going aboard the transport. I wanted to look at her myself."

"Sorry if I misunderstood. Shall we go exploring?"

The chaplain gave a nervous laugh. "Only if you insist. Now that I'm standing at the gangway I'd prefer to go back. To tell the truth I've a mortal terror of fog."

The man's eyes brushed Paul's as he spoke: he seemed to

grow shyer with each word he uttered—yet he continued
to stand on the stringpiece. There was a sturdiness in his
manner that contrasted oddly with his almost timid utter-
ance: Paul wondered how much he had guessed about his
real reason for visiting the pier. He put down the wonder
and took refuge in brusqueness.

"You're right to turn back. This old tub may be taking
us both to immortality. Why should we go aboard before
our time?"

"Yet we were both drawn to this pier tonight," said the
priest quietly. "I wonder why."

"You said that God sent you."

"It's quite true, Doctor. An hour ago I was dozing in my
billet at Port Headquarters. Some force outside myself
brought me to the gangway of the *Millard Fillmore*. Don't
ask me to give it a name. God will do, for now."

Paul was glad that the yellow-white mist continued
to swirl between them: he could only hope that it had
softened the mocking laughter he had just choked down.
"You really mean that, don't you?" he managed at last. The
words were lame enough, but he felt that some retort was
needed.

"Of course I do, Doctor. May I ask your reason for being
here?"

"Perhaps I'm a masochist at heart."

"My guess is that you're the truest patriot of all. One who
can lock his fear of death away and still serve his country.
To say nothing of his creator."

That, thought Paul swiftly, is quite enough offbeat for
one evening. He decided to end this jabberwocky with no
further thought of manners. "I *have* served my country,
Padre. For twenty months of combat in Europe. I brought
back a broken tibia to prove it, and a good many shattered
ideals. Right now I'm not in the least afraid. Just regretful
that another doctor isn't taking my place on that transport."

"Forgive me, Dr. Scott. I didn't mean to offend."

"I'm sure you didn't." To his astonishment Paul found that his resentment had left him, now that he had put this little bumbler in his place. Perhaps it was the guileless look the priest offered him: when he smiled the quiet radiance in his face seemed out of place in the world. For no reason that made sense Paul was suddenly reminded of a shell-blasted church in St. Lô—and a head of St. Francis that had rolled, unbidden, into the corner where he was setting up a field hospital.

Again he took refuge in a shrug. "Since we aren't tempting fate by going aboard—shall we guide each other to dry land?"

"We can try, Doctor."

They walked down the pier together in a silence that was oddly without strain. "Why do you fear the fog, Padre?" he asked.

"It's not easy to say. Perhaps because it is a symbol of the forces of darkness. Is that too mystical for a man of science?"

"A bit, I'm afraid. Didn't it take courage to come this far?"

"You made it, Dr. Scott. I felt that I could follow."

In another moment their heels rang on the cobbles of the waterfront. Here, because of a dozen brightly lighted bars, the universe seemed in perspective again—including the Army jeep parked at the curb. The driver (whom Paul recognized as one of the battalion runners) saluted briskly.

"Where to, Chaplain?"

"I'll settle for the USO canteen, Corporal," said Father O'Fallon. "Why don't you join me, Doctor? They've a special show tonight—a unit that's about to go overseas."

"Whatever you say, Padre."

It was almost a relief to step into the jeep, to let his unwanted companion take over for a while. Only later did Paul wonder at the presence of the jeep at that particular corner in San Pedro—and the fact that the driver seemed to take his appearance for granted, no less than the chaplain's. The age of miracles, like the age of saints, belonged to the more credulous past. He could hardly thank Father O'Fallon for saving his life—when that humorless neophyte was clearly unaware of the service.

v

Long before he had settled into the empty wall booth at the USO center Paul realized that it had been a mistake to come here.

He made no protest when Father O'Fallon hurried to the row of vending machines: for the moment he was too busy making himself small in the booth. There was no rule against his presence at a servicemen's canteen (several ensigns and their girls were in the crowd tonight, as well as a few juniors like himself). Still it was felt that officers were paid enough to provide their own diversions. . . . He would only stay a moment, Paul promised himself, just long enough to make this overzealous cleric happy. Then he'd take refuge in his hotel room: there was enough nembutal in his Val-Pak to insure oblivion until morning.

"You'll like this place, Dr. Scott."

Paul accepted a Coca-Cola from the chaplain. "I can't stay long—"

"The girl who's singing is a friend of mine. I'll invite her over when this number ends."

For the first time Paul turned his attention to the band-box stage above the dance floor. The singer who was belting out "Night and Day" at the microphone seemed like a hundred other synthetic blondes—not bad, though she was certainly no Doris Day. He pulled his eyes away from the spotlight with no effort and gave Father O'Fallon what he hoped was a disarming grin.

"She's working too hard," he said.

"Exactly what I've always told her," said the chaplain. "She could be a sensation if she'd only sing naturally. Her voice was made for chamber music. Folk songs—or perhaps the *lieder* of Schumann."

Paul cocked an ironic eye at the priest, who had cupped both hands beneath his chin and was listening entranced. He did not speak again until the girl paused for an intermezzo and looked out over the audience with one of those show-business smiles that might have been painted on her too-bright lips.

"She's a nice person, Doctor, even nicer than her voice."

"I'm sure of that, Padre." This obviously was not the moment to enlighten the priest on one of life's fundamentals. Paul was still admiring his own forbearance when the song ended and the singer bowed to rather tepid applause. The master of ceremonies, a bald young man in a sharp tuxedo, bustled to the microphone, clapping just a bit louder than the audience.

"That was Kay Storey, fellows. A little lady who's going places fast. Let's give her another big hand."

The GIs (who packed every table around the dance floor) stepped up the tempo of their applause a trifle, and the girl took a second bow. She was on her way to the dressing room when Father O'Fallon bustled out of the booth.

"Miss Storey!"

Even in the depths of his apathy Paul noticed that the girl's face had brightened at the sound of the padre's voice.

"This is a surprise, Father O'Fallon."

"Tonight I'm here with deliberate intent. There's someone I'd like you to meet."

The smile on the girl's overpainted lips was still quite genuine as she permitted the chaplain to lead her toward the booth: Paul saw her face go blank when he rose in response to the padre's introductions. Not that he could

blame her too much: he could imagine how dour his own
face must seem at the moment.

"Won't you join us, my dear?"

For a split second, Paul saw, the blond singer contemplated a refusal. Then, just as mechanically, she put down
the urge. That, too, he could understand. The metal crosses
on Father O'Fallon's tunic were insurance against most
rebuffs.

"I was just going to have a Coke in my dressing room—"

"Have one here instead." By some private legerdemain
the padre had already produced a third bottle: he pressed
it into the girl's hand and ushered her into the booth. "Dr.
Scott, will you entertain this young lady a moment while
I visit with our outfit?"

A duenna out of Dickens, thought Paul, would have
been less gauche. He watched the padre bustle into the
crowd—and felt the emptiness of the night invade his
heart again, the void to which he had all but yielded on
the pier. . . . Detached as he was, he could admire Kay
Storey's poise as she settled beside him and lifted the
Coca-Cola in a parody of a toast.

"I won't keep you," he said quickly. "Not if you'd rather
rest awhile. Father O'Fallon has yet to learn the facts of
the theater."

"I've a few minutes, Doctor." Her voice, like her aplomb,
was disarming—and much friendlier than he deserved,
Paul added gloomily. "Would you be surprised if I said I'd
seen you before?"

Now that they were side by side he noted that Kay
Storey was much smaller than she had seemed in the spotlight's glare: her voice was pitched low, with a deeper resonance than the microphone had revealed. A voice for
folk songs, or Schumann *lieder:* could Father O'Fallon's
ear be keener than his own? Paul found himself looking
into her smoky green eyes with genuine appraisal.

"Forgive my poor memory. Where did we meet?"

"We didn't. I was singing at the Kit-Kat last summer, in Altadena. My car was sideswiped and they brought me to the Holt Clinic."

"Nothing serious, I hope."

"Just a cut scalp. They were taking the last stitches when you came through the emergency room."

"I'd pretend to remember if I dared," he said politely. "Apparently I didn't officiate."

"Hardly. You were in a tail coat, and looked as though you owned the world." Kay Storey's generous lips widened in a smile that held no hint of mockery. "I could guess why: I'd seen your picture in the *Examiner* that morning, with Daphne Holt."

"I'm afraid tail coats belong to the past," he said. "May I compliment you on your song?"

"Don't bother. You've heard better singers—and you needn't deny it."

"Are you really going overseas?"

"Not quite so soon as the 141st Battalion."

"Has our chaplain been talking *that* freely?"

She gave him a level look. "Is it tomorrow, Lieutenant— or the day after?"

"The day after, I'm afraid. You aren't a North Korean spy, by any chance?"

Kay Storey laughed lightly, but her eyes were still serious as she continued to study him with that same disarming interest. "Father Tim will endorse me, I'm sure. And you mustn't blame him for talking out of turn. The first night we met here we told each other our life stories. Isn't that what a chaplain's for?"

"I don't blame him at all," said Paul—and this time, he almost meant it. "In fact, I'm hoping we'll meet in Korea."

"Shall we make a tentative date for April?"

"April in Seoul," said Paul. "It hasn't the lilt of April in Paris."

"Did you win those service ribbons in France? You've a lot for a lieutenant."

He saw that she was keeping a standard USO conversation moving. It was hardly her fault that she had touched him on a sore spot. "Most of them were earned in combat," he said evenly. "Right now, I'm a casualty of the doctors' draft."

"Has it made you as unhappy as you sound?"

"Need you ask?"

"At least you'll have prospects when you get out. Don't forget I've seen both the Holt Clinic and your fiancée."

"Daphne Holt was never my fiancée," he said. "And I'm no longer employed by the clinic. Dr. Holt felt that he couldn't wait for my discharge in *this* war." It was incredible that he could speak so calmly of Daphne and her father. The sensation was remarkably pleasant. So pleasant that he decided to prolong it. "Odd as it sounds, the Holt Clinic doesn't seem too important—now."

"What I saw of it that night looked pretty important. So, for that matter, did you."

"Let's say I was on my way up—and took a fast tumble."

"Would you believe me, Doctor, if I say I'm sorry?"

"Of course, if you'll prove it."

The green eyes did not flicker. "What's your idea of proof?"

"Shall we say dinner—after your last number?"

"Do you have your chaplain's approval for this invitation?"

"By no means. And I'm not asking him to make a third."

"I'll weigh your proposition," said Kay Storey. "How well do you know Father Tim?"

"I don't know him at all. In fact, I've rather avoided him since I joined his outfit."

"Why, Doctor?"

"What do you make of him? Don't stop and think—answer straight off."

"I think he's sweet."

"Sweet—and a bit too naïve?"

"Not nearly so naïve as he seems."

"Surely he's a little nosy."

"Isn't that part of his job?"

"Don't think I'm complaining," said Paul. "Shall we dine at Chasen's—or Romanoff's?"

"You needn't be so grand," said the girl. "I suppose you've already labeled me a Hollywood siren, but I live on the wrong side of Pico Boulevard."

"You'll accept, then?"

"I'm still not sure, Doctor. Why do you dislike Father Tim?"

"How can I dislike him? He's brought us together."

"*Together*, Dr. Scott?"

"For dinner, at least, if you'll trust me that far."

"I might—if you'll answer me. What don't you like about your chaplain? What has he done to hurt you?"

A trifle nettled by her perception, Paul withdrew his hand, which had been on the point of covering hers. "Is Father O'Fallon by any chance your confessor?"

"I'm a backsliding Methodist," said the girl. "What are you?"

"How did you guess *I* wasn't a Catholic?"

"No good Catholic would use his priest to help along a conquest."

"Isn't that rather a strong word?"

"I don't think so, Doctor. If anything, it's an understatement."

Their eyes held. When he dropped his glance it was only to lift her hand and kiss one finger tip gently. "Can you blame me?"

Kay Storey took back her hand with no appearance of haste. "The answer is no, Dr. Scott."

"You mean, you *don't* blame me?"

"I'm refusing your dinner invitation—politely but

firmly." She got up as she spoke, taking a cigarette from his pack and accepting a light.

"Any particular reason for the refusal?"

"Just one. It seems only fair to save your time." She left him on that to vanish briefly through the curtained entrance to the dressing rooms.

He was still pondering that exit when he spied Father Tim approaching the booth. Not that he had been too startled by Kay Storey's abrupt departure: in fact, their brief passage at arms had been stimulating—almost elating. He just missed laughing aloud as he grasped the reason for that lift. However briefly, the girl *had* teased him out of his own selfishness. Her refusal to dine with him had given him a problem outside himself—and the challenge had made him want life again. . . . He was still chuckling over the discovery when the chaplain slipped into the booth.

"I'm afraid the lady has left us, Father."

"She'll be out directly, Doctor. She has to change for the next number."

"That isn't what I meant. I drove her away."

"I'm sorry to hear that, Dr. Scott. When I introduced you I was sure you could help each other."

"Father O'Fallon," he said a little testily, "did it ever occur to you that most foot-loose men and women are interested only in helping themselves?"

The priest smiled across the table—another of those gentle smiles that began and ended in the eyes. "I refuse to believe that about either you or Kay, Paul. May I call you that, since you've opened your heart to me?"

"How could I when I've said nothing of myself?"

"You've told me that you have a grudge against the world. So, I fear, does Kay Storey—though hers doesn't show quite so plainly. I was hoping you'd both have a go at solving those grudges. It's been done before, you know."

"Are you suggesting I try again?"

"Believe me, Paul, she's a fine girl. Give her a chance to prove it."

Paul shrugged. "If you wish, Father Tim, I'll give her every chance."

"She's going on for the last time now. It won't be long before she can join us again—"

"Apparently she's run into heavy weather."

Both of them turned to the bandstand: as Paul had just said, Kay Storey had become the focal point of one of those sudden brawls so characteristic of wartime canteens. At first glance he could not identify the reason for the fracas, though it had already involved most of the dance floor.

"Do you have this sort of blowup often?"

"Almost nightly, I'm afraid. I'm sure she can handle it."

Standing on his chair for a better view, Paul saw that the troublemaker was a large, rather beefy officer who was evidently determined to join the musicians. Several noncoms were doing their best to dissuade him. Kay, with one foot on the dance floor, was working hard at her role of peacemaker. While Paul watched, the intruder shoved the noncoms aside and climbed to the stage; with a bellow of triumph he snatched a saxophone from one of the musicians and turned to face the dance floor. Paul felt a prickle of unholy rage along his spine when he recognized Colonel Jasper Hardin, his battalion commander. Despite Kay's persuasions Hardin had already launched into a rendition of the dance tune—a braying travesty that suggested he had studied music via the mail-order school.

"What's our C.O. doing here?"

Father Tim sighed. "He's visited us before, Paul. You see, he usually dines—and drinks—at the officers' club."

The officers' club stood only a few doors from the canteen. More than once Paul had observed Hardin's antics at the bar; tonight it was evident that his libations had been more prolonged than usual. "Isn't there some legal way to keep him out?"

"I'm afraid not. Usually he pretends he's sober until he reaches the bandstand. Then he *always* wants to lead the orchestra."

Hardin had kept his footing; when Kay attempted to deprive him of the saxophone he prisoned her with one arm and planted a highly inaccurate kiss on her cheek. The hall rang with booing now. And yet, intimidated by the silver eagles on Hardin's shoulders, no one had ventured to approach the bandstand. Paul got to his feet, feeling the worst of his rage dissolve in action.

"I'm going to break this up, Padre."

"Believe me, Paul, she can manage. It's happened before."

He shook off the chaplain's hand and reached the bandstand in a dozen long strides. The enlisted men on the crowded floor outdid each other to let him pass; the colonel, his arm still about Kay's waist, gave him a glassy stare of nonrecognition when he stepped up to the stage.

"The lady promised me this dance, sir."

Hardin's answer was a prolonged bray on the horn. Confident that his whim was law, he had already turned his back on the intruder and made a second attempt to kiss Kay Storey.

"If the colonel pleases—"

"*As y'were, shavetail!*"

The parade-ground bellow had struck terror to hearts from Fort Dix to Manila: tonight it only translated resentment into action. Paul's elbow, smashed into Hardin's midriff, was all the help Kay needed to free herself. Deprived of that support, the colonel sat down heavily on the platform, missing the snare drum by inches. The hall shook with cheers as Paul handed Kay down to the floor and spun her into a waltz turn with the sudden revival of the orchestra.

"Thanks, Doctor," she whispered.

"It was a pleasure."

"I could have handled him, you know—"

"It was still a pleasure."

There was no time for more. Because of the crowd Paul had been able to dance Kay only a few steps from the bandstand. Too late, he realized that Hardin was on his feet again with the saxophone raised.

A sergeant tried to bar the way, but the drunken officer flailed him from his path: there was barely time to push Kay aside before the blow descended. For a split second the horn seemed to hang in mid-air, a grotesque, golden bludgeon. . . . Paul saw that Hardin was glaring at him insanely: the red hate that glowed in those eyes assured him the C.O. had recognized him. He heard Father O'Fallon's cry of protest from a great distance as the saxophone connected solidly with his head.

vi

When Paul opened his eyes he was in a strange bed; the flawless California sunlight patterning the carpet told him that some time had elapsed since his brush in the canteen.

He tested his reflexes cautiously and was gratified by the result. Whatever their other faults his forebears had bequeathed him a solid skull; save for a decided headache and a tenderness in the area of the left temple, he was feeling fit enough. A second glance assured him that this was not his room at the Hollywood Hotel—nor were the somewhat flamboyant pajamas his own; the bed (though it was made up with hospital precision) was a living-room divan. The room itself, he surmised, belonged to a person of taste and little present means.

Kay Storey's humming reached him through one of the two closed doors; the situation fell into perspective before she could enter with a coffee service. In slacks and a powder-blue pull-over, she looked much younger than he remembered—and her smile was part of the sunny morning.

"Sleep well, Dr. Scott?"

Paul sat up in bed and rechecked the lump behind his temple. "Is sleep the proper word?"

"Indeed it is. I gave you a rather strong sedative before I tucked you in—three grains of seconal. Don't look alarmed, please: I was a R.N. before I decided to have a career." Kay Storey settled on a leather-covered cushion beside the divan and hugged her knees. "You look wonderfully rested."

Paul sipped his coffee gratefully. What she had said was true enough: even the headache was dissolving rapidly in the fragrant steam from his cup. "It would help if I knew just what you've done for me," he ventured. "Whatever it is, Miss Storey—"

"If I call you Paul, will you return the compliment?"

"Do I deserve it, Kay?"

"I think so, after your bout with Colonel Hardin."

They surveyed each other, across the counterpane of the day bed. "Is it proper to ask how I got here?"

"It seemed the best place to bring you. Father Tim wasn't sure of your hotel—"

"Don't tell me I arrived under my own power?"

"Partly. Two enlisted men helped you to my car."

"And afterward?"

"Don't you even remember climbing my stairs?"

"My last clear image is a tenor saxophone connecting with my ear."

"Your colonel was a mad dog last night," said Kay. "There's no other name for him."

"What became of *him* afterward?"

"The noncoms spirited him out ahead of the Shore Patrol." Kay smiled as she took Paul's empty cup. "He's still sleeping it off."

"How come you're so well informed?"

"Father Tim phoned an hour ago. He's dropping around later."

"*Here*, Kay?"

"I'd promised to show him Hollywood: he hasn't had time to make the tour—and today's his last chance. Care to join us?"

She left him before he could frame an answer and took the cup into her tiny kitchen. On her return with fresh coffee, she opened the second door and went in to tidy the bedroom where she had obviously slept. Kay Storey, Paul gathered, was not a girl to waste words. Only the pajamas he was wearing remained unexplained.

"Perhaps I should apologize for the trouble I've caused," he said, when she had settled again on the cushion. "Obviously I behaved like a knight-errant with delusions of grandeur. Still, I couldn't stand by and let that drunken goat maul you."

"Do you think he recognized you?"

"For just a moment, I'm afraid. Probably the liquor washed out the memory."

"You've made a lifetime enemy if it hasn't."

He shrugged. "Hardin has hated me from the moment I reported for duty."

"Any special reason?"

"People like him *need* someone to hate. As his newest officer, I'm a natural victim."

"Are you sure he doesn't hate himself most of all?"

"What's this, Kay? Freud in reverse?"

"You must see what I mean, Paul. Father Tim told me the colonel's been passed over twice on the promotion lists. That's slow death to a West Pointer."

"Don't tell me you're *sorry* for Hardin?"

"A little. Can you imagine feeding on hate to nourish your own self-esteem?"

"You wouldn't make such excuses if you were in his command."

"I can still pity him because he's failed so badly. Maybe that's because I'm on the edge myself."

Remembering Father Tim's words in the canteen last night, Paul sat up in the day bed. He was pleased to note that he was not dizzy, proving that the slugging last night had left no permanent effects.

"Move over then while I join you," he said quietly.

"*You* haven't failed, Paul."

He studied himself in the glass of a wardrobe door. The pajamas, he noted, were of white silk decorated with a pattern of crossed scimitars. He wondered why he did not feel more awkward wearing them.

"I failed to make a date with you last night," he reminded her.

"Yet here you are."

"Only because I stopped that horn with my skull. And the chaplain's arriving any moment now to keep us respectable—even if I am wearing your husband's pajamas."

"I have no husband, Paul."

"Then you're making your point the hard way."

"Perhaps I am." She got up from the cushion. "You'd better dress before Father Tim *does* arrive. The bath's in there —and so are your clothes. If you like you can finish your life story through the kitchen door while I wash up."

He found his uniform on the shower rail, neatly folded on a hanger. The sting of cold water banished the last of his hangover: he was himself again when he walked into the living room and stood at the wardrobe mirror to knot his service tie. Kay was busy in the kitchen: he wondered if she had taken that refuge deliberately, and was careful to keep clear of the open door.

"I told you my life story at the canteen," he said. "In a way I'm a worse failure than Hardin: only mine has come in a single installment."

"How can you call yourself a failure? You've always had what you wanted."

"Only by fighting every step of the way."

"Why stop fighting now?"

The question seemed preposterous in the clear light of morning: Paul spoke mechanically to gain time. "So I'm to accept Korea—*and* Hardin—and make the best of both?"

Kay emerged from the kitchen, dropping an apron en route. "Is it too much to ask?"

"Must I keep a stiff upper lip, too?"

"You'll finish this job, Paul—the way you finished the others. What's more, you'll be the better for it; your satisfaction will come in a way you least expect. Once you've seen it's the work that matters, not the reward, you may even discover you're a happy man."

"Are you quoting the chaplain, by any chance?"

"Word for word," she said. "You see, he's given me the same advice."

Kay was leaning against the doorjamb as she spoke. He moved toward her slowly, giving her time to avoid him before he lifted her chin and kissed her gently. It was not a lover's kiss. Yet he sensed that it had set off (as definitely as a comma) a second clause in their relationship.

"Thanks, Kay."

"What have I done now?"

"You may not realize it but you've set me on my feet again. Can I do as much for you?"

"Is this my cue to identify the pajamas?"

"Only if it will help."

She moved a little away from him. "They belonged to Eric Lindman."

"*Lindman?* The director with all the Oscars?"

"At one time he was a visitor here."

Now that she had surmounted the first hurdle, her story was both honest and matter-of-fact. She told it without hesitation, as though speaking of a stranger. A girl who had come to Hollywood all of three years ago via the beauty-contest trail. A too-eager, too-credulous girl whose talent had been submerged in the tidal wave that inundates the film capitol. . . .

"Maybe it's symbolic, Paul—but I was born in Mc
Pherson, Kansas. It's the geographical center of the United
States. When you're dead center you have to break
free—"

"I was dead center too," he said. "So far, we're two of a
kind."

"Last year they gave me a bit in *Sirocco*—Eric's best picture. A street scene in Cairo—I was a bazaar dancer. It
was a fill-in scene: one of his assistants directed it. But
Eric saw the rushes. That night he rang my doorbell. He—
offered to help me. If I'd accept his help."

"Help you—with your acting?"

"With my acting," she said firmly. "That's all I ever took
from him. When he came here—which wasn't often—it was
only to get away. Do you believe me so far?"

"Of course. When did you fall in love with him?"

"I—respected Eric's genius. There's no one like him."

"Even his worst critics admit that."

"I was grateful for his help, Paul, and he *did* help. He
made me believe in myself as an actress. But I wasn't in
love with him. Not even at the beginning."

"Are you sure?" He wondered a little at the relief in his
voice.

"Absolutely."

"Where is he now?"

"On location in Africa. He's been gone for six months but
he writes steadily. He says he'll have a part for me—whenever I feel I'm ready."

"Meanwhile you're to sink or swim on your own?"

"Isn't that what makes an actress? Eric has helped me
all he can. I've got to prove I can make it from there."

"Have you worked regularly?"

"Enough to have my own apartment and be independent. I've done the small night-club circuit and kept my voice in training. And when there were no bookings I could always find other jobs. I've sold real estate in Beverly Hills and I've been a barker on a tourist bus. I've been a car-hop at a drive-in more than once—" She gave him a smile that was only a trifle strained. "Don't feel sorry for me, Paul. I've my own prescription for survival."

"Does it include naming yourself a failure? That's a dangerous ingredient."

"I *am* a failure by all reasonable standards. Be honest: what did you think of my singing last night—really?" Her fingers closed briefly on his before he could answer. "No— I won't embarrass you. Perhaps I'm exactly what you saw. A platinum blonde with no assets but her youth. Another contest winner who's too stubborn to take the Hollywood brush-off. On the other hand there's Eric and his faith in me. He *will* give me a chance if I ask for it—"

"Of course he will." To his astonishment, Paul found that he meant it.

"Only I won't ask until I'm ready. Until my talent really comes through. And I *do* have talent: that's one thing I'm sure of."

"You've made your point, Kay. Where does your R.N. degree fit in?"

"I went into training to get away from McPherson. One of my aunts paid my way through Barnes Hospital in St. Louis. It seemed only fair to *be* a nurse until I'd paid her back. I was good at it, too—"

"You'd be good at anything you do, Kay."

She gave him a grateful smile. "Like you, Paul. I guess we're a couple of mavericks, cut from the same pattern." This time it was she who bent forward to kiss him—and this time, he knew, there was an invitation in the kiss she could not quite bring herself to utter.

"Thanks for putting me in your class," he said. "It's an honor I'll try to deserve."

"Still like to tour Hollywood with Father Tim and me?"

"There's nothing I'd like more—if you'll both promise to dine with me at Romanoff's."

"Father Tim has a six o'clock service at Port Headquarters."

"The two of us, then?"

There was a flush at her cheeks when she answered: he felt his heart leap at the knowledge that she understood him perfectly. "It's your last evening here, Paul. Are you sure you want to spend it with me?"

"There's no one I'd rather spend it with."

"It's a date then," she said quietly. "*After* we've shown your chaplain Hollywood." Her color was still high—but she did not avoid his eye as she moved to answer the buzzer downstairs. A discreet ring that could be only Father Timothy O'Fallon.

vii

When Paul wakened the next morning he had no need to ask his whereabouts: his mind rang out the news as joyfully as a carillon.

After they had put the chaplain on the San Pedro bus Kay and Paul had gone hand in hand to their tour of the Hollywood fleshpots. They had dined royally at Romanoff's and danced at Mocambo and Ciro's, secure in the knowledge that they had earned these hours together. Afterward they had gone back to the apartment on Pico Boulevard: there had been no hidden tensions when the lock of her apartment door had clicked shut behind them. . . . Now, rousing in earnest, he knew that he had never been happier, never more deeply content.

"Where are you, Kay?"

There was no answer to his shout: he roamed the tiny apartment twice before admitting that he was alone there. On the second tour he saw that the coffee service was ready on the range. A note was propped against the percolator: like Kay herself, it was to the point:

> Leaving for an early rehearsal call. (Our final workout before we join forces with the Korean unit.)
> I'll be at the pier—if they let me out in time. If not, it's April in Seoul. Remember— we're *both* seeing this war through.

He wrote his own hurried farewell while the coffee boiled over: a glance at the clock had reminded him of the tyranny of time. At the Hollywood Hotel he collected his Val-Pak and paid two nights' rent on an unused room. While hailing a taxi he remembered Daphne Holt: in another hour she would be stepping off a plane from New York. It was good to remember, beyond all doubting, that his bondage to Daphne's world was ended.

There was hardly a moment to spare before he boarded the transport. It was only when he ascended the gangway with his surgical unit that he realized he had neglected to write down the address of the apartment on Pico Boulevard. Father Tim would have it, of course: he would send Kay his APO later. . . .

He needed a half hour to check in at quarters, to assure himself that the enlisted men under his command were well billeted. A post band was blaring at the pierhead when he returned to the deck, and the transport had begun to back ponderously into the harbor.

Somehow the gala air was forced, though there were sweethearts and wives by the dozens on the pier, and the band's rendition of "Aloha" could not have been more spirited. Paul found the chaplain at last, in the press of uniforms at the bow. A glance told him why Father Tim was waving so wildly: Kay Storey's runabout had just nosed into the crowd and she was running to the stringpiece of the pier with all the skill of a halfback determined on a touchdown.

Already the strip of water between ship and shore was too wide to shout across. Evidently she had realized she might be unable to wish him the usual good-by; when she reached the stringpiece the placard she lifted told its own story in foot-high block letters.

CARRYING THE TORCH TO SEOUL. HAPPY LANDINGS!

All over the transport voices roared an answer to that message, on the assumption that it was a general tribute. Crushed among the windmilling arms in the coaming, Paul felt his throat tighten at the energy of that response. Thanks to Kay Storey, the tepid ceremony of leave-taking (which the blaring of the post band had only underlined) was now transformed into a genuine farewell, a blend of tears and wholehearted cheering.

Now that these vigorous young voices had taken over he was reminded once again that youth is eternal, that the young will always live down the evils devised by their elders. . . . America's wars, he added solemnly, will always be won—so long as there is a Kay Storey waiting at the war's end.

"The girl next door," said Father Tim. "That's what I called her the day we met. D'you understand why, Paul?"

"Yes, Father Tim. I understand perfectly."

He cupped his hands to add his farewell shout to the others, knowing in advance that she could not pick out his voice. But he was sure that she had found him in that cheering multitude, that she was waving to him alone. And he knew that he loved her beyond reason—even though he had not yet put his love in words.

The Presidio

THE IMAGE of the troopship dimmed, though he could half hear the wail of the siren. Alone in his room at the Bachelor Officers' Quarters, Captain Paul Scott saw that dawn was waiting behind the fogbound eastern sky.

The silent prayer had helped; so had his familiar communion with the past. He was glad that he had gone back to the beginning with Kay—and happier still that he could face that beginning with no regrets. Until their meeting he had not quite realized that he was a member (in reasonable standing) of the family of man. The lesson had taken a deal of learning; he had passed his last exam in the hell of the prison camp at Pyongyang. But he had learned to forget the demands of self with Kay. For the first time he had discovered that being in love was only a short cut to the admission that it is more blessed to give than to receive.

Only a few hours ago, in the lounge of the BOQ, he had tried to thank Kay for the part she had played in his education. There had been no words to convey his thanks—not even to the woman he loved. . . . Paul turned to his Spartan cot now with a sigh. Wondering if sleep would elude him again, he found himself dropping into oblivion as his head touched the pillow.

ii

"Will you read the charges—or shall I?"

"Fire away, Hi. You can explain as we go along."

Hilary Saunders glanced up sharply while he emptied
the contents of his brief case on the rumpled blanket covering Paul's cot. The question was deliberately prodding, in
the hope of shattering his friend's inattention.

"I stopped counting clients years ago," said Hi, "but you
win the blue ribbon for sang-froid."

Paul was seated in the window frame, breathing deep of
the flawless morning. The fog had burned away with the
sunrise and San Francisco was as clean-washed as its sky.
Maybe it's a hangover from two years behind barbed wire,
thought Hi. Maybe freedom has made him a little balmy.
So balmy that he doesn't realize he may be facing another
prison stockade tomorrow. . . .

"Is it wrong to enjoy a little sunshine?"

"You know what I mean," said Hi. "No one can be so
cool. Not when he's fighting for his life. Is it something
you learned from Confucius?" (He regretted the fumble
at humor instantly. Paul's captors had been largely Chinese: for all Hi knew, a perverted Confucianism had
been part of the brain-washing.)

"My only credo comes from a more recent teacher," said
Paul. "An unsung philosopher named Father Timothy
O'Fallon. Remember *him?*"

Hi nodded. "A runty priest with his nose in everyone's
troubles—and a line of malarky that might have been
funny, if it had been less crude. Of course, I never really
knew him. That might make a difference?"

"It would," said Paul. "I can remember when my reaction was identical with yours."

"Shall we skip the padre for now? We'll be walking into
your court-martial in just twenty minutes. It might help
to remind you of the charges."

"We've been over them, Hi."

"Let's repeat them again—in the ineffable prose of the
Army." The lawyer picked up a blue-bound dossier that
lay among the notes on the blanket. "Charges and Specifi-

cations," he intoned, in a bailiff's voice—enunciating each word clearly, but dwelling on none:

"CHARGE 1: Violation of the Uniform Code of Military Justice, Article 105

"*Specification 1:* In that Captain Paul R. Scott, U.S. Army, 141st Battalion, while a prisoner at Pyongyang, North Korea, on or about September 1, 1951, without proper authority and for the purpose of seeking favorable treatment from his captors, did offer and give medical treatment to enemy personnel in a prison camp maintained by North Korean and Chinese military forces near the said city of Pyongyang.

"*Specification 2:* In that Captain Paul R. Scott did use captured medical and other supplies in the treatment of enemy personnel for the selfsame purpose.

"*Specification 3:* In that the same Captain Paul R. Scott did freely confess and sign a statement that he had personally helped to load bombs with bacteria to be dropped upon the enemy—said confession being, to the accused's own knowledge, false and without basis and made solely to obtain favorable treatment for himself.

"*Specification 4:* In that Captain Paul R. Scott, having been offered release from prison, following the signing of an armistice, did refuse repatriation and chose, at the time, to remain with the enemy though later, and of his own accord, he did seek and receive repatriation.

"CHARGE 2: Violation of the Uniform Code of Military Justice, Article 133.

"*Specification:* In that Captain Paul R. Scott did, while a prisoner at Pyongyang, act in a manner unbecoming to an officer of the United States Army

and did, directly because of such conduct, give aid
to the enemy through the publication of propaganda
material.

"CHARGE 3: Violation of the Uniform Code of Military Justice, Article 134.

"*Specification:* In that Captain Paul R. Scott
did, while a prisoner at Pyongyang, conduct himself
in such a manner as to bring about the prejudice of
good order and discipline in the armed forces and
in such a manner as to bring discredit upon the
armed forces of the United States."

The lawyer was silent for a moment after he had intoned
the last syllable. A smile of sorts played about his lips.
"Shall we plead guilty to the lot?" he asked finally.

"Do you believe a word of that jargon?"

"Your prosecutor does—and Jim MacArdle's a smooth
lawyer. If he gets your scalp he'll probably win his eagles
—so he'll use every trick in the book. First trick, the
grapevine tells me, will be to move for dismissal of some
of the charges. Probably the first two items in Charge One.
Maybe the Army won't accuse you of aiding the enemy
sick, or using captured medicine—"

"Why not?"

"Because it will look better in the headlines if Jim can
nail you as a Grade-A collaborator—and skip the fact that
you're also a Grade-A doctor. There's no point in saying
that you stopped a few epidemics with captured U.N. supplies. It might make you seem a shade too human."

"Shouldn't we insist on keeping the charges as they
stand?"

"We can try. It probably won't stick—but I can hold
Mac's feet in the fire until I've made the point." Hi took a
list of names from his brief case. "We've just time to go
over your judges."

"Is that cricket?"

"Once we're in that star chamber, pal, *anything* is cricket that doesn't land us in clink." The lawyer checked a name on the list. "I've told you that Colonel Sellers will preside. Old regime, but fair as they come. So's Major Duggan: as second officer he'll sit on Sellers' right. He's a Korean veteran and he knows the score." Hi checked a third name, with a visible pucker. "I can't say the same for Captain Carter—he's bucking for a permanent place in the judge advocate's office. The rest are run-of-the-mine Army boys—remote from reality as monks. All but Major Betts, the law officer—*he's* a walking encyclopedia of protocol and as full of crotchets as a National League umpire. You can forget him. He's my headache—"

Hi let his voice trail and marveled again at his friend's apparent unconcern. Had they been about to attend a routine classroom lecture, Paul could hardly have seemed more relaxed. An unwanted phantom rose in the lawyer's mind—the suspicion that his client might really be guilty as charged. He dropped his eyes before Paul could notice his distress, and closed the clasps of his brief case.

"We can walk over now," he said. "It'll be better if we're early—wouldn't look well to make an entrance."

"Lead the way, counselor," said Paul. "From now on, I'm taking orders."

"No more questions?"

"Just one. Do we have a chance?"

"We could use a few witnesses," said Hi carefully. "I'll do what I can to make MacArdle's boys work for our side but I'm afraid they've been too well coached." He looked hard at Paul. "I won't say this again—but it might be easier if you'd plead guilty—throw yourself on the court's mercy—"

"I'm not guilty, Hi."

"Have it your way. Want to say a prayer before we go?"

"I said it last night. This is your show now."

iii

Early as they were, they found the courtroom jammed.
Marching in behind a wedge of white-helmeted military
police, Paul had an impression of hot, glaring lamps, of
Brobdingnagian cameras, of clustering faces blank as dinner plates. In a corner someone was chanting a litany
in a tongue that was not quite English—he would learn
later that this was a network technician, checking his
moniters to make sure that the nationwide television
coverage was complete.

Paul recognized several of the men at the press tables,
writers from the wire services and the great dailies of the
East; most of them had pounced on him in Tokyo after
his repatriation and he felt himself bridle under their staring. Larry Kirk, throned in their midst and doodling on a
scratch-pad, had not lifted his eyes: there was something
in the famous commentator's boredom that was more
damning than the newsmen's X-ray appraisals.

Since they had entered by a side door, Paul had only a
distant look at the audience—and audience, he reflected,
was the proper term.

People were seated in the aisles, and there was a dense
mass of standees behind the last row of benches. Outside,
at the gateway of the Presidio, he could hear loud-speakers
urging the crowd to disperse. Since it had been the decision
of the Secretary of the Army to admit both spectators and
television, Paul could understand the interest in the court-
martial. Just the same, it had shocked him to learn that
people had waited outside the court since early morning
and that thousands had been turned away for lack of
space.

There was no sign of Kay Storey; after their last meeting
he had not expected to find her here. Instinct told him
that she was nearby—waiting, like the unseen audience

that could be counted by the millions, to follow the trial on radio or television.

The courtroom itself was drab enough: the only spot of color was the flag between the two tall windows that let in a blaze of sunlight. The railed enclosure, with its chocolate-brown dado and plain wooden tables, could have been duplicated in a dozen dusty Army posts. So could the half-moon of desks on the dais, and the seven chairs where the court would sit. (The dais, Paul noted, was placed between the two casements, so that the sun glare would fall on the witness box, a lonely eminence facing the president's chair.)

Major James MacArdle and the lieutenant who was his assistant were sorting papers at the prosecutor's table; Paul gave the trial counsel a cautious glance before he settled in his own chair. MacArdle was hardly forty: his face gleamed with the special ferretlike intelligence that is the hallmark of the successful lawyer. The fact that such a man could be content with the rewards of a judge advocate's office was an endorsement of his zeal. So was the spark that illumined his pale eyes. (They were a trifle protuberant in a too-thin face, and seemed equipped with invisible magnifiers.) Torquemada himself, thought Paul, could not have enjoyed his work more. . . . He dismissed the comparison as unworthy and snapped to attention with the others as a master sergeant bawled the order from the doorway.

With Colonel Sellers at its head, the seven-man court took its place on the dais. Studying each face with care, Paul felt his heart sink. Reason though he might, he was certain that these solemn martinets had already sealed his fate.

Sellers was a head taller than the others, a handsome saturnine man with deep-set brooding eyes. Major Duggan, a mahogany-dark campaigner, needed no service ribbons to advertise his veteran's status. The others, Paul

admitted, were unmilitary by contrast, despite their beautifully tailored uniforms and ramrod airs; stripped of their
insignia, the lesser members of the court could have passed
for lodge brothers ready to officiate at a weekend ritual.
Sellers and Duggan, he realized, would be his real judges—
with an assist from the overeager captain at the president's
left, a buoyant young man with all the gusto of a college
football manager.

For an instant the court remained frozen behind the
seven chairs while a small, tubby man arrived at a special
table beside the dais. The late-comer, Paul gathered, was
Major Betts, the legal light who would interpret the Army
code for those court members who were not lawyers.

Colonel Sellers lifted his hand for silence and spoke in
a voice that seemed, to Paul's anxious ears, incredibly mild.

"At ease!"

Army and spectators settled in their chairs. Only Mac-
Ardle remained standing, his chin lifting a trifle when he
saw that the TV cameras were turning. Sellers gave him a
curt nod and opened the file on his blotter.

"The court will come to order."

Paul, watching the television go into gear and the scrib-
blers at the press tables, held his breath in the expectation
of shattering drama. Not even Shakespeare, he reflected,
had commanded a fraction of MacArdle's present audience. Actually the proceedings of the next half hour were
freighted with boredom.

There was a long recital of names, the swearing-in of
court reporters, a statement of the qualifications of the
Honorable Hilary Saunders (the only civilian present
within the railed enclosure). Members of the court were
sworn, including Betts, the trial counsel, and his assistant.
Thanks to last night's insomnia, Paul was half dozing in
his chair when the president announced that the court was
now in session.

MacArdle rose and stated the source of the charges.

There was a final hiatus while he offered Hi the right to challenge any of the judges. When this privilege was waived a subtle change in the prosecutor's manner told Paul that this, at last, was the first true attack.

Striding to the clear space between the lawyers' tables, MacArdle faced the bench with his eyes half closed and a notebook seemingly forgotten in his hand. He spoke diffidently—and so rapidly that the stenotype operators seemed hard put to catch the words.

"By direction of the convening authority, the prosecution withdraws the first and second specifications of Charge One, and will not pursue the same further in this trial."

"Objection!"

Hi Saunders' voice had stopped the prosecutor's half-audible drone. Colonel Sellers opened his eyes wide for the first time. Paul noted that they were a clear light blue: they seemed completely innocent in their careworn setting.

"Does defense counsel *object* to withdrawal of charges against the accused?"

"I do, sir. Charges and specifications, in their entirety, are general in nature. Later I intend to move their dismissal *in toto*. To withdraw any part of them now will prejudice the prepared defense of the accused."

MacArdle kept his poise. "If the court please, this is irregular to the extreme."

"The handling of this whole case has been irregular," said Hi. "I repeat that withdrawal of any part of the formal charge will deprive Captain Scott of a full opportunity to clear himself."

The president leaned forward: his eyes were magnets now, drawing both lawyers to the bench. After Major Betts had joined the whispered huddle the court rose as a body and filed from the room to deliberate the objection.

"Don't look so puzzled," said Hi, when he had returned

to the defense table. "All I said was that you're ready to
take your punishment—and mean to fight back. It regis-
tered on TV—that's all we care about."

"What will happen?"

"Nothing. A distress call will go to the convening
authority, and they'll rule for MacArdle."

True to Hi's prediction, the court returned in a few moments to uphold the withdrawal of the first two specifications of Charge One. When Hi had protested (and the
protest had been recorded), copies of the revised charges
were passed to each member of the court and to the press
tables. After this solemn obeisance to justice the court-
martial ground into motion again.

"With the consent of the accused," said MacArdle, "I
will omit the reading of the charges. As the court knows,
they are sworn to by Colonel Jasper Hardin, who is thereby
subject to the military code as the accuser. Charges and
specifications, the name and description of the accused, his
affidavit, and the reference for trial will be copied verbatim
into the record."

"The accused consents," said Hi.

"On September twentieth last," said MacArdle, "the
charges were served by me on the accused. How does he
plead?"

"The defense moves for a dismissal of all charges and
specifications," said Hi.

"On what grounds?" asked the president.

"On the grounds that the accuser publicized the charges
at a time when Captain Scott was still in Korea. On the
grounds that copies of an alleged confession, signed by
Captain Scott in the enemy prison at Pyongyang, have
long since found their way into the newspapers—with the
result that this case has been tried by headline before the
accused could prepare a defense. On the further ground
that these charges are false in their entirety and were made
solely for the purpose of discrediting Captain Scott—the

aim being to prevent him from making known the truth about his conduct in Korea."

Colonel Sellers' gavel enforced silence. "Mr. Saunders, the accuser in this case is an officer of the United States Army. He has sworn to the charges. Are you implying he committed perjury?"

"It is our intention, sir, to prove that the charges *do* constitute perjury."

"The court will withdraw to discuss the motion and vote on it."

Hi assumed a grave face for the television as he stood at attention and watched the seven judges leave the room. But his eyes twinkled when he settled beside Paul.

"I'm improvising," he admitted. "But it was too good a chance to miss. In any case, we'll want these protests on the record in case we appeal."

It was a suffocating thought, but Paul could see it made sense. With the charges as grave as they were, conviction at the present court-martial was all too likely. Hi was already laying the groundwork for a possible second trial before the Court of Military Appeals. Composed of civilians, it was a final resort in such cases, short only of the Supreme Court itself.

This time, Paul's seven judges filed back after the briefest of recesses.

"The motion is denied," said Sellers. "Proceed, Major MacArdle."

"How does the accused plead?" the trial counsel asked.

"The accused pleads not guilty to all specifications and charges," Hi Saunders announced.

MacArdle addressed the court. "The prosecution states at this time that it will introduce in evidence a confession by the accused."

Hi barked an instant objection. "The accused will deny making any confession that would prove valid in a court of law. The statement by the prosecution at this point tends to indicate that a valid document of such nature exists, which the accused denies."

"The objection is sustained, subject to objection by any member of the court," said the president. "The reporter will strike from the record all reference to a confession. Has trial counsel any further statement?"

MacArdle's eyes were modestly lowered before Sellers' glare, but his lips were tight with anger. "None, sir."

"Are you ready to call your first witness?"

"I am. The prosecution calls as witness Corporal Harold Jackson."

iv

Corporal Jackson marched stiffly into court: a rangy, horse-faced regular who had once seemed as familiar to Paul as a foster brother. He felt the expected pang at his heart when Harry favored him with a totally blank stare. He had guessed that Jackson would be the first to testify against him. In his way, the corporal's reactions summed up the case from the prosecution's point of view.

After the witness had been duly sworn MacArdle handled him with friendly competence, establishing the fact that he had served in Korea with the 141st Battalion, and that he had been captured after the surrender of Hill 1049, in the summer of 1951.

"You were, I believe, a member of the medical detail under Captain Scott?"

"Yes, sir, I was."

"Did he ever say or do anything while in the front line that suggested he was thinking of co-operating with the enemy?"

"Well, I heard him say once 'I'm going to make the best of this that I can.'"

There was a stir of interest among the spectators; the

prosecutor let it run its course. "You're sure that Captain Scott used those precise words?"

"Yes, sir. I heard him."

"What did you think?"

"Nothing at the time; I figured it was just a front-line gripe. But I remembered it later—when we were prisoners at Pyongyang. When Captain Scott began to co-operate with the Chinese——"

"Objection," said Hi. "Prosecution has offered no proof of co-operation."

"I intend to do so through this witness," said MacArdle.

"Any reference to co-operation will be struck from the record," said Sellers. "Proceed, Major."

"Think carefully, Corporal. Did you notice anything different in Captain Scott's conduct after you reached the prison camp?"

"He was running the camp hospital."

"Was there anything unusual in that?"

"Well, they had Chinese doctors there before."

"Were you ever admitted as a patient?"

"Yes, sir."

"How would you describe Captain Scott's position at the time?"

"He was head man; they all did what he said."

"You would say, then, that he was co-operating with the enemy?"

"I would, sir."

"Did other prisoners share your belief?"

"Everyone in my barracks called him a canary."

"Canary?"

"A progressive. Someone who's gone over to the Commie side."

"No further questions."

There was an edge to Hi Saunders' voice when he rose to cross-examine. "Corporal, what were your duties on Hill 1049?"

"I was a first-aid technician." The deference had gone
from Jackson's manner; it was evident that he resented the
presence of a civilian lawyer. Remembering the months
they had shared in the lines (when Hi had also been in
uniform) and how friendly the lawyer had been with the
members of his surgical team, Paul wondered if Jackson
had put that camaraderie from his thoughts deliberately.

"Did you assist Captain Scott with operations?"

"Yes, sir."

You did indeed, thought Paul; not too long ago, you
helped to save your questioner's life on Hill 1049. A great
sense of frustration claimed him as Jackson's surly voice
went on. Already the monstrous blackening of his past was
underway. Could he keep his mask of unconcern unbroken
while the lie took shape and depth until it was a living
thing?

Paul felt his eyelids droop as a familiar alembic began
to function in his brain; it was a trick of disassociation that
had saved his sanity in Korea, and it seemed only fair to
use it now. In another moment the drone of the corporal's
testimony had grown fainter, along with Hi's sharp efforts
to break down his veracity. . . . There would be time
enough later to measure the success of those efforts. For
the present it was simpler to let his mind go back—to the
very scene that Harry Jackson was distorting so fatally.

Hill 1049 had been the place where his faith in his fellows had had its first real testing. It was worth a visit in
memory—now that Major MacArdle's trap had begun to
close about him. The prosecutor need never know that his
victim (thanks to that knack of immersion in the past)
could escape the trap at will.

Hill 1049

THE CREST of Hill 1049 dominated the long funnel of the valley below it. For this reason a series of observation posts had been scooped in its spine the last time it had changed hands. After the United Nations lines had been pushed down the northern slope the posts had been largely abandoned by the lookouts, who could now spy out enemy maneuvers at closer range. This afternoon the lone observer who squatted in one of these two-man foxholes was lost in his own musings—though he was alert enough to keep his head down. The crest of Hill 1049 was still within sniper range. Not ten minutes ago (when Captain Paul Scott had scrambled in from the far side of the ridge) a bullet had whined across the sandbags.

It had become Paul's custom to watch the sunset from this vantage point, whenever his presence was not required at the aid station. The communion with death that he shared down below was a burden no man could discard for long—a surgeon least of all. For that reason he had begun to prize these rare moments of solitude—and today, after all, was a milestone of sorts. Just six months ago (he could almost name the hour) the 141st Battalion had first set foot in Korea. In that interval, he felt, he had earned these brief retirements from his job.

Six months to the day, he added, with a trace of bitter pride. Add three weeks for the crossing and yet another month for final indoctrination in Japan: it's more than half

a year since Kay Storey waved good-by to you from a pier
in San Pedro.

ii

His fingers touched the packet of air-mail envelopes in
the upper pocket of his shirt; he always reread Kay's letters
at this hour, though he could have recited their contents
verbatim. Going through them one more time, he felt the
familiar tug at his heart; the need for her living presence
was as real as it had been on the deck of the *Millard
Fillmore*—and the chances of reunion seemed remote as
ever.

The troupe for which Kay had qualified (thanks to one
of the last-minute switches so dear to the Army) had not
sailed after all. Instead, it had gone on a nationwide tour
to boost morale in the cantonments. Paul's letters (which
he had somehow managed to keep cheerful) had followed
Kay all over the United States; they had been answered
promptly from such unlikely addresses as Key West and
Pocatello and Seattle. His last, however, mailed a good six
weeks ago, was still unanswered. So far, he could not even
assure himself that this was a hopeful sign and that she
had really embarked at last. . . .

There had been no word of love in their correspondence,
no sentiment beyond a playful tenderness; by unspoken
agreement they had both avoided serious topics. After all
—and he had reasoned this out a hundred times—he had
no right to assume that his desire, which had grown so
steadily in their long separation, would find an answering
chord in Kay. A night of shared rapture (he reminded
himself wryly of this obvious fact) is a common thing in
wartime. In granting him that boon, Kay had remained
herself: perhaps, in her mind, it had been only a patriotic
duty. Certainly it did not prove that she had felt more than
a friendly interest in him.

He put the chilling possibility aside and looked through the observer's slit at the scarred landscape below. As always, he was stirred by the sinister beauty of this mountain terrain. It was a beauty that transcended such manmade artifacts as bunkers, gun mounts, slit trenches, the black slashes on a northern hill where aircraft had loosed napalm fires at low-level range. Even there, new grass had already begun to clothe the ravaged earth. . . . Perhaps it was a fact that the truce talks (begun a few weeks ago, after the war had ground into a second year of stalemate) would bring results. At least it was comforting to note that nature was already working to erase the thumbprints of Mars.

So far, Paul told himself, you've kept your head and survived. You've earned a captain's bars and a firm place as battalion surgeon. Never mind what that promotion's worth in a foxhole—or the psychotic ragings of Colonel Jasper Hardin. The C.O.'s enmity is a thing you've learned to take in stride. . . . His nerve ends sprang alive as a pebble rolled into the observation post—and eased again when he saw that it was one of his technicians. The friendly horse-face of Corporal Harry Jackson restored Paul to the problems of the everyday. Thanks to willing helpers such as Jackson, most of those problems had solved themselves.

"Litter case comin' in, sir. Figured I should warn you."

"This is too fine a day for casualties, Harry. Why couldn't you tell me they've declared a truce at Kaesong?"

"Cap'n, if there's a truce comin' up, this sector ain't been alerted. Or maybe the gooks across the way just can't read."

"The front's been quiet as a church since dawn."

"Easy Company don't think so. They just had a killed-in-action—guy stepped on a mine coming back from patrol. The fellow with him got some iron in his tail: they're sending him to us for repairs."

Paul jammed his helmet over his ears and lifted himself

carefully until his head was level with the sandbagged rim
of the post. Behind him, Jackson followed the move without orders: Jackson was a regular who had been in this
war from the beginning.

"No snipers when you came in, Harry?"

"Nary one, sir. Maybe they *can* read, after all." They
exchanged a grin when a bullet sang across the crest, near
enough to pull their heads down together, like puppets in
some Punch and Judy booth.

"Maybe they don't believe their own propaganda," said
Paul. He was glad that Jackson had come here to fetch
him when he might easily have sent a runner: he had always liked the corporal and felt that the liking was returned. Both Sergeant Furness (his senior NCO in the
medical detail) and Jackson had welcomed him from the
start. So, for that matter, had the other medics, the battalion aid men and the stretcher-bearers—mere boys, for the
most part, who risked their lives daily in his behalf. Perhaps it was because of this shared danger (and the will to
ignore it) that the aid station was a close-knit unit, a
striking contrast to the battalion it served.

He repeated the conviction solemnly while he crawled
out of the post in Jackson's wake and scrambled down the
ridge. Friendships such as these (when the stakes of the
game were life and death) could never be valued too
highly. Without them, he would have long since broken
under Hardin's goading.

iii

Well down the southern slope, protected by the walls of
a deep ravine, the aid station occupied a roomy bunker
the Chinese had dug there months before. Compared to the
usual station in the lines, Paul had found these quarters
almost luxurious. Even in the nightly barrages the surgical
bunker had never been shelled too heavily. This, obvi-

ously, was an ominous proof that the enemy intended to
bag Hill 1049 in his next push and wished to keep the
shelter intact for his own use. Meanwhile it permitted the
medics to catch up on sleep.

Two litter-bearers were approaching when Paul
dropped into the ravine. The casualty, a rawboned boy
still in his teens, was dozing comfortably under the morphine administered by the company aid man, and there
was a clean dressing over his wounds. At Paul's direction
the stretcher was placed on two empty oil drums outside
the bunker entrance. The boy's pulse, he noted, was strong
and his color good; the medical tag indicated that the
wound itself was scarcely a half-hour old.

One look at the injuries completed the clinical pattern:
Paul had treated scores of these cases during his long
months in the bunker. The mine boxes the Chinese used
were always hard to spot—but this soldier had been lucky.
Both thighs were badly chewed (there was no better way
to describe the gnawing cruelty of the wounds). Bits of
muscle hung from the jagged lacerations, showing that
part of that burst of scrap metal had buried itself beneath
the fascia. But this, after all, was only a minor mishap.
Given prompt surgery and a few weeks in a rest area,
Private Ewell Hansen would live to fight again.

"How'd he get off so lightly, Harry?"

"The other guy stepped on the box. They're scrapin' *him*
off the rock."

The boy's eyelids had flickered at the sound of voices:
he stared up at them sleepily from morphine-tight pupils.
"Is it bad, Doc?"

"You've some iron in your legs," said Paul. "It's nothing
serious, Hansen. You've bought a rest ticket at a bargain."

Sergeant Furness had already heaved up from the
bunker, like an outsize mole emerging from its burrow. The
chief technician, a tireless, grizzled veteran whose build
had always reminded Paul of a Japanese wrestler, carried

an extra blanket: his hands were surprisingly gentle as he swathed the casualty.

"We're ready when you are, Cap'n."

"Keep him warm, Tom," said Paul. "I'll see if we can get him back to MASH." The Mobile Army Surgical Hospital was ten miles to the rear, and chances of transport at this hour were slight. Still, it was an inflexible rule that a call must go through in such a situation.

"I've set up to operate here," said Furness.

"He must go back, if they'll take him."

"Cap'n, you're better than those jokers at Regiment."

Paul spoke for the benefit of the stretcher-bearers: this, too, was a routine that seldom varied. "As you were, Furness. The colonel doesn't approve of front-line surgery."

"If you ask me, sir, the colonel can——" The rest was lost when Furness popped back into his bunker. Paul closed his ears to the burst of profanity the walls could not quite muffle: during these months in the lines, Colonel Jasper Hardin had been cursed in many tongues.

Battalion headquarters was located well down the slope, in a steel-and-concrete bunker—another legacy from the Chinese, which Hardin had spared no pains to make even safer. Paul had always found the place a trifle grotesque after a tour of the lines, and the dress-parade manners that the C.O. insisted on there were, to him, just short of macabre. From the first day he had established himself in this heavily sandbagged retreat, Hardin had insisted that his officers report to him in person, no matter how small the request. The colonel himself rarely ventured outside. When the shelling began the steel door slammed—and orders were transmitted to the forward posts by telephone.

This afternoon the door was open wide, and a spruce sentry gave Paul a model present-arms as he moved into its shadow. (The soldiers on the far slope of this same hill might resemble sullen mud turtles—but Hardin's own quarters were always spotless.) The room where the colonel worked was at the far end of the bunker, a compact nest piled high with maps and heavy with field phones. Hardin did not look up when Paul came to attention before the desk. The corner of the comic book he had been reading still showed under the map he had pushed forward to conceal it: comic books (of the gorier sort) were the C.O.'s one relaxation besides the bottle. . . . Sniffing the lifeless air of the bunker, Paul concluded that Hardin was sober. After all, it had been a quiet day on Hill 1049.

"You may speak, Captain."

"Easy Company just sent in a casualty, sir. A land-mine burst."

"The fool got what he deserved. Every member of this battalion has gone through a course in mine detection."

"The man who stepped on this one was KIA," said Paul. "The boy they brought in was the innocent bystander."

"Will he live?"

"His wounds aren't dangerous if he undergoes surgery promptly. I'd like to call for an ambulance to take him to MASH."

"Request is denied, Captain. Our MSR is under fire again."

The main supply route to the rear, though it had been bombed sporadically, was usually navigable. The fact that it was now under steady fire was bad news indeed—the probable overture to an all-out attack on their position.

"May I order a 'copter, sir?"

"The word is *helicopter*, Captain. You're supposed to be an educated man. Don't speak like a juvenile delinquent in my presence."

Since he had been given no order to stand at ease, Paul's shoulders were still painfully braced, his arms rigid at his sides. Feeling his fingers curl, he kept his voice level. "Sorry, sir. Request permission to call helicopter evacuation unit."

"Permission granted, Captain. Dismissed."

Paul gave the colonel a model salute, which the other acknowledged with a flick of his hand: the about-face that took him from the C.O.'s presence would not have disgraced a West Pointer. The communications center was in the room behind Hardin's sanctum; in a few moments the enlisted operator had put through a call to regimental headquarters. The chief surgeon at the mobile hospital unit, a friend of long standing, informed Paul that all available helicopters were busy elsewhere.

"It sounds like a routine casualty. Can't you operate there?"

"Certainly, Major; I'd prefer it that way if he can be evacuated later."

"Go ahead, then. I'll send an egg beater to the hill tomorrow."

What Paul had said was no vain boast. As soon as the divisional surgeon had learned of his qualifications he had sent up enough special equipment to the battalion station to transform it into a small but highly efficient hospital. Somewhat to his surprise, Paul had learned that this was routine practice in the Korean War, when large groups of infantry were often cut off for days from communication with headquarters and unable to evacuate wounded. Because of this early and adequate surgery, fatalities on Hill 1049 had been held to a minimum.

He had never quite understood why Hardin should object so strongly to his using the battalion aid station as a hospital: perhaps it was involved with the dark suspicions that gnawed at the C.O.'s brain whenever he was forced to accept a deviation from standard operational procedure. Like all small-souled men, Hardin was a slavish follower of the book, and any threat to S.O.P. (those hallowed initials, Paul suspected, had been burned into his psyche at West Point) was a threat to his own shaky pride. Then too, it was a reminder that Paul took orders—as well as help—from higher authorities, particularly the regimental and division surgeons—and was therefore not always responsible to battalion headquarters for his actions.

In any event, Hardin had fought furiously to keep his chief medical officer from functioning as a surgeon. As he knocked for a second time on the C.O.'s door Paul knew that he was girding himself for the inevitable battle—and prayed that his badly frayed temper would not betray him.

This time there was an appreciable pause before the shouted permission to enter. The stale air of the bunker room held a tangible reek of whiskey now. Sunset (which brought the first gun flashes from the north) was usually the time of Hardin's first potation.

"You may speak, Captain."

"Efforts to evacuate the casualty have been negative, sir. All helicopters are absent on other missions."

"Hold him overnight, then. We can't ask for an ambulance with the MSR under fire."

"Waiting doesn't help wounds of this kind, sir. Bits of clothing are always driven in by the mine fragments. It's a prime spot for a gas-bacillus infection to develop." Paul had mentioned the threat deliberately, hoping that it would rouse an echo of Hardin's own experiences in World War II. Actually those vicious germs had been largely conquered in the present conflict, due largely to front-line surgery.

"Would you like to be a hero, Captain, and take out an ambulance yourself?"

"That won't be necessary, sir. The regimental surgeon has ordered me to operate here."

"Since when does Major Williams exercise command over troops? His is a staff function only."

"Part of his staff function, Colonel, is to be responsible for the medical welfare of the troops—just as mine is here."

"Your function is to obey my orders, Scott." Hardin was

really shouting now. "Do you understand that much, you conceited fool?"

"I understand, sir," said Paul quietly. "I'll make the notation on the man's medical tag. I hope that higher commands will realize why I did not carry out my duty."

It was a calculated risk, but the implied threat struck home. (Actually he had no intention of letting Private Hansen pass the night without surgery. If the official record had gone forward tomorrow with such a notation, his head would have rolled, rather than Hardin's.) When the C.O. did not answer at once Paul knew that he had won. This time, at least, Hardin had been shrewd enough to yield, though his reply was bellowed in a voice that shook the casements.

"Very well, Scott. Stick out your neck again if you must. D'you take full responsibility?"

"Of course, sir."

"Then operate—and be sure you know what you're doing. It's against all regulations to give surgical aid in the front lines."

"Not in this war, Colonel."

"Dismissed, damn it, *dismissed!* Get out of my sight!"

Another dress-parade salute and a precise about-face took Paul through the door: as ordeals went with Hardin, this one had been mild enough. As he turned to the incline leading to the outer world, the technician at the battalion switchboard gave him a wink of pure sympathy. There was no impertinence in the gesture: it was simply Sergeant Luppino's way of telling a friend that he, too, was bearing his burden as best he could.

Outside, an ominous purple light had invaded the sky; an alien burst of flame had just violated these dregs of sunset. The explosion that followed was strong enough to shake dust from the bunker roof.

"Concert's early tonight, sir," said the technician.

"You ought to sleep through it here, Angelo."

"After six months in these hills," said Luppino, "I could sleep anywhere. Wish I could say as much for the old man."

They exchanged another wordless look as they heard the unmistakable *wheet* of a cork from the colonel's sanctum. There was no other sound to advertise a human presence, save for the whisper of the chair leg that Hardin had just propped against the already locked door.

"You're a doctor, sir," said Luppino. "Tell me what a man does when he's scared—and still can't sleep?"

iv

On his return to the aid station, Paul was pleased to find Father Tim standing above Hansen's stretcher. A stole lay across the chaplain's shoulder and there was an open Bible in his hand—but Paul knew that the phrases pouring from his lips were recited from memory. The battalion surgeon had heard that prayer for the recovery of the wounded a hundred times and knew better than to interrupt. The few minutes that Father Tim needed to minister to Hansen would make no difference in his treatment—and he had profound respect for the balm that litany could bring to war-torn nerves.

When the priest had closed his Bible and folded the narrow stole inside the cover, Paul saw that the boy on the stretcher had quieted visibly: as always, he was grateful for this mysterious therapy, without attempting to diagnose its cause.

"You'll be all right now, Hansen," said Father Tim. "You may not realize it, but the surgeon who's operating on you tonight is the finest in the whole Eighth Army."

Paul stepped aside to give Sergeant Furness a path to the stretcher. "Thanks for the vote of confidence, Padre," he said. "Who told you we were operating?"

A faint smile lit Father Tim's tired countenance. "Colonel Hardin's voice carries when he's really roused. I won't

keep you from your work, Paul: we'll be meeting again
tonight before the concert's over."

"Seems they're tuning up now, Father," said Sergeant
Furness. The three men lifted their eyes to the brow of the
hill, where a series of garish orange flares continued to vio-
late the afterglow of the sunset. With each burst the earth
rumbled faintly, as though an unseen colossus were stamp-
ing in anger, far down the valley.

"Is the table ready, Tom?"

"Ready and waiting, Cap'n."

"Take him in, and get your anesthetic started. I'll be
with you in a moment."

Paul linked an arm with Father Tim's and walked the
priest down the ravine to the door of the officers' shelter.
It was a custom he followed whenever possible, for the
frail young padre's nerves were none too steady when these
bombardments opened. Yet unlike Hardin—who merely
burrowed for cover when danger threatened—Father Tim
seemed to risk exposure deliberately. On occasion Paul had
been forced to speak sharply, lest the chaplain stop a bullet
in his haste to reach a dying soldier's side. Had it been
feasible he would have insisted that he administer last rites
in the safety of the aid station.

"Get what rest you can, Padre," he said. "So far,
they're only feeling each other out."

Experience had told Paul that the present "concert" (as
Hill 1049 had dubbed the nighttime bombardments) was
only a prelude for another of those senseless head-on
charges that had proved nothing, so far, but the enemy's
disregard for his own man power. In a few moments more
the stepped-up tempo of the salvos confirmed his guess.
Far back in the American bastions the 240s and the 155
Long Toms were barking steadily: a symphony filled with
dissonants, counterpointed by individual bursts from M-1s
on the northern slope. . . . It was music from hell—and

although he had memorized every note in the infernal cadence, it could still rattle the teeth in his head.

And yet, when he had gone back to the aid station and finished scrubbing, Paul felt his panic slip away. On the flanks of Hill 1049 men might go on slaughtering each other until dawn. Here, at least, he was above the din. His job was clear-cut, and a life depended on his skill.

Hansen was on the table now; Furness had begun to inject the ampoule of sodium pentothal. Jackson, who would serve as Paul's assistant tonight, stood waiting at the instrument table. Doctor and medics had stripped to the waist: they would work thus through the summer night, when the artillery duel brought its harvest to their door.

"Ready to go to sleep for a while, soldier?"

"Sure thing, Doc. Reckon they'll evacuate me tomorrow?"

"Regimental HQ promised to take you out in the morning."

In a few seconds more the boy was snoring peacefully. Above the table the gasoline lamp hissed faintly, bathing the dugout in a white glare. Paul had dropped the blanket flap over the entrance when he came in, shutting the world of healing from the world of war. . . . The business of probing the wounds was a ticklish affair: he approached it carefully, with a hemostat in his free hand, wary for signs of hemorrhage. It was a tedious process as well, but a vital one. The smallest scrap of cloth, hidden in those gaping lacerations, could set up a focus for later infection that would mean untold trouble. Minutes spent now in removing such fragments might save months of hospitalization later.

Now and then the forceps grated loudly in the quiet of the bunker; the gleaming jaws lifted from the wound to drop splinters of steel into the basin that stood beside the table. Furness, the syringe of pentothal cradled in his palm, steadied the patient with easy competence. With each dart of the forceps, Jackson was ready with a swab, sponging away the bright ooze of blood that inundated the wound with each removal.

"That makes thirteen, Cap'n. This guy owes the Russkis something—hope our fellows pay it back."

Hansen moaned under the anesthesia, and the sergeant pressed gently on the plunger of the syringe: the injection, flooding the blood stream with its soothing contents, quieted the movement almost instantly. Once again Paul rejoiced in the easy magic of sodium pentothal: in cases like these he liked the patient to be carried as lightly as possible.

"'Bout through, sir?"

Paul glanced at Furness in mild astonishment. So intense was his concentration, he had been unaware of the passage of time. A whole half hour had slipped by unnoticed while he proceeded with his meticulous cleansing of the wounds.

"Almost. Retractor, please, Harry. We'll make a final exploration and call it a day."

Jackson slapped the metal strip into his palm and stood ready with fresh sponges. Enlarging each wound with care, Paul swabbed it from end to end and studied the exposed fascia minutely. There was no trace of cloth or metal: the last possible focus of infection now lay in the basin.

"I'll bandage him, Sergeant. You can let him out."

Furness eased the needle from the vein and stood by to assist in taping the long spiral bandage that Paul had begun to wind around the patient's leg. The activating dose of tetanus toxoid had already been injected: by tomorrow Hansen's resistance to the once-dread lockjaw would have risen to a point where he would be amply protected. When he had bandaged the other leg Paul injected a heavy dose of penicillin as an added precaution—and stood back while his two assistants transferred the boy to the far side of the bunker where a half dozen cots always stood ready.

Hansen's pulse was only a trifle faster than before the operation, but Paul decided to take no chances. A unit of plasma was opened at his order: so skilled were his technicians in this routine, it took only a moment before the dark brown liquid was flowing into a vein. Not even a base hospital, Paul reflected, could have provided more complete assurance of recovery. Yet the operation had been performed only a stone's toss from enemy trenches.

There had been no more casualties while they worked: the battalion had grown adept at taking cover during these nightly assaults. However, though losses would be held to a minimum, Paul knew that he could expect a dozen wounded before morning. At least he could use his own initiative at this time, with Hardin safely under cover. Frequently he had operated from dusk to dawn, here in the harsh glare of the gas lamp.

"Better chow up while you can, sir," said Jackson. "Me and Tom had ours early."

Paul nodded and turned to the door. As always, he felt a warm glow of satisfaction in the knowledge that his two medics (thanks to their months of teamwork) could solve most postoperative problems without him.

"Take a breather yourselves," he said. "You know where to find me."

This, too, was part of the nighttime ritual. On the step of the dugout he paused to slip into his shirt (there was no chance of an encounter with Hardin, but the precaution was automatic). Furness had already cut off the gas lamp above the operating table: with only a small oil lantern to illumine it, the bunker had a curiously homelike air. Paul put down the impulse to linger and forced himself to step over the sill. It was always a slight wrench to break free of this little world.

v

Outside, Paul found that the artillery duel had rumbled into silence, though heavier pieces still quarreled far down the valley. Evidently the attack on Hill 1049 had been a feint, to hide a thrust elsewhere. Only a few whispers broke the eerie silence while he groped toward the mess. It was hard to believe that the slope was thick with men, still waiting behind their guns to repel an advance that had already recoiled on the northern slope.

Hearing the chatter of static from the portable radio inside, he paused for an instant on the sill of the headquarters bunker. A wiry form, disengaging from the blackout curtain, spoke his name as he was about to move on.

"Evenin', Cap'n. Operation over?"

"Wrapped up for delivery in the morning," said Paul shortly. He had never liked Master Sergeant Bates, the chief figure in the camarilla that insulated Hardin from his battalion. There was nothing on which he could base his dislike, unless it was the man's carefully controlled impudence. Bates did his job efficiently. True, the battalion had a special (and unprintable) label for the Sergeant Major and his genius for currying favor with the colonel—but that, too, was only inevitable.

"Enjoy tonight's concert, sir?"

"I was too busy to listen."

"Didn't care for the selections myself," said Bates. "Not that they hit us too hard. It's another story on the MSR."

"Is that why the colonel is using the radio?"

"Phones went out an hour ago. The gooks are behind us, all right."

The surgeon shrugged off the news and moved on. In this queer war of thrust and counterthrust Hill 1049 had been isolated before: the main supply route had always been reopened in time, after determined regimental action. He could hear Hardin on the radiophone, bellowing for a

relief column. Even at the distance he could catch the
man's strident note of panic—and understood all too well
why Bates was standing guard. . . . Paul shrugged off
Colonel Jasper Hardin in turn. Bates had his uses after all.
At least the fears that churned in Hardin's brain would not
infect the men who stood guard beyond.

In the warm, Spam-flavored haven of the battalion mess
Paul felt his nerve ends unwind as a cook ladled stew
into his mess kit. "Better eat hearty, Captain. I hear we
might have fried gook for breakfast."

It was an old joke and a stale one, but he found that he
could laugh at it nonetheless. The chance that the hill
might be swept before morning had never disturbed this
stolen half hour of rest.

"Mine if I join you, Scott?"

Paul smiled up into the soot-blackened face of Major
Hilary Saunders—a liaison officer from the battery on the
next hill. Like himself, Saunders looked tired but happy as
he dropped into the place beside him: the face was slack
with fatigue, but the eyes in the coal-black mask were
sparkling with good humor. Save for the trench knife and
the .45 attached to the webbing of his belt, Hi could have
passed for an end man in a minstrel show, about to unburden himself of a sure-fire joke.

"What brings you here tonight, my friend?"

"Who but your C.O.? Ever since sundown he's been
shouting for artillery support. As a result I've been giving
an imitation of a blacksnake to get here. I can assure you
it's rough going in the country between your hill and mine.
Grenades all the way: some of those Chinese noncoms can
pitch like big-leaguers."

"Why come over in person?"

"Colonel Hardin insisted. Wanted a gunnery officer
whole on the hoof." Saunders glanced at the drowsy cooks
and lowered his voice. "How can you stand him on a round-
the-clock basis?"

"I sometimes wonder, Hi."

"The man's a psychotic. You can't deny that."

"I've known it from our first interview."

"Back home he might be bearable: discipline and the old Army routine could keep him in line. Out here he must be hell on wheels."

"I'm hoping he'll sweat it out."

"Sure he will—if he can dissolve his fear in booze. If he can hold this hill he may even emerge a hero. The fact remains he can't stay in that bunker forever." Hi Saunders yawned and rubbed the worst of the soot from his forehead. "Not if the enemy *really* means to smash our present line. Ever wonder what might happen if Hardin really blew his top?"

"I've tried not to dwell on it," said Paul.

"Funny, isn't it, how death gets to be a commonplace here? Most of us discover we can bear it—so long as *we* aren't the ones to die. Hardin is a different breed of cat. He would sacrifice the lot of you without turning a hair."

"What are you suggesting? A round robin, asking for his removal? You know how higher authority would react."

Saunders nodded soberly. "It's no picnic, watching the wheels of tradition turn and measuring the waste with a civilian's brain. The irony of it is, Hardin might have been a success if he'd been born the same year as Napoleon—"

"When wars were fought by the book?"

"Exactly—when a man could exist by the code, without thinking at all."

Paul found that he was chuckling at Hi's low, earnest whisper. He knew that he should stop this flow of words, that such relaxation bordered on mutiny. But it was a profound relief to hear an analysis that matched his own.

"The colonel himself has a standard lecture on that subject," he said. "From his viewpoint the trouble began after Pearl Harbor. World War II was the show that really fouled up the Army—putting a lot of civilians in officers' uniforms, with jobs they couldn't handle. Today even the dogfaces are given comforts the *old* Army couldn't spell—recreation centers, education, psychiatric help—"

It was Hi Saunders' turn to chuckle. "You were in the last big one, Paul. *All* old-school officers aren't like Hardin."

"Far from it. Call him the eternal throwback every profession is cursed with."

"In another minute you'll say he's more to be pitied than blamed."

"Oddly enough, I *do* think he's to be pitied."

"So does the chaplain," said Hi. "Of course, he has a perspective that's denied us."

"Father Tim would forgive Mao himself if he could get within hailing distance," said Paul.

Hi Saunders looked at him keenly. "Are you picking up his viewpoint?"

"Not quite. I'm in this business to get what I can out of it—particularly a whole skin." Anger had lifted Paul's voice: he broke off when he saw that Corporal Jackson had come into the mess for coffee. "Let's secure this patter," he said. "You aren't being paid to hear my gripes."

"You hear mine," said Hi. "So it's fifty-fifty. Speaking of angels, here's your chaplain now."

Father Tim, who had paused at the cook's counter for a word with Jackson, dropped into a seat beside them when the corporal left the mess. Watching Hi's offhand welcome, Paul could envy the artillery officer his aplomb. Harvard had helped, he reflected, as well as the silver spoon. Still and all, his friend had made his own life: a born lawyer, with a vast practice in Los Angeles, it was ironic that he should have been chosen for heavy-weapons duty in Korea —simply because he had served with the ordnance department in the last world war.

"You've arrived just in time, Chaplain," said Hi. "Paul is insisting that all men are brothers—including your C.O. I was about to enter a minority opinion."

Father Tim stirred his coffee. "Give me time to collect myself," he said.

Paul spoke as severely as he could; it was always hard to bear down too heavily on the padre. "Were you listening to the concert out of doors?"

"Yes, Paul. On the brow of the hill."

"I've warned you before to stay under cover until you're needed."

"If I'm in the open I can follow the stretcher-bearers."

"You could do as well if you'd stay in the first-aid bunker. The men will call you whenever you're needed."

Father Tim smiled. "If tonight's show had gone on another ten minutes I'd have scuttled for this burrow like a rabbit."

"Fear is man's oldest emotion, Father," said Hi. "There's no cause to feel ashamed if you yield to it."

"You and Paul have never yielded."

"Tonight we've nowhere to run," said Paul. "Or hadn't you heard that we're surrounded?"

The priest knotted his fingers. There was something touching in the fact that he made no effort to hide their trembling. "What's to become of us?"

"We'll hold the position—I hope. Tomorrow a regimental combat team will clear our supply route."

"I believe you, Paul, but I'm still afraid. I'm the one who comforts the dying and speaks of life after death. Yet I'm afraid of dying myself."

"Maybe it isn't *dying* you're afraid of, Padre," said Hi Saunders. "Could be your anger kicking back."

"I've long since put anger behind me, Major Saunders."

"Twentieth-century man has every reason to curse the history that's been forced upon him," said Paul. "Suppose we die here, with no chance whatever to write our names on the honor roll. Haven't you ever dreamed of being a cardinal someday? Or another Albert Schweitzer?"

"My only desire is to serve my fellow man, to outlive the

demands of self." The priest looked up at the step that had just sounded outside the dugout. Paul had guessed Sergeant Furness' errand before he could put in his head.

"Call from Able Company, sir. Infiltrator just knifed a sentry."

"Can they bring him in?"

"Afraid not. He's too badly hurt."

"I'll come at once," said Paul. "Sorry to end this metaphysical discussion, gentlemen, but duty calls. Did you bring my pack, Sergeant?"

"It's right outside, sir. I'll show you the way down."

"The company aid man will be with the casualty. I can go alone."

"Not with Fu Manchu on the loose: you'll need a pair of eyes looking backward."

"You're to stay in the aid station, Tom. We're sure to have other cases."

"But, Captain——"

"That's an order, Sergeant. Help me with the pack."

Absorbed in the business at hand, they had moved outside the dugout: Furness bent to lift the pack containing the equipment a surgeon would need for an emergency dressing in the field. It was a familiar summons if a risky one: Paul had ministered to dozens of wounded on the spot, when expert care was needed.

"Let me take the sergeant's place, Paul."

Looking into the chaplain's troubled eyes, Paul saw that they were blank with terror. "Thanks, Padre," he said. "I can find my way alone."

"The sentry may need a priest."

"Wait at the aid station: I'll bring him back."

"What if you can't move him? Besides, I *want* to go."

"In God's name, why?"

"Because I *am* here in God's name."

Their glances locked—and the padre's eyes won, for all

the panic that lurked in their depths. It was not the first
time Paul had yielded to similar pleas.

"Are you trying to prove I'm wrong, Father?"

"About forgetting self, Paul—or about dying?"

"Never mind. Just hang on to my pack strap and keep
your head down."

vi

They whispered the first password where headquarters
company guarded the approaches to the bunkers. From
that point a ditch snaked toward the lines on the lower
slope, a furrow so deep that it was possible to move downhill at a slight crouch, without exposure. Below, a foxhole-
pitted slope led in turn to the outposts: they traversed it at
a swift crabwise gait, repeating the password a dozen times
in response to whispers in the dark. Twice they froze to
the earth when illumination shells spouted up from the
enemy lines, bathing the slope in a greenish glare. On
each occasion there was a spatter of machine-gun fire from
the nests that commanded this terrain by daylight.

"Easy does it, Padre—we're almost there."

Paul had worked on the slope so often he could have
found every outpost blindfolded. Five minutes later, he
dropped into a rifle pit and exchanged the password one
more time. He had not yet dared to glance back at Father
Tim, who had labored in his wake, with a death grip on the
pack.

Together they bent over the wounded sentry, who lay on
his back in the pit. The company aid man (distinguishable
in the starlight because of his white brassard) lifted a
plasma bottle against the night and gave the surgeon room.

"Knife wound, sir—severe. Doesn't seem to gain—"

Paul felt for the man's pulse: as he had feared, it was
hard to time the rapid, fluttering beats. His flash lamp
showed the red crater of the knife wound. Blood bubbled

at the sentry's lips with each anguished breath, a sure sign
that the knife point had found a vessel inside the lung.
The miracle was that he had lived so long.

"*Mother of God—I want a priest!*"

"I am here, my son."

Paul moved to one side as the chaplain knelt beside the
dying boy. Father Tim was no longer the white-faced,
trembling misfit he had led down the hillside: in his stead
was a man of God, whose command was absolute. The
mortally wounded sentry felt the priest's power instantly,
and the sense of communion was transferred to his pulse
beat, which slowed even as it became stronger.

Hearing the chaplain's voice as he whispered the
prayers for the dying, Paul marveled anew at a phenome-
non that was almost unbelievable even as the proof was
translated by his finger ends. He was aware that the chaplain's effect on the dying man was purely psychological.
Deep in the victim's chest, the collapse of the soft, spongy
lung (caused by the pressure of air sucked in with each
breath) was slowing the hemorrhage; it was barely possible that the plasma dripping into the blood stream would
step up the circulation rate in time. . . . Unemotionally
the surgeon's part of his brain rejected the thought in advance: the puncture had been far too severe to justify such
wild hopes. Yet the sentry clung to life with all his senses
as the prayer continued.

In another moment the pulse had resumed its ominous
flutter: the hoarse gasp of the sentry's breathing slowed
and finally ceased. Paul disengaged the plasma needle
from the collapsed vein and rose to his feet. The company
aid man, packing his equipment with a few quick motions,
spoke in an angry whisper.

"Didn't have a chance—did he, sir?"

"Not a chance. The diagnosis for his tag is *wound, pene-
trating, thorax*. If we can we'll send him back for burial
in the morning."

"I'll stand by until his relief comes through," said the aid man. "Better watch yourself going back, Captain Scott. That infiltrator is still on the loose."

The exchange restored Paul's sense of proportion, which Father Tim's transfiguration had jolted badly. Concentrating on the business of reaching the hilltop alive, he gave little heed to the slight figure stumbling in his wake: he needed no second glance to tell him the priest, now that he had fulfilled his God-given function, was only a badly frightened man again.

"We're over the top, Padre. You can stand up again."

They were in the headquarters area once more, with the spine of the ridge behind them. Paul could see the battalion aid station clearly, and the silhouette of Sergeant Furness moving about some routine task within. At the same moment he was conscious of the newcomer approaching the dugout from another angle, via one of the many short gullies that led down from the ridge.

The man wore an American uniform: even by starlight he could see that much clearly. But there was no mistaking his unfamiliarity with the terrain or his hesitation as he drew abreast of the ravine that opened to the aid station. Perhaps he was a runner from another company, fumbling his way to the headquarters area for the first time—but Paul was taking no chances.

"You there—give the password."

The newcomer, marking their position by the muttered challenge, did not answer. Instead, arm and body described a sweeping arc; the object that cannoned toward them was a grenade, the kind that GIs called an ink bottle.

"Down, Father!"

Paul had spread-eagled to earth with his own warning, conscious that the priest had blundered a few steps nearer the ravine and that the grenade had already landed at his feet. Exploding in that area, it could kill them both instantly—to say nothing of guards from headquarters company whose shallow foxholes were within range.

Had he been a stride closer Paul would have caught the priest in a flying tackle, hoping to fall into the ravine, where the rocky outcrop offered cover of a sort. As things stood he was too far away to intercept Father Tim when he charged the lethal missile, like a shortstop fielding a slow-rolling grounder. Rizzuto in his prime could not have set up a double play more accurately. The padre's snatch at the grenade and the sweeping underhand pitch that sent it winging were part of the same fluent motion.

Paul was still on his feet with seconds to spare: his tackle sent the priest sprawling. Dropping at Father Tim's side, he was in time to see the North Korean (still in sharp silhouette against the stars) in the act of dodging to avoid the expected destruction below. The thud of the grenade striking the man's chest at the moment of detonation sounded clearly in the night, before the thunder of the explosion blotted out the world.

Fragments of metal screamed overhead, to send rock splinters flying; the shock of the concussion smashed Paul into the earth with giant fists. Deafened as he was by the blast, he scarcely heard the machine-gun bursts as a dozen nests enfiladed the hill in the belief that a sneak attack had been launched against the line.

"Fire one round illumination!" The voice seemed to rise from the earth at Paul's elbow. He saw now that he had plowed down the slope as he tackled Father Tim, so that they were sprawled at the doorframe of the communications shack.

The exploding shell, bathing the whole hill in its glare, gave convincing proof that the attack (a strictly one-man affair) was over before it began. Brief though the illumination was, it gave Paul a ghastly glimpse of the infiltrator. Lifted by the force of the blast, his body had been literally demolished. The pulpy-red remnant smeared against the outcrop at the crest resembled the pelt of some freshly skinned animal, plastered to a barn door by a not-too-skillful taxidermist.

Father Tim was unconscious: there was a dark bruise at his temple but no other sign of injury. Furness and Jackson (who had come out on the double) eased the priest onto a litter. In another moment they were safely within the bunker, where Paul could examine him thoroughly.

The chaplain's body showed no sign of a wound, but there was no mistaking the depth of his coma. Meeting the sergeant's eyes above the cot, Paul shook his head in silent disbelief. It was an astonishment that both Jackson and Furness echoed after he had told his story.

"Now that you mention it, Doc," said Jackson, "he *did* play shortstop at the seminary. A good glove man, he told me. But he could never hit in the clutch."

"He proved it tonight," said Paul.

"What's he got? Concussion?"

Paul shook his head. Concussion could destroy a man without leaving a mark on the victim—but he, too, had been close to the explosion and had escaped unharmed.

"Bed rest until morning may bring him out of it. I'll stand by until my trick is over."

Father Tim still slept as soundly as before when a bleary-eyed Furness stumbled in to relieve Paul. He sent the sergeant for coffee while he pondered the case—and asked himself if he might use a novel therapy to help his diagnosis. When Hi Saunders (who had passed the night in the officers' bunker) looked in to say good-by he ventured to bring his idea into the open.

"He'll get a bronze star for that throw," said Hi. "But you'll have to rouse him somehow before they pin it on."

"Has it occurred to you that he may not *want* to waken?"

"Psychic block, eh?"

"For a lawyer turned artilleryman," said Paul, "that's a

good snap diagnosis. Tell me, Hi, have you ever killed a man?"

"Dozens. Why?"

"How did it feel the first time?"

"Bad, Paul: the stuff nightmares are made of. Happened last year on the big push for the Yalu. I was leading a patrol and fresh as new paint. We must have overreached our mission, because I'm sure this fellow didn't think there was a Yank in miles. There he was at a crossroad, bigger than life and a perfect target. And yet, when I got him in my sights, I couldn't pull the trigger."

"A lot of men have had combat paralysis," said Paul. "Nothing could be more natural."

"Two seconds later he started shooting at *me*. I blew his head off then."

"Something of the sort happened to Father Tim, I'm sure. When that grenade came rolling down the slope he used a set of reflexes he'd buried years ago. I never saw a sharper fielding play. If that Chinaman had been wearing a baseball uniform he'd have been hit letter-high."

"Then Father Tim knows he's killed a man?"

"His instinct for self-preservation made him aim the toss. The discovery must have cut through his soul. The result is identical with your experience. Only you got your paralysis before you dropped your enemy. Father Tim got his afterwards."

"Are you a surgeon or a psychoanalyst?"

"Working this close to death, I'm a bit of both. Besides, I must get the padre on his feet before Hardin sleeps off his hangover. You know what he'd make of it if I gave Father Tim a rest ticket. Hardin hates his chaplain as much as he does his medical officer—for the same reasons."

"How *can* you start him ticking again?"

"He seems in good shape physically," said Paul. "My problem is to break through his mental trauma—if that's the proper term. I'm going to try a little experiment and keep my fingers crossed."

Five minutes after Hi Saunders had reluctantly taken his leave Paul reached for a tourniquet and the sodium pentothal. Mixing the yellowish solution with sterile water and drawing a light injection into a syringe, he pondered his chances. The technique (called narcosynthesis) had been used frequently in World War II with excellent results: even if it failed today it could not harm the priest.

Narcosynthesis, he reminded himself, was based on the fact that the conscious mind could not always be controlled by the will. In cases like Father Tim's its withdrawal from reality could be complete, often for an extended interval. In France Paul had seen soldiers rigid with paralysis on the eve of battle. Others had gone temporarily blind. Still others had dropped in their tracks, like zombies. . . . These men were not malingerers. Theirs was a profound wound of the mind as definitely as a bullet through the leg was a crippling wound of the body. Rest and quiet usually cured them in time. On occasion special drugs had been used to hasten the process—and one of the most effective of these was sodium pentothal.

Normally a small dose of this anesthetic put the conscious mind to sleep, relieving the brain from the psychic block it had established and permitting the deeper subconscious portion to reveal itself. Usually this release took the form of a monologue in which the patient poured out the problems that had brought on the attack. Often the victim himself was unaware of the cause of his paralysis —and the mere voicing of that cause was enough to free him of its spell.

Now as he injected the pentothal slowly into a vein Paul began to speak to the priest in an even voice. At first there was no response. Then, as the drug took hold, Father Tim opened his eyes and stared up at Paul with a smile of recognition. This, too, was part of the clinical picture: Paul had seen many patients go into stupors during which they seemed oblivious of externals. At a later date (when they chose, for reasons of their own, to become conscious), they could recall everything that had gone on around them.

"Why am I here, Paul?"

"A grenade exploded, Padre. The concussion knocked you out."

"A grenade? I remember now. It came rolling down the slope—"

"Fortunately you fielded it in time."

"*Fielded* it, you say?"

"Like Rizzuto making a play at second."

"*Like a play at second.* Yes, Paul; it's much clearer now."

"Why didn't you tell me you were once a star shortstop?"

"It was only softball—at the seminary. I haven't played in years."

"The fact remains, I never saw a finer underhand toss."

"Where did I throw the grenade? I can't quite remember—"

"You tossed it over the hill," said Paul quietly. He was careful not to mention the North Korean soldier. "It had just landed in the middle of headquarters company. A dozen men owe their lives to that play at second."

"I wish I could remember more. I *do* have a picture of scooping up a grenade. Then my mind blacks out."

Paul had continued to inject the drug slowly. He stopped now, lest it pile up in the padre's blood stream and bring genuine unconsciousness. So far, Father Tim was responding favorably.

"What sort of grenade was it, Paul?"

"An ink bottle, I think. It banged off at the crest of the hill. You were lucky you weren't hit."

"I remember that you pulled me down beside you." Father Tim had been staring at the bunker wall; now he turned his head and looked into Paul's eyes. "What's this you're giving me? Plasma?"

"You don't need plasma, Father. You weren't even scratched and you've slept the night through. This is sodium pentothal."

"Isn't that an anesthetic?"

"You've been unconscious ever since the grenade went off. I'm trying to find out why."

The priest closed his eyes and his slight body trembled. "If my memory won't function, I must have sinned grievously."

"I've said you saved a dozen men from death. That's hardly a sin."

"What *really* happened, Paul?"

He had hoped that Father Tim would answer that question of his own accord. But he could hardly hesitate now. "An infiltrator threw a grenade at us, Padre."

"A man in an American uniform. I remember. Did I— toss it back at him? *Like a play at second?*"

"Like a play at second. You put him out—for keeps."

The priest's face was drawn now, and there was hell in his eyes. "I *wanted* to hit him, Paul. It's a dreadful thought but it's true."

"What you did was pure instinct. He meant to kill us both, but you hit him first."

"You can take out the needle, Paul," said Father Tim quietly. "I'm all right now."

"Most facts can be faced, once they're put in words," said Paul, as he removed the needle and strapped a pad on the slender arm.

"Only yesterday I'd have said the confessional was my task, rather than yours." The priest managed a wan smile. "Still, it's good of you to take over my office."

"You mustn't blame yourself. Self-preservation is the first law of nature."

"*Thou shalt not kill* is a law of God."

"Which is older, Padre? Nature or God?"

"If my religion means anything it means that God is

the beginning. Hate may be older than love—but love must conquer if the world is to endure."

"I wish I could share that hope."

"You'll share it some day, Paul, I promise you. If you can't, then your chaplain has failed."

"Right now it's enough we're both alive. Can't you thank God for that?"

"First I must ask God to forgive me for killing another human creature."

"Doesn't the Bible say *For a man's blood shall a man's blood be shed?*"

"*Whoso sheddeth man's blood, by man shall his blood be shed,*" the priest corrected gently. "Perhaps that will be my atonement before this war is ended."

"You mustn't say such things, Padre. Remember, that's the Old Testament God we've been quoting."

"The *lex talionis*," said the chaplain with another smile. "For an unbeliever, you do know your Bible."

"Jesus taught another way, Padre. Wouldn't He forgive what you did last night?"

There was a long silence in the bunker: Father Tim had not ceased his trembling. "I can see the man so clearly now," he said at last. "His arms were spread wide: the grenade must have struck his chest. The explosion silhouetted him for a second—then there was nothing."

"You took an enemy's life to save your friends. How often must I tell you that?"

"A man of God can have no enemies, Paul. It was hate that made me throw back the grenade—that made me choose *him* for my target. I could have tossed it aside as easily."

"I've told you there was no time to think."

"That's just the point. Hate had taken over: when hate rules the mind it leaves no room for God."

"Have it your way, Padre," said Paul resignedly. "We'll still make sure you're awarded the bronze star."

"You mustn't, Paul. I couldn't accept it."

"Not even for heroism above the call of duty?"

"Soldiers have the right to be heroes, I suppose. And the right to kill when they're ordered to kill. *My* orders are to save souls, including my own. What I did last night was the most grievous of sins. I must pray for absolution before I can do my work again."

"Sleep on it, Padre. You'll feel differently when you awaken."

"I'll feel the same—now you've helped me to face the facts. Still, I *would* like to sleep awhile."

"You're going under now," said Paul soothingly. "That's another reason for the syringe."

"I wanted to record my confession. I suppose it can wait until I've rested."

"We're still cut off, Father. They can hardly bring another priest to the hill."

Father Tim smiled drowsily. "I don't need a *human* confessor, Paul. Surely you've seen me writing in the diary I keep in my duffel bag?"

Like his brother officers, Paul knew it was the chaplain's custom to make copious entries in a notebook with a special lock, which he kept hidden in his quarters: he had often wondered what the padre was writing there. Usually Father Tim made his entries at the day's end when he had time to himself. But he was not above writing in the diary at odd moments in a kind of frowning concentration that discouraged questions.

"I won't pretend I wasn't curious," Paul admitted.

"That diary is my confession book."

"*Confession* book?"

"It's a dispensation my bishop allows me when no priest is available; God can read what I write there, even with the covers closed. I try to put something down each day— when I have sinned or been found wanting. If anything happens, I'll be ready."

"Nothing will happen to you now, if you'll stay inside this bunker," said Paul. "At least I can rely on the pentothal to keep you quiet for a while."

"It's a true wonder drug, Paul. Thank you again for using it—and saving me from being a coward."

vii

> . . . in the first world war, I'm told, the address was "somewhere in France." For now, I've had to settle on "somewhere in Korea" to describe my present whereabouts—though it isn't half so romantic. (Or was it *you* who said that first, Paul? Bits and pieces of our talk keep coming back to me. They're a help in making you stay real.)
>
> Do I have to say I'm eager to see you again? And hoping against hope that you'll have some leave coming up, so you can watch our unit perform?
>
> I can't tell you where we'll be when you receive this. Only that we have come overseas at last—and that the show (after a fairly rugged start) has succeeded beyond all my dreams.
>
> Don't try to answer this until you've seen a special messenger I'm sending with the latest news. Again I can't mention dates or names. But he'll be with you in a few days' time—rely on that.
>
> How have you been making out with the promise you gave me? I've been making out right well with mine.

The letter had reached Hill 1049 ten days ago, and Paul had read it through a hundred times. He read it once more now, between chores in the aid station, by the light of the hissing gasoline lamp. Like Kay Storey's other letters, it was short and to the point—but this time he could feel her affection in every line, her solid belief that he would fulfill his promise.

With a little effort he could even put that promise into words. . . . It was quite true that he had done his job here with all his heart and soul. From what Larry Kirk had just told him, Kay had done hers too, even more brilliantly.

The visit of the famous television commentator to the front lines had not been entirely unheralded. Kirk had arrived only yesterday, preceded by a helicopter loaded with cameras and nervous public-relations officers who had taken over the headquarters bunker on orders from above. Kirk (spruce in brand-new suntans, with the green crescents of a war correspondent shining at each shoulder) had proved far more regular than his build-up had suggested. Within an hour Paul found that he was chatting with the journalist like an old friend.

Even Colonel Hardin (a far calmer C.O., now that the enemy had ceased punching at his sector for a while) had been on his best behavior. Kirk, as Paul now perceived, had the knack of penetration, of seeing beneath mud and resentments to the essentials. If he had slipped a bit on Hardin, it could be put down to the colonel's protective coloration—a defense in depth so massive that it was sometimes hard to decide where officer ended and man began. (Now that Kirk had flown out with his film and his notes, Paul could only hope that he himself had not spoken too freely.)

As for Kay Storey, the news Kirk brought was both amazing and heartening.

The show that had taken its brassy routines across the United States had been completely revamped after its first performance in Pusan. Now, with Kay as its focal point, it had perfected a special technique for making the audience part of the performance—with the accent on nostalgia. Kirk had been purposely indefinite on this point: he had informed Paul that it would only spoil his pleasure if he divulged the plot of *The Girl Next Door* in advance. Not that an hour of genuine home-grown entertainment, combining the best features of *commedia dell' arte* and an old-fashioned American picnic, could be said to have a plot. . . .

"Even up here we've heard of 'The Girl Next Door,'" Paul admitted.

"You should have," said the journalist. "She's the best thing to hit Seoul since the liberation."

"Why couldn't Kay write sooner?"

"I can answer that with a direct quote," said Kirk. "Miss Storey didn't want to build your hopes up in advance— if there was no chance of your getting leave."

"Couldn't they have billed her by name?"

"The fact they haven't is part of the show's charm. Headline entertainers give the boys one sort of lift. Kay Storey is each man's sweetheart when she sings—because she *is* anonymous." Kirk had broken off abruptly on that, with the all-American grin that had warmed millions of living rooms. "I won't say another word—except I wish someone was looking forward to seeing me as she is you."

"Apparently she's hit her stride at last," said Paul. "I couldn't be happier."

"You can say that twice," said Larry Kirk, and departed in a whirl of helicopter blades and glory two days before the enemy had begun to probe lazily at Hill 1049 again, with all the offhand assurance of a tiger teasing an exhausted mouse.

viii

The battalion surgeon had meant every word at the time. He meant them today as he folded the letter away and began to check the setup for an emergency call that had reached him from the next hill. Kay's summons still upset

him a little; he could put his confusion down to the ac-
cumulated fatigue of these months in the lines.

The fact that orders for a week's leave in Seoul had just
been cut at regimental headquarters—and the still more
amazing fact that Hardin had approved—seemed only appropriate nods from fate, now that Kay was in Korea. He
hardly minded the fact that her arrival in Seoul and his
long-overdue leave were strangely coincidental. Nor did
it matter if "The Girl Next Door," with Larry Kirk's help,
had expedited the orders in high places.

What really mattered at this moment was the fact that
his own desperate need might betray him. . . . For six long
months, he told himself, he had fulfilled her belief in him:
he had done his job on Hill 1049 and done it well. Thanks
to Father Tim (and friends like Hi Saunders), he had kept
his sanity, after a fashion. But the thing that had really
sustained him had been the memory of Kay Storey and the
hours they had shared in Hollywood. How could he be
sure that love and that brief encounter were synonyms in
Kay's dictionary?

Perhaps he could find the strength and the wisdom to
keep things in proportion when they met. To realize that
"The Girl Next Door" was not his special sweetheart—until she made the first move of her own accord. . . . He was
reaching for Kay's letter again to search for hidden mean-
ings, when he heard the litter-bearers in the ravine.

Paul was not too surprised when he saw that the man on
the stretcher was Major Hilary Saunders—Hi's group on
the next hill had been beating off a flanking thrust for the
past two days, and its casualty list had been heavy. What
disturbed him immediately was the artillery officer's chalk-
white face and the way his hands compressed his abdomen: he had observed these ominous portents far too
often.

"What happened, Sergeant?"

"Seems he stopped a tank with a bazooka," said Furness.

"A whole gook company was tailing it. Major took a ticket home before the M-1s could wipe 'em out."

Harry Jackson, who had hurried ahead of the litter-bearers, had already set up a plasma unit in the bunker: between them, the two medics transferred Hi to the operating table. A runner was waiting in the doorframe for Paul's report. He gave it quickly, knowing that Hardin would not dare object to front-line surgery on an emergency case: the C.O. had been almost co-operative since Larry Kirk's visit and the journalist's evident interest in Paul.

The morphine Saunders had received in the field had blunted his perceptions: when Paul sank a second needle in his arm, he stared up at the surgeon from a deep well of sedation, with eyes that barely took in his surroundings. Jackson had slashed away the uniform to permit an evaluation of the wound, an innocent red pucker just below the rib cage. Closer inspection revealed a somewhat larger wound of exit, lower down the right side.

"Think it missed the spleen, sir?" asked Furness. He had already begun to sponge the evident area of operation while Jackson swung the instrument table under the lights.

"Let's hope so; the exit was low enough to skip the liver too, if we're lucky." Paul had not paused to complete the clinical picture that was forming with such merciless clarity. Between those two vital organs lay the whole coiled length of the small intestine, with the U-shaped larger colon arching above it. Inevitably this area had been damaged as the bullet passed through, probably by multiple perforations. The boardlike rigidity of the abdominal wall could only come from irritation of the peritoneum when the contents of the intestine (acid, base, digestive juices, and, if the colon was injured, teeming malignant bacteria) were suddenly sprayed against it.

Part of the shock that had turned Hi's skin an ashen white was due to this grave insult to the sensitive peritoneal lining. But there must be internal hemorrhage too—

and this would continue until the injury was corrected. Nor
would the inflammation cease until the contamination was
sponged away and the perforations sutured.

"Will you do a laparotomy, Captain?"

"I'm afraid we'll have to, Sergeant."

"No chance of sending him back to MASH?"

Paul glanced at the emergency cots in the bunker annex
where a BAR man was snoring peacefully under a booster
shot of morphine. An hour ago they had saved his life
by tying off an artery in the groin. With the main supply
route closed, and the 'copters busy with even more urgent
evacuations, Paul had fallen into the habit of operating at
once on cases such as these. The fact that Hardin no longer
opposed such judgments was, of course, only a temporary
windfall, but he meant to reap its benefits tonight.

"Put through a call to division," he said. "They'll understand this case can't wait till morning."

While Furness relayed the message to another headquarters runner, Jackson started the pentothal; one of the aid
men, who had volunteered for emergencies of this sort,
came forward at Paul's nod to inject a double dose of
penicillin and set up a second plasma unit. Some of the
color had returned to Hi Saunders' cheeks by the time
Furness had painted the operative area with two layers of
bright red antiseptic and draped it with towels. Despite
the fact that the operation he was about to perform was
surgery whittled to its essentials, Paul saw with satisfaction
that the patient's response was encouraging.

"You can discontinue the pentothal, Harry," he said. "It's
time to start the ether: we want this one deep under."

"Ether coming up, sir."

Paul watched narrowly as Jackson placed the cone
above Major Saunders' face and began to drip in the pun-
gent liquid—and saw at once that the man's technique was
adequate. There would be no time later to correct the mistakes of a fumbling anesthetist. In a few moments Hi's

profound snore at the end of each respiration advertised a
depth of anesthesia sufficient to relax the muscles of the
pharynx, an absolute necessity in abdominal surgery.

"About right for now, sir?"

"Just about, Harry. We may need more when we get
inside."

Furness had drawn on a fresh set of gloves; now he
slapped a scalpel into Paul's hand and arranged several
forceps and a strand of catgut on a towel spread across
the patient's thighs. From chest to knees, Hi was blanketed
in sterile linen, with only the operative area exposed, a
rectangle of cherry red that glowed in the lamplight as
intensely as freshly spread lacquer.

"Ready, everyone?"

Three heads nodded in unison as the knife described a
lateral slash across the rectangle. "Since there can be perforations anywhere along the track of the bullet," said Paul,
"I'm making a transverse incision. I'll make it only large
enough to explore—and enlarge later as needed."

The knife cut deeper; as the skin parted, droplets of
blood appeared where the superficial vessels of the abdominal wall had been severed. Paul and Furness worked
rapidly, sponging the incision clean and tying off the open
mouths of the vessels with catgut after they had been
clamped. Then, using a second scalpel, the surgeon cut
through the tough whitish layer that surrounded the mid-
muscles of the abdomen and severed the red fibers themselves whenever they appeared in the depths of the
rapidly widening wound.

Here, as was to be expected, the bleeding was more
severe. In a few moments the incision was thick with
forceps. The muscle barrier had now been penetrated completely, and only the glistening membrane of the peritoneum showed in the nest of clamps.

"Step up the ether a little, Harry," said Paul. "I'll need
full relaxation before I go in."

When Saunders was completely relaxed under the anesthetic Paul tented the peritoneal membrane with a slender forcep and nicked it with a sharp tap of the knife. The sergeant held the forcep while Paul inserted a second clamp. Surgical scissors were used to slit the membrane, a precise technique that opened it for a distance only a little smaller than the dimensions of the wound itself— perhaps twelve inches in all. As Paul had expected, the incision was promptly inundated with a whitish fluid mixed with blood. It was an ominous advertisement of the damage he would find within the abdomen itself.

"Too bad we haven't a suction machine," he said. "Towel, please."

Three sterile towels were needed to sponge the incision clean. For the first time he dared to peer into the abdomen through the formidable window he had opened in its wall. The whole complex of the alimentary tract was clearly visible—the pinkish, tight-packed loops of the small intestine, the fanning mesentery which supplied blood vessels in this area, the descending curve of the colon itself. To the layman's eye these vital organs might have seemed undamaged; yet somewhere in that convoluted mass were perforations that could be Hi Saunders' death warrant.

Paul slipped a gloved hand into the abdomen, reaching under the left end of the transverse incision. "I can feel the wound of entry," he said. "It's clean and closed tight by muscle contraction. The spleen is undamaged and so is the kidney on this side. Hold him just as he is, Harry, while I check the colon."

The three-man operating team hung motionless above the table as the surgeon continued to explore organs he could feel but not see. "The left side of the colon appears uninjured," he said, letting some of his relief come through with the announcement. With this organ unpunctured, the task ahead was simpler.

"I'm now following the transverse colon, across and

down the right side. There is no injury there, nor in the right kidney." With each word he spoke he could feel Hi Saunders' life expectancy rise. "The bullet was too far forward to injure the spinal cord. I'll check the small intestine now."

This check was made by direct vision, starting at the lower end of the small bowel where it joined the massive dilatation of the colon called the cecum, with the appendix hanging from it like a small, forgotten finger. Paul's hands moved swiftly, lifting the intestine loop by loop, then dropping it into the abdominal cavity. Over six feet were stripped in this way before he found what he was seeking— a reddish nick that seemed superficial until he discovered the telltale pout of the inner lining.

"Perforation number one," he said. "Not large, but definite." A gauze pad soaked in water came into his hand; taking the loop gently between thumb and forefinger, he showed the sergeant how to hold it clear of the wound.

"Sutures, sir?"

"Not yet. We can't close this one until we see what else is damaged."

Another foot of intestine, delivered from the cavity with the same testing, revealed the first severe injury. Here the bowel had been cut entirely across—and there were five separate punctures just beyond. Paul covered this section with a moistened, sterile towel. A painstaking exploration of the remaining convolutions failed to reveal another injury.

"How's he bearing up, Harry?"

"Pulse is a hundred, Doctor," said the corporal. "He's breathing well."

"What about the plasma?" With his whole being concentrated on the ruptured organ, Paul did not even lift his head to examine the bottle above the table: until those ruptures had been mended they represented the boundaries of his world.

"On the last third of the second flask, sir."

"Good: he should continue to hold up. I'm going to re-sect this portion of the intestine: it's too badly damaged for separate repairs."

No one spoke around the table: there was nothing for the assistants to contribute. Since this was a command decision, the responsibility would rest on the surgeon alone.

"I'll need extra forceps, Sergeant," said Paul, as he took the length of damaged bowel from Furness' hands. "Just drop them on the towel with the sutures." He had already slit the fanlike mesentery; now he took a loop of catgut and pulled it through the opening. Several inches farther along he pushed the forcep through again—and, lifting one end of the catgut, placed a loop around that section of the mesentery. Tightly knotted, the catgut constricted the dangerous vessels in this area; across this captive portion he clamped a forcep on the side toward the intestine and cut cleanly, freeing the bowel completely from the tissue that nourished it.

With the extra forceps that Furness had placed within his reach it was a simple matter for Paul to repeat this maneuver; the section of intestine he intended to remove was now completely free and was easily lifted into the incision. Extra-large clamps were fastened firmly at each end of the damage area. Placed in pairs, they enabled him to cut between them, severing the intestine cleanly but retaining its contents. Several feet of injured bowel, still gleaming pinkly, and flaccid as a torpid snake, was lifted free of the wound and dropped in the basin beside the table.

Moving his fingers gently, Paul brought the two clamped ends together, so that they were resting side by side in the wound, like the two barrels of a shotgun with the muzzle down. A catgut-bearing needle came into his hand: the point bit firmly into the intestinal wall (first on one side, then on the other) in the area just behind the forceps. It was a delicate technique, but a vital one: working at the side away from the forceps, and holding the two severed sections firmly together, Paul continued the joining until the needle reached the twin forceps themselves.

Now, taking his time to make sure that he had fashioned the joining accurately, he turned the forceps completely in the wound, until the matched ends of the bowel projected upward. A few more stitches, and the resection began to take on a definite pattern: when the steel clamps were almost hidden he freed them gently. There remained only two more bites of the needle to cover the spot where they had disengaged their grip.

The suturing was now virtually complete: Paul permitted himself a shrug as he felt the admiration in Corporal Jackson's eyes. "It's a technique you learn early in surgery," he explained. "Actually, it's as simple as a housewife's darning. But I'll place another row of sutures, just to be sure."

The reserve stitches were quickly placed: two complete rows of sutures now encircled the junction point—one of them the absorbable catgut, the other black silk that would fix this area permanently. One minor manipulation remained, and it was pure pleasure to perform it. Using the gentlest of pressures, Paul pushed his finger through the opening—now completely concealed within the intestinal wall. As though it possessed a separate life, the bowel assumed its normal shape, as naturally as a toe might invert a sock.

ix

The operation had succeeded with that final probe of the surgeon's finger: Hi Saunders would survive, with luck on his side and the therapies of modern war to sustain him. The business of closing the incision was a tedious anti-

climax, but Paul took pleasure in every stitch: it was only
when he had stripped off his gloves that he realized how
tired he was—and how wonderfully relaxed. Hi would
pass a quiet night, he hoped, along with the bandaged
automatic-rifle man: they could both be delivered to the
collecting station tomorrow—and would probably sleep in
a Toyko hospital before the day's end. It was a heady triumph to take into the night.

On the dugout step he breathed deeply of the late-
summer air. For once, the night above Hill 1049 was silent:
the clean stars that studded the Korean sky were shining
brightly, unclouded by the smoke of the usual bombard-
ment. For an instant Paul paused above the headquarters
bunker and put down the impulse to report the operation
to Hardin: even in his present mood, it would not do to
press the C.O. too far. (In time, of course, there would be
a showdown with Hardin: this was not the moment.)

The sense of quiet gladness persisted—tinged but faintly
with panic—as he thought of his impending meeting with
Kay Storey. The achievement of tonight was definite, and
no tomorrow could spoil it. Hill 1049 had been a synonym
for hell in the months that he had labored there—but he
had worked hard at his chosen calling and he had found
a new dedication there. Come what may, he told himself,
you've earned a week's leave in Seoul.

The Presidio

THE SCREEN of memory faded, and he was back in the crowded courtroom in San Francisco—dimly conscious that the court had risen to vote on another question of law. Captain Paul Scott summoned a grin for his counsel —and admitted privately that the experience had been a refreshing one. At least he had been spared the preliminaries.

"How's it going, Hi?"

The defense lawyer returned the grin. "I saw you woolgathering, pal. Can't say that I blame you. To the lay mind, it's been damned dull so far."

"I wasn't exactly woolgathering," said Paul. "It's a trick you learn in Communist prison camps. You might call it shutting off the present—when the present begins to drive you nuts."

"You haven't missed a great deal. So far, MacArdle and I have been rolling with each others' punches. I got Jackson to admit that he and Sergeant Major Bates were cronies in prison—and that he joined Hardin's group because the food was better. He still insisted the real reason for the switch was because you operated on the camp commander. So does Bates, of course—"

Paul glanced at the master sergeant, lolling at ease in the witness chair while he awaited the return of the court. Bates returned his stare with heavy-lidded insolence; the surgeon was glad indeed that he had missed the first part of that born conniver's testimony.

"I gather you made no headway there?"

Hi shook his head. "MacArdle has rehearsed him like a straight man in a Broadway play."

"When will they introduce the confession?"

"My guess is that Hardin himself will read it from the stand. MacArdle knows I'll keep it off the record as long as I can. He's too smart to muff *that* big scene."

"Why let Hardin read it?"

"The colonel brought it out of Korea, remember? It's his big stick: obviously, he plans to use it for your *coup de grâce*."

"What about Kay? Will they try to drag her in?"

Again Hi shook his head. "Not MacArdle—things are going the way he wants them so far, except for a few tricks I've pulled on the witnesses to show a selfish motive in the food. If I leave it to *him*, he'll hardly mention her— except as a prisoner who shared your captivity."

"And Father Tim?"

"They've dodged him too, pretty successfully. So far as the court knows, they both went along for the ride because they couldn't help themselves. The fact that they were also your friends has gone unmentioned."

"Isn't it time you brought it out, Hi?"

"I'm saving that element for the afternoon session," said the lawyer calmly. "Mac will probably put Hardin on the stand after lunch as the final witness for the prosecution. Don't bite my head off, Paul—but I've got to open our own case with Kay."

"You said we could keep her out."

"Only because you wanted her out. Now that I've seen MacArdle in action I'm afraid she's essential."

Paul stirred uneasily. He had foreseen this change of front on Hi's part and, since he had given the defense lawyer a free hand on strategy, he knew he was powerless to combat it. "MacArdle will only crucify her," he said quickly.

"She won't mind if it'll help our case," said Hi. "Don't be such an exclusive martyr."

"How can she help?"

"By getting to the root of this court-martial. By telling the court that Hardin's persecution of you goes back to his cowardice on Hill 1049 and even further."

"Can't you bring that out another way?"

"Maybe you *should* have listened," said Hi. "All morning long I've tried to break that very barrier. It's been a struggle even to get Hill 1049 on the court record: MacArdle keeps insisting you're being tried for what happened *after* your group was captured there." He stared unhappily at the seven empty seats on the bench. "That's why they've recessed now—to decide how far they'll limit my questioning."

"Surely I can go into Hardin's past when I testify?"

"To a point, if we move fast. I can't let you go too far: we mustn't seem to be matching your word against his. That's another reason we need Kay up there. *She* can speak her mind. With luck we can even make them listen."

"Can't you forget Kay?"

"I'll forget her for now," said Hi cheerfully, "but I'm calling her this afternoon. On your feet, boy—here come Sellers and company. And I can read their ruling in advance."

ii

Hi's prediction was confirmed: in a tone that seemed even frostier than usual, Colonel Sellers announced that the last objection of trial counsel had been sustained by a vote of the court. Henceforth, Hi was instructed to confine his questions to matters pertaining directly to the charges and specifications. On this note he resumed his cross-examination of Master Sergeant Bates.

"Before the court retired, Sergeant, we were discussing your arrival as a prisoner of war at Pyongyang. When was

Colonel Hardin appointed commander of prisoners in the compound?"

"Straight off, sir. He was senior officer."

"And when was Captain Scott put in charge of the prison hospital?"

"Maybe two or three weeks later. It was a few days after he joined us."

"Then he did not travel with Colonel Hardin's group?"

"No, sir. We were captured separately. The two groups came together for just one night—at Sinmak. Next morning, the Chinese gave the colonel truck transport."

"Captain Scott did not ride in the truck?"

"There wasn't room."

"So he was forced to march from Sinmak to Pyongyang?"

"So I'm told."

"Who marched with him?"

"Three people from his group. I think they were Miss Storey, Sergeant Furness, and Corporal Jackson. And one from ours—Lieutenant Crosby."

"Will you identify Lieutenant Crosby for the court?"

"He was a recent replacement on Colonel Hardin's staff. We'd been under heavy pressure on Hill 1049 and lost several of our officer personnel. Lieutenant Crosby was second in command when we made our withdrawal."

Paul, studying Bates narrowly, marveled at the precision of the man's coaching. Though he had described Crosby accurately, he had naturally failed to mention that the lieutenant had been in command on Hill 1049 for almost twenty-four hours before the mad scramble that he had called a withdrawal—or that Hardin himself, for most of that interval, had been too drunk to stand. . . .

Hi had taken the witness quietly, so far—permitting his description of Crosby to register with the court before he attacked from a new angle. "Isn't it unusual for a staff officer to be parted from his C.O., even when they're prisoners of war?"

"Not in this case, sir."

"Say what you mean, Sergeant. You must know that Lieutenant Crosby gave up his place at Sinmak so that Chaplain O'Fallon could ride in the truck?"

"I believe he did, sir."

"Because the chaplain was ill?"

"That may have been the reason."

"After Colonel Hardin had refused to make room for him?"

MacArdle, sensing the trap, was on his feet now. "If it please the court—what is the purpose of this random questioning?"

"Charges and specifications make much of an alleged confession which Captain Scott signed at Pyongyang," said Hi. "Defense will establish the fact that he signed this document for just one reason—to obtain the release of both Miss Storey and Chaplain O'Fallon from solitary confinement, where they were in grave danger of death. Surely it is germane to prove that Father O'Fallon's health was already failing on the prisoners' march to Sinmak."

"Trial counsel's objection is overruled," said Sellers.

"Now, Sergeant," said Hi, in a tone that was deceptively mild, "isn't it true that Captain Scott had already requested a place on the truck for the chaplain, because of his illness?"

"I believe he did, sir."

"And did not Colonel Hardin refuse the request?"

"The colonel was riled that morning at Sinmak. Dr. Scott had taken the best billets; he'd made the colonel sleep in the barnyard—"

"He relented, then, only because Lieutenant Crosby gave up his place to the chaplain?"

"That is correct, sir."

"Do you know where Lieutenant Crosby is today?"

"He died a few weeks later at Pyongyang. In the meningitis epidemic."

"The same epidemic that Dr. Scott treated?"

"Yes, sir. The lieutenant was one of the first to go."

"But the epidemic was checked?"

"It was in time."

"Because Captain Scott administered a drug, sulfadiazine, to everyone in camp. Didn't you take a dose of that drug yourself?"

Bates' voice rose a trifle: he spoke rapidly, as though to forestall interruption. "Colonel Pak had put the doc in charge. He was dosing everyone—gooks and prisoners both. We had to follow orders."

"What were the sanitary conditions in the camp, Sergeant, when you arrived with Colonel Hardin's group?"

"Bad, sir."

"You have said that Colonel Hardin was put in immediate charge of all prisoner discipline. Did he take steps to improve these conditions?"

"Objection!" said MacArdle. "Colonel Hardin is not on trial."

Hi faced the court. "Defense considers it vital to show that Captain Scott, and none other, was responsible for the good health record of this prison camp. His forthright action in controlling epidemics and improving sanitary conditions—"

MacArdle was shouting now. "If the court please!"

"*Quiet!*" Sellers had barely raised his voice, but the murmurs among the spectators died out, along with the contending voices of counsel. "Objection overruled, subject to review by any member of the court. You may answer the question, Sergeant."

Bates swallowed hard but kept his composure. "There was nothing the colonel could do. It wasn't his line."

"But there *was* an improvement in the health of the prisoners after Captain Scott arrived."

"I believe so."

"Wasn't there a marked improvement—with a lowered sickness and death rate?"

"For a while. Things got worse later."

"Because the captured medical supplies were exhausted. Isn't that correct?"

"I believe that was the case."

"Then United Nations prisoners did benefit from Captain Scott's medical skill, regardless of whether he received preferential treatment at the camp hospital?"

"I think you could say that."

"Thank you, Sergeant. Speaking of preferential treatment, you have already testified that Captain Scott received favors from the Chinese commander, Colonel Pak. Just where was the captain quartered?"

"I'm not sure, sir."

"You were Colonel Hardin's assistant. Didn't your duties include constant camp inspections?"

"Of course, sir."

"Then you must know that Captain Scott slept in Barracks Four with the other prisoners and had his meals there."

"So it seemed."

"*Seemed,* Sergeant Bates?"

"Everyone said he got extra food at the hospital and took long rests there."

"But you've no personal knowledge that he did?"

"No, sir. How could I?"

"Let us move on to the moment when the camp was evacuated after the armistice. Did you hear Captain Scott state that he did not wish repatriation?"

"No, sir."

"Isn't it true that your only knowledge of his wishes is based on Colonel Hardin's report?"

"That's correct, sir." Bates was still intact under pressure: he seemed the picture of innocence, buffeted by waves of protocol beyond his ken.

"Didn't you know that Chaplain O'Fallon was gravely ill at the time?"

"I'd heard he was sick."

"Wasn't he in the last extremity? And was that not Captain Scott's true reason for remaining in Pyongyang?"

"I can't say I thought of it that way, sir. Speaking for myself, I was too anxious to get home again. So was every Joe in the compound."

"That is all."

MacArdle rose for his rebuttal. "Did you have personal knowledge of the chaplain's illness, Sergeant?"

"No, sir."

"Not even when Captain Scott refused to be repatriated?"

Hi objected vigorously. "Nothing in the testimony had proved a refusal."

"I'll rephrase the question," said MacArdle, with a side glance at the court. "You have testified that you saw a report made by Colonel Hardin in which Captain Scott declined repatriation?"

"Yes, sir. It was part of my duty to file those reports."

"Does the file exist today?"

"It may. Colonel Pak confiscated it when we were sent to Panmunjom."

"Do you recall the notation?"

"Not exactly. It said something like 'Captain Scott refused repatriation in my presence, and in the presence of Colonel Pak. Reasons undisclosed.'"

"Did Colonel Hardin comment on this at the time?"

"He did, sir. He said, 'I hope that son-of-a-bitch never goes home, except to face a court-martial.'"

"No more questions."

iii

A perfect witness to the end, Master Sergeant Bates walked out on a ripple of amusement from the spectators. There was something in that undercurrent that ran like ice water down Paul's spine. Nor did it help when Sellers made no immediate move to restore order.

"I'm sure no such report existed," he whispered to Hi. "Why didn't you challenge it?"

"It's too early to start calling Hardin a liar," said the lawyer. "Wait till he's on the stand himself. We've planted a reasonable doubt. As of now, we can hardly hope for more."

"Still think I've a chance, Hi?"

The lawyer took the question in stride. "An outside chance—when I bring in Kay. Already we're proving this isn't the open-and-shut case the papers are calling it. One good rooter for your side could make all the difference."

"Are you sure that Kay would be such a witness?"

"If we move fast, she can brand Hardin as a drunken poltroon. She can surely tell the court why you signed that phony confession, and make it stick. All *we* can do between us is make you look too self-sacrificing to be true."

"MacArdle will ruin her chances for a picture career. You must see that."

"Kay's quite a girl, pal. I don't think she'll mind ruin in the slightest if it saves our case." Hi gave a wry grimace as Sergeant Furness marched toward the witness chair. "Maybe you're *both* too good to be true. I've suspected it for some time."

Sergeant Furness took the stand with only a stony stare for Paul. (Like the other witnesses, it was obvious that his indoctrination had been complete.) Under MacArdle's guidance he repeated most of Bates' story. Unlike Bates, Paul could see that his belief in each statement was absolute.

"While you were a prisoner, Sergeant," said MacArdle, "were you closely associated with Captain Scott?"

"I was a member of his medical team."

"For how long?"

"Over a year. Until I asked the C.O. to reassign me."

"Why did you make that request?"

"It was after Captain Scott operated on Colonel Pak."

"What was the nature of the operation?"

"Closure of a perforated ulcer."

"Was the operation a success?"

"It was."

"What were your feelings after Colonel Pak recovered?"

"I thought he deserved to die. I couldn't take it—standing by and watching Captain Scott keep him alive."

"So you went to Sergeant Bates and asked for a transfer."

"That's it, sir."

"No more questions."

Hi Saunders rose. "About that transfer, Sergeant. You say you couldn't take the fact that the commandant recovered. Did you mention your unhappiness to Captain Scott?"

"No, I didn't. We'd stopped speaking."

"Did the captain ever treat you badly?"

"No, sir. We were good friends before—"

"Before what?"

"Before he started handling gook patients like they were *human!*"

Hi shrugged off the outburst. "Did it occur to you that you were making his job much harder by leaving?"

"I couldn't go on helping *them*."

"Was that your only reason, Sergeant? Corporal Jackson has already said that he was tempted by the better food served in Colonel Hardin's quarters. Did you yield to a similar temptation?"

"Maybe I did eat better afterward. That wasn't the reason at the time."

"Did Sergeant Bates suggest that you request the transfer? Or was it your own idea?"

For the first time Furness looked uncomfortable. "It was his idea too—in a way."

"Cast your mind back, Sergeant. At the time of your transfer how many prisoners from Hill 1049 were alive in the Pyongyang compound?"

"Well, there was the colonel and Sergeant Bates. Corporal Jackson and myself. And a Sergeant Luppino, on the C.O.'s staff: he died early in '53, as I remember."

"That was the colonel's group, I take it. Can you name the others?"

Furness looked faintly aggrieved. "Of course. There were three others—the chaplain, Miss Storey, and Captain Scott."

"The chaplain and Miss Storey were in solitary confinement when you transferred, weren't they?"

"Yes, sir."

"In other words, Captain Scott had two sure friends at the time—both of whom were expected to die—and four against him?"

For once MacArdle was caught napping. His objection when it came, was stentorian. "Counsel had no right to use the word *against*."

"Surely it describes the situation."

Colonel Sellers leaned forward from the bench. "I must warn defense counsel against making reckless allegations."

"If my allegations are reckless," said Hi, "the court has my apology. The fact remains that the witnesses for the prosecution are Colonel Hardin, Sergeants Bates and Furness, and Corporal Jackson. At the moment the only witness for the defense is Captain Scott himself."

"The court will retire to vote on the propriety of your last question, Mr. Saunders."

Hi settled at the defense table while the seven uniformed backs vanished through the door. "I think we've shaken

them a bit," he said. "Not that we've established collusion
—but they do realize that Hardin has snake-charmed your
technicians. Which means *everyone* who could help you—
except Kay. You must see why I'll have to use her."

Paul covered his eyes for a moment. "You're a good lawyer, Hi," he said. "I wish you wouldn't play psychiatrist
too."

"Every good lawyer's a bit of a head-shrinker," said Hi.
"What are you trying to prove here, after all? That all men
are brothers, regardless of who's shooting who?"

"You might call it that."

"Then why are *you* alone in court?"

Paul let his hand fall: with the gesture, he knew that he
had yielded. Despite his fears for Kay, he could not keep
down a surge of gratitude. Hi was right, of course: no man
(not even Father Tim) could fight the whole world singlehanded.

"Have it your way," he said. "Just spare her all you can."

iv

Hi Saunders had studied Paul narrowly while he spoke.
Now he was both startled and pleased at his friend's ca-
pitulation. *At least it's something to know you're lonely,* he
told Paul silently. *Lonely and frightened enough to forget
that martyr's mask. Human enough to be less than perfect,
when the chips are down.*

When he had agreed to take the case Hi had seen clearly
that Paul's chances were slim indeed, so long as he continued to stand alone against the juggernaut of the Army's
legal code. If he had seemed to agree, at first, to the exclusion of Kay, it was only because he had sensed that Paul
would yield in time. . . . Ever since it had come by messenger that morning, Kay's note had burned his pocket.
For an instant he considered showing it to Paul, but restrained the impulse. A mystic is always difficult, he told

himself soberly. When he's fresh from the hell of a Chinese prison camp, he needs kid-glove treatment.

Hi got briskly to his feet as the court returned. Clearly that was not the moment to inform Paul that the girl he loved was waiting to see him at this very moment. Or that her eagerness to testify in this trial was no less intense than Hi's need of that testimony. . . .

As he had expected, Sellers upheld the objection of trial counsel and his last question was stricken from the record.

"Let us return to Colonel Pak, Sergeant," he said. "Do you think Captain Scott should have refused to operate?"

"I can't blame him for operating," said Furness. "They'd have shot him if he hadn't. He could still have let something happen."

"D'you realize what you are saying, Sergeant?"

"It's what they said all over camp."

"That Captain Scott should have used his surgical training to commit murder?"

"We didn't call it that."

"What did you call it?"

Furness did not budge. "We figured gooks like Pak were better off dead."

"I believe you gave the anesthetic at the operation. If anyone could have caused Colonel Pak's death and gotten away with it, weren't you the one?"

"I couldn't do it. Captain Scott was too smart to let me."

"But you expected *him* to kill a patient on the table?"

"We all expected it."

"Sergeant, are you familiar with the Hippocratic oath?"

"I know most of it."

"Can you say, from your own personal knowledge, that Captain Scott has ever broken that oath?"

"No, sir, he hasn't."

"Thank you, Sergeant. I have only two more questions. Did you see Miss Storey and Chaplain O'Fallon when they were brought from solitary confinement?"

"I did, sir."

"What was your opinion of their condition?"

"They both seemed to be dying."

"That is all."

Hi smiled inwardly as he watched MacArdle charge up for rebuttal. The violence of the trial counsel's attack told him that he had scored this time.

"Sergeant, from what medical school did you graduate?"

"None, sir. I'm just an MC technician. You have my service record."

"Never mind your service record. By what authority do you give a medical diagnosis?"

"Objection," said Hi. "The witness *thought* the two prisoners were dying. He gave no diagnosis—nor was he asked to do so."

From the bench, Sellers upheld the objection with asperity. MacArdle resumed, with a stain of red at each jowl.

"Sergeant, do you consider yourself competent to make a diagnosis?"

"Objection," said Hi. "Trial counsel is badgering his own witness."

Sellers leaned forward. His brows were knitted and he resembled an outraged eagle more than ever. Hi masked his elation when he observed that Major Duggan (the Korean veteran on the president's right) was frowning just as darkly.

"Trial counsel is warned against such outbursts."

But MacArdle had already recovered his poise. "Sergeant, could you decide, beyond a doubt, if a person were dying?"

"No, sir."

"No further questions."

"We are about to recess for lunch," said the president. "Does any member of this court wish to query the witness?"

Major Duggan thrust forward in his chair. "Sergeant, you and Corporal Jackson were the only members of your barracks who transferred to Colonel Hardin's quarters—is that correct?"

"Yes, sir."

"Then you can compare the food in both places. Was it better in the colonel's quarters?"

"Yes, sir."

"In quality or quantity?"

"In—both."

"I'll give you three choices, Sergeant. Was it simply better, much better, or very much better?"

There was a gleam of sweat on the sergeant's forehead, and he answered in a voice that was just above a whisper. "Very much better, sir."

"No further questions."

MacArdle, with a line between his brows, dismissed the witness at the president's nod. There was a great scraping of chairs as the court rose.

"Call that our inning, Paul," said Hi. "Not that it means the game, of course: the enemy's just warming up. But that major could be our entering wedge. *He* was captured too, four months before the war ended: he knows what passes for food in North Korea."

"Speaking of food, will you lunch with me?"

"I've a date at Tarrantino's," lied Hi glibly. "Take my advice, and have a tray sent to your room at the BOQ. This afternoon promises to be rough going."

"What about Kay?"

"Kay's my headache now; forget about her. You've done your damnedest to keep her out of this: you can rest your conscience."

Hi delayed a little longer at the defense table while the familiar wedge of MPs shepherded Paul down the aisle. His friend moved easily in that cordon: he seemed unaware of the flash bulbs, the jab of the reporters' questions. Shaking his head in pure wonder, Hi stole a glance at Kay's note:

> "I'll be in maroon convertible, parked at
> ocean end of Highland Avenue, Sausalito, wait-
> ing for the court's luncheon break. Will you
> meet me there alone—and tell me the quickest
> way to get into this fight?"

Paul had just gone through the side door with his head
high: a prince of the blood en route to the guillotine could
not have seemed calmer. Whatever brand of salvation Father Tim was selling in Korea, Hi thought, Paul has absorbed the essence. His need for Kay Storey is still the chink
in his armor.

v

Kay had written to Hi Saunders an hour before dawn,
when sleep was clearly impossible: she had not paused to
weigh the words. Once the note was in a messenger's
hands, she had felt a strange peace descend upon her, the
fatalism of a warrior committed to a battle she could not
vision clearly.

Even when she was breakfasting with Eric Lindman
(just before his plane left for Hollywood) it gave her a perverse satisfaction to keep her own counsel. Eric would
surely have jumped out of his skin had she confessed that
she was determined to testify in Paul's behalf, no matter
what the cost; but she was in no mood for the wonder boy's
glib arguments—and she had no excess strength to combat
them.

Now, parked in Sausalito, with the car radio purring out
its version of the trial at the Presidio, she was profoundly
glad to be alone. When she had driven across the Golden
Gate Bridge her eyelids had been heavy with weariness,
but her mind had never been more wide-awake; she could
even rejoice in the spot she had chosen for her meeting with
Hi. Sausalito, a San Francisco suburb clinging to the pen-
insula across the Golden Gate, was a perfect backdrop for

her mood. The wheels of her convertible (cramped at the curb where Highland Avenue ended at the sheer drop above the Pacific) were set at a precarious angle: had she released the hand brake, the car would have plunged for the spouting waves below her. . . . The sense of danger gave an added fillip to her pulse beat.

The euphoria had not endured. She had reckoned without her own impatience—which had forced her to arrive here a good hour before Hi could join her. Nor could she pin her mind to the radio and the long wrangles of the lawyers—though she had understood perfectly when the court had refused to permit questions on events prior to the surrender of Hill 1049.

Her anger had subsided when she realized that no questions from Hi could bring out the true story. The fact that a line officer of the Army could be a fool and a coward was a possibility this court would never admit, even in the abstract.

Somehow (she told herself bitterly) there must be a way to break the tissue of half-truth that MacArdle was weaving. Between us, Hi Saunders and I must turn the hard, white light of reality on this case, or Paul is lost. . . . Perhaps the true story of Hill 1049 would never be told. Yet her mind returned persistently to that battle-scarred ridge and the terror she had met and conquered on its slope. Of course she had been mad to venture there: she had deserved every aftermath of that visit. Yet she could not regret the impulse that had brought about her reunion with Paul and Father Tim, in the very shadow of catastrophe.

Her eye moved for the tenth time to the dashboard clock, and her hand darted forward impatiently to twist the dial of the car radio. Back in San Francisco the court-martial seemed on the point of adjourning—but it would be some time before Hi could cross the bridge to join her. The lawyer would want the details of her Korean adventure exactly as she remembered them. There was still time to rehearse that story once again—beginning with the night in Pusan that had witnessed the creation of "The Girl Next Door."

That strange, hybrid dream girl had been her special triumph; as "The Girl Next Door," she had felt that she could do no wrong. There had been no sense of trespass when she had pulled wires deliberately to bring Paul to Seoul on leave—or, later, to arrange a visit at his surgical bunker on Hill 1049. . . .

On the car radio the court-martial at the Presidio had been replaced by a disk jockey who was retailing the star dust of yesterday. Appropriately enough, the record he was playing now was "Night and Day." Kay found that she was murmuring the words of the lyric as "The Girl Next Door" had murmured them—speaking rather than singing, as she had done at that ancient piano in the cantonment at Pusan. Her eyelids drooped, shutting out the stark, bright colors of Sausalito. She was deep in the past again, with every sinister overtone as clear as it had been halfway across the world.

The Girl Next Door

IT WAS a song she had shouted from a hundred platforms, in barracks from Governors Island to San Diego. She had sung it in theaters as well equipped as any Broadway show shop—and in unlighted, unheated barns. Tonight's theater in Pusan was somewhere in between—a drafty cave that boasted nearly a thousand seats, a switchboard of sorts, and acoustics that could almost be described as adequate. . . . She had expected the house to be packed: audiences were ready-made in a staging area and presumably eager to be entertained. The fact that the present audience was not even mildly amused had baffled the troupe of which Kay Storey was a featured, if not a vital, unit.

Whirling into the final chorus (in a serpentine dance step that lifted her flaring sequin gown to thigh level), Kay wondered numbly at the lack of response from those tiers of khaki beyond the footlight trough. The song was a Hit Parade favorite; the special lyrics she was using were knowing and naughty: they had raised gales of laughter in stateside cantonments. Tonight the risqué rhymes fell like wet pennies in the mud. Even the glimpse of her legs, in black opera-length nylons, had produced only a few wolf whistles.

Kay had played to tough audiences before; she could gauge her applause expertly, long before the number ended—and braced herself for the scolding that would await her in the wings. As she had expected, Danny Dietz was at the prompt table—but the fox-faced director (who doubled as a stage manager and a straight man for the comic) gave her no more than an harassed grimace. Danny's own number had fared just as badly as her song: the director's gloomy visage hardly suited his checkerboard zoot suit and bright scarlet tie. Off stage, behind the plywood door of a dressing cubicle, Kay could hear the cursing of the star. Bugs Jordan was a comedian who took his art seriously, and his drinking even more so.

Regardless of its lack of applause, the show rolled smoothly on. Kay stood back to let the six-girl chorus line scamper on stage for its burlesque of "The Easter Parade," a strip-tease routine that had delighted a California air base three weeks ago. Waiting for the laughs that did not come, she shivered just a little, despite the thick bathrobe Dietz had tossed over her shoulders.

"What are we doing wrong, Danny?"

"Nothing," said the director. "You were in there punching."

"Did I punch too hard?"

"Don't try to take it apart, Kay. Last week they had Bob Hope—and they howled their heads off. Does anyone work harder?"

"Maybe they've had too much Hope," said Kay. "Maybe these unit shows are too alike. If we had a change of pace—"

"Don't *you* worry about our pace, darling. That's my department—and I'm stuck with it."

"We can't lay eggs all over Korea, Danny."

"Starting tomorrow," said the director, "we're cutting down to size. You for looks, me for laughs—and the quartet for background. The rest fly back to Tokyo: maybe they'll sound better with cherry blossoms."

"What about Bugs?"

"*He's* going back for sure. I always figured Bugs Jordan was a Lambs' Club actor. Now I'm sure of it." Dietz bit off the words as the comic (exuding a mixture of despair and bourbon) stalked from his dressing room, like Hamlet on a rainy Monday, and moved to the wings to await his cue.

"Shall I go cheer him up, Danny?"

Dietz shrugged. "What can you say to an actor who's just fallen on his face? Go swear a bit yourself if you like —you deserve it."

"I don't feel in the least like swearing," said Kay. "I think I'll write a letter to Paul."

ii

But no words would emerge on paper when she switched on the naked bulb in her own dressing cubicle and opened her writing kit. She had looked forward to surprising Paul with the news that she was in Korea at last. Now that she had set foot on the perimeter of his war, the space that divided them seemed wider than ever. It was absurd to imagine (even for a sentimental moment) that the divinity that watches over lovers would miraculously arrange their meeting.

The divinity that watches over lovers. Had they really been in love, those two days in Hollywood? Was she guilty of the sin of pride when she hoped he loved her still?

In fairness to Paul, she had not put that love into words. She would wait (she told herself) until she had looked into his eyes and seen if her love was returned. For that reason she had kept her letters brief and gay, with no overtone of the emotion that gripped her. . . . Tonight she could ask herself if the show's failure was a portent. Had it been presumptuous of her to force her way into this world of fighting men, a gray existence she could never share?

Puzzling over her failure, she continued to stare down at the empty page in her writing kit. Somewhere, she pursued, there must be an antidote for that grayness, for the boredom of these boys in khaki (most of them were really no more than that). A reminder, however fleeting, of a happiness they had left behind them—a universe of football rallies, midnight sodas, love-making in jalopies. . . . A universe, in short, where they had been themselves.

Tonight's show had forgotten to bring back the color and shape of that universe. The clowning of Bugs Jordan and company had merely repeated the ennui of other evenings when these GIs had watched other Broadway maestros go through their imitations of Hope and Berle and Jolson. Since she had been only an assistant in that routine, she could hardly blame her audience for its polite parody of applause.

Now that she had failed to prove herself, had she been wrong to take the job? Her voice was unsuited to torch singing: she had done far better in the smaller night clubs, where she could work in the midst of her audience. With a more compact troupe, it might be possible to perform at canteen level. . . . Or was this, too, only another hopeless fancy—since USO entertainment, by its very nature, was geared to a vast audience?

If Korea was the end of the road, she would return to Hollywood and accept what jobs were available. If Eric Lindman had overestimated her small but steady talent, she would take the defeat in stride. With that resolve to steady her, Kay closed her writing desk and prepared to leave the theater.

Outside, a raw rain was lashing the cantonment. She turned up the collar of her trench coat and followed a boardwalk that led to the guest wing housing the female members of the troupe. In America there had usually been rehearsal pianos available in such quarters: it had been her custom to strum idly for an hour after the last show—a kind of busman's holiday that had brought its special relaxation. Tonight a glance told her that her billet was only a segment of an officers' wing. There was not even a sitting room for the convenience of weary Thespians, and the heavy breathing that reached her ears suggested that the ladies of the chorus had long since called quits on the evening. Knowing that she could not sleep, Kay followed a second boardwalk and a sign pointing to the canteen.

The recreation center was a pair of converted loading sheds joined by a tin corridor that served as a sounding board for the rain; the nearer of the two held a half dozen chairs and a battered piano. Beyond, in the larger room, a half hundred GIs were at checkers or flipping the pages of ancient magazines. Most of the loungers seemed lost in apathy—a basic emptiness that isolated each man from his neighbor; to the girl's appraising eyes, it seemed a sloth more paralyzing than despair.

Daring to enter the smaller room, she found that there was a droplight above the piano. The keyboard of the instrument was yellowed with age, scarred by a hundred cigarette burns; but the strings were true when she struck her first lazy chord. Thanks to her high collar and overseas cap, she might pass for another of those weary boys, provided she could keep her distance. If she glided into her first tune more emphatically than usual, it was only to underline the fact that she (no less than these sullen young effigies) was lonely enough to scream.

> "As I walked out in the streets of Laredo
> As I walked out in Laredo one day. . . ."

Why had she picked a cowboy's lament out of her endless repertoire? And when had she begun to hum in the husky contralto that had always been her natural singing style? It hardly surprised her when several voices (not all of them Texan) picked up the words: in the female barracks she had shared so often, it was customary to join in during the last half hour before bedtime. . . . Kay let her fingers slip into a long arpeggio, not too different from the riff of a cowboy's guitar, and went to the next verse without conscious thought.

"I see by your outfit that you are a cowboy.
These words I did say as I boldly walked by. . . ."

A score of voices had picked up the melody now—and most of the singers had begun to converge on the piano. So far, the group was neither an audience nor a crowd of rebellious young men who might, conceivably, get out of hand. The sharing of the tune was all that mattered.

"What's your name, sister?"

"I'm not your sister," said Kay. "I'm the girl next door."

"D'you know 'Sometimes I'm Happy?'"

"I know them all."

She had been a natural by-ear pianist since childhood, with nearly total recall. Gliding into the old musical-comedy favorite, she could bless her easy gift and the boon it had brought to this plywood haven. Her audience was with her this time—though it was not an audience at all, in the usual sense, and she felt none of the nervous tension of a performance. When she finished the first request number GIs were banked ten-deep around the keyboard and the requests were coming too fast to sort.

"'Night and Day,' sister!"

"She isn't your sister, yardbird—and *we* want 'Star Dust!'"

"'St. Louis Blues!'"

"'Melancholy Baby!'"

"D'you know 'As Time Goes By,' lady?"

"D'you know 'The Missouri Waltz?'"

For an interval that could have been a night or an hour Kay ceased to measure time while she ranged through the whole rich field of the American folk song. Scores of forgotten musicals came back to her, entire. Together they sang the songs of Romberg and Kern and Gershwin, of Porter and Rodgers and Coward; they explored the melodies of Hoagy Carmichael and Irving Berlin. For the most part, she played with her eyes half closed, sure that the vigorous young voices would sustain her; between numbers she talked to them as easily as she had once chatted with friends on her porch in Kansas. . . . As the improvisation continued, she could pretend she was singing to Paul alone (the dim lights helped, and a tall noncom who stood a trifle apart from the others made a fair stand-in). The nonsense she spoke was for his ears. The jokes she traded were part of the fun they might have shared, had fate dealt different cards.

This, she told herself, was entertainment in its purest form—the element of make-believe that lifted them all outside their drab surroundings; this was a family party where she had become, quite by accident, the guiding spirit. As the song fest continued, she found that she had answered every request—and, in response to the clamor, repeated a score of favorites. She sang "Margie" and "Let Me Call You Sweetheart" as happily as she gave them "Someday I'll Find You" and "Tiger Rag." She sang "The Foggy Foggy Dew" to a basso-profundo counterpoint, and "Night and Day" as it was meant to be sung—a sentimental threnody rather than a torch song.

Toward the end she was aware of Danny's presence in the front rank of the singers and realized that the male quartet had mingled with the crowd to set the pitch for the more difficult numbers. Aside from these gentle assists, it was her show alone. When the lights went up at last and she left the canteen with Danny's arm in hers she was genuinely startled by the thunder of the applause—and touched, no less poignantly, when none of her listeners pressed forward to meet her in person. The illusion she had created, she saw, was too precious to spoil by contact with an actual performer.

It was only when she paused in the portal of her billet that the magnitude of her success struck home. Oblivious of the teeming rain, she faced Dietz with shining eyes.

"What happened, Danny?"

"Shall we say a star was born, darling?"

"Don't talk nonsense. That wasn't *me*."

"So you were singing off the cuff," said Danny. "All really great acting is spontaneous—and don't contradict your director."

"Can we try it again?"

"We can and will, right up to the Thirty-Eighth Parallel —if the brass will give us clearance."

"Promise to let my ad libs ride, and never rehearse me?"

"After tonight, Kay, you've got a deal."

"What shall we call it?"

"You've named your act, darling. Can you think of a better label than *The Girl Next Door*?"

"I didn't invent it," said Kay soberly. "The first man to call me that was a chaplain at San Pedro. Funny, isn't it, that *he* should see where my talent lay?"

iii

The pride of achievement lasted in the busy weeks that followed, while the reorganized unit (with Kay as its focal point) repeated the success of that first impromptu song fest in canteens from Pusan to the edge of the combat zone. Riding a wave of self-esteem no less heady than the wine of success, she was strangely content to hold the thought of Paul at arm's length—now that she could name the time and place for their reunion. She could even put off the summons deliberately: it gave her an odd thrill to realize that the growing fame of "The Girl Next Door" must reach him in time, though the girl herself was anonymous.

She had made that stipulation from the beginning, in spite of Danny Dietz's protests.

"Give me another month—I'll make you the toast of the whole Eighth Army," said Danny. "Think what *that'll* be worth to Kay Storey in Hollywood."

"It isn't *me* they love," Kay had insisted. "I'm not that

vain, Heaven knows. It's the memories I bring back. If I had a name, it might spoil everything."

"You've turned your torch down low, darling—all you've used so far is the back burner—but the kids always catch fire. Won't you take some of the credit?"

"Be smart for once, Danny. Let 'The Girl Next Door' call the tune. Don't bring show business into the act."

Dietz had capitulated, of course—and the show moved north on the note Kay had established in Pusan. As he had done on the memorable first performance, Danny mingled with the crowd in each canteen, getting things under way with a few adroit impromptus. The male quartet (inconspicuous in ODs) was also part of each group, helping to set pitch and tempo. Otherwise it was Kay's night—and the Army's. The Army continued to enjoy it to the hilt.

Playing to one-night stands (with extra performances when a barracks boasted more than one canteen) the troupe had used no press agent or other formal drum beater to advertise its coming: the word of mouth that preceded it was enough to assure packed houses.

"Larry Kirk's at the PRO," Danny told Kay at the end of their first thundering success in a camp outside Seoul. "So's the AP man, and a feature writer from the King syndicate. You've *got* to give those boys some time. It's in the cards."

"I don't mind—if you'll keep my name under wraps."

"They may recognize you from your pictures."

"I wasn't *that* famous in Hollywood, Danny."

She was still enjoying her anonymity when she arrived in the Army public-relations headquarters and submitted to mass questioning from a group of newsmen that had swollen to the proportions of a mob. Afterward Larry Kirk had insisted that Dietz bring her to the Hotel Chosun for a drink—and a more exclusive interview. Despite the artful pumping of that famous television commentator, Kay had refused to give an inch—until he had mentioned his impending tour of the lines.

"The boys will be wondering how soon you're coming north. What can I tell them?"

"I'm ready to sing anywhere," said Kay. "The Army knows that." She had thought of Paul then—and yielded to impulse before she could quite arrange her thoughts. "Could you find time to visit the 141st Battalion?"

"With the friends I have on staff," said Larry Kirk, "I can go anywhere short of the Yalu. Is there someone special in the 141st you'd like to flag down?"

"Will you deliver a note to the battalion surgeon—a Captain Paul Scott?"

"If you like, I'll ship him back in person."

"Things can't be that easy, Mr. Kirk. Not even for you."

"Just put me to the test, young woman," said Kirk. "You've given this man's Army a great deal. It's time they reciprocated."

iv

Her mass interview in Seoul made the front pages in America. A few weeks later word reached Kay that there were features in more than one magazine—and a front cover on *Life* (a candid-camera shot) that showed her singing out her heart. She found that she could take such publicity in stride. Korea, after all, was far from the bustle of the home front. Regardless of this civilian hubbub, "The Girl Next Door" would continue to serve her purpose.

She could hardly keep her cloak of mystery now. Her first real shock was a cable from Eric Lindman. It addressed her as casually as though they had parted yesterday:

```
ALWAYS KNEW YOUD HIT YOUR STRIDE WHEN
ARE YOU COMING HOME TO BE FAMOUS?
```

Such a wire would once have opened the gates of paradise. Today (with a show to give in ten minutes) it was only a tribute, to be pasted in her memory book. She did not even show the cable to Danny—though the USO director was bustling with plans for her future. So long as the war continued she would stay on in Korea—moved by a compulsion far more complex than the need to share the same continent with Paul Scott.

A few nights later, when she was singing in a camp just north of Seoul, it seemed quite natural to look up from the keyboard and find herself looking into his eyes at last.

Apparently he had entered the hall after the song fest began; now, he stood on a table top that made a natural vantage point. Two bulky enlisted men shared the perch with him, and the three had linked arms for balance. It gave her an odd sense of her importance (if that was the proper word) when Paul made no immediate attempt to catch her attention. Even when he called a request of his own, toward the concert's end, he did not quite meet her eyes.

She pretended to misunderstand, though she had heard perfectly. "What was that again, Captain?"

"'Night and Day,' please."

The night they first met in San Pedro she had sung the Cole Porter classic with all the brass of the orchestra behind her: here in Korea she sang it simply—and if the song was addressed to Paul alone, no soldier in the jam-packed room was aware of the exclusion. When it was over at last, she permitted Danny to fold her trench coat about her and whisk her out as he always did—with only a finger-tossed kiss for her farewell. Nor was she disturbed when Paul (obeying the unwritten law that had surrounded her with a magic circle no man had crossed) let her depart with no outward sign of recognition.

It was after midnight, and she had given two more shows in the interval, before she returned to her hotel to

find him waiting in the lobby. This time, when he held out
his arms she came into them as naturally as though she had
never been away. He held her for a moment before their
kiss—and the kiss was worth all her months of waiting.

"It's been so long, Paul—"

"It's been an eternity," he said. "I wonder how we've survived—but we have."

"Now you're here, it seems as though you've never been
away."

He smiled down at her as she tossed aside her trench
coat and settled before the fireplace, on the sofa with the
broken spring. It was a smile she remembered well—but
there was an added depth she did not recognize. It was
like looking again at the painting of a loved one, she told
herself. Each feature was in place—yet there was a difference she could not define.

"You've changed, haven't you, Paul? I think it's for the
better, war or no war."

"*You* haven't," he told her, "except to grow more beauti-
ful."

"After the day I've put in I must look a fright."

"Don't talk nonsense—you understand me perfectly. *This*
beauty is something from within. If Father Tim were here,
he'd call it an added richness of spirit—"

She savored the phrase for a moment: after all, it was
an exact description of the light in Paul's own eyes when
she had walked into the lobby. As lovers will, she wondered if this empathy was a special magic—which she,
alone among mortals, was privileged to share.

"How is the padre?"

"Much the same," said Paul. "A little more frail, I'm
afraid—and a great deal wiser. Or so it seems, now I know
him better." He looked at her with a rather sheepish grin.
"Perhaps I'm the one who has grown up."

"*Must* we talk of Father Tim?"

"Of course not. I'm using him as a shield, to avoid mentioning 'The Girl Next Door.'"

"We can forget her for tonight: she won't give her next show until tomorrow."

"Doesn't fame make a difference?"

"Not if you'll promise never to confuse me with that girl at the piano."

"Come off it, Kay. Dietz showed me a copy of *Life*. We both know what's waiting for you in Hollywood. So does Eric Lindman."

"Hollywood's a whole world away—and I haven't changed a bit. That's one observation you can't withdraw."

"You're sure of that? When people like Larry Kirk run errands for you? I realize that you arranged my leave between you—"

"Didn't you deserve a leave?"

"That's beside the point. Not that I don't thank you for separating me from Colonel Hardin, however briefly—"

"Has it been bad, Paul?"

"Not too bad to endure. I'm prepared to stick it out."

"And so am I, darling. 'The Girl Next Door' is signed on for the duration—and she's happy that she's needed. Her happiness would be complete—if you need Kay Storey too."

With only a glance to make sure the lobby was deserted, he took her in his arms with all the hunger she had awaited from their first kiss. It was a savage embrace—but she did not cry out at the hurt. This, after all, was the answer she had sought across half a world.

v

If the week that followed was a blissful one, it was not because of physical passion; the new, warm relationship between them was sufficient in itself. At San Pedro their coming together had been an inevitable end product of their frantic searching for shelter in the midst of chaos. Here in Seoul, while Paul's leave ran its course, they discovered that liking could be as precious as love.

At nightfall Paul was forced to share her with the thousands who thronged to her song fests. Usually (so great was the demand for *The Girl Next Door*) the performances overlapped the official lights-out—and it was a weary, happy Kay who returned to the Hotel Chosun in the dawn. But the days were theirs alone—and they made the most of the hours she could steal from her work.

Twice in that week there were cables from California— a second teaser from Lindman, an outright offer from Barney Gould, the head man at Eric's studio. Kay had left both of them unanswered with hardly a pang. It was true that Paul had said no word of marriage. But she knew, quite without words, that they were already wedded, that the final, legal seal must come when this business was ended.

On their last afternoon together they borrowed a jeep from the motor pool and drove into the country for an outing, complete with a picnic hamper (procured from the officers' mess) and a bottle of contraband champagne. It had taken searching, but they had found a green hillside, with a grove of pine trees and a meadow at its foot. For a time they rested quietly in the shadow pattern of the pines, half afraid to spoil the perfect afternoon.

"When will I see you again, Paul?"

"I'd give a great deal to answer accurately."

"Everyone says the war may end at any moment."

"Perhaps it will, Kay. But I won't mind serving my time, with no more favors. It's something I'm not sure I can explain."

"Won't you even try?"

He drew her close. "This will sound pompous, I'm sure. Like a one-worlder praising the brotherhood of man. But

I've learned to call myself a member of the human race on Hill 1049. Here with you I'm enjoying a happiness I haven't paid for. It's like buying something on the installment plan. Maybe I *have* made the down payment—but there's a lot of earning ahead."

"Darling, do you *want* to go back?"

"Only to make those other payments, Kay. Now we've had this week together, I can endure anything."

She lifted her head from his shoulder and met his eyes. "Including the fact that I might do a picture for Eric someday?"

"Of course—if it's what you want."

"I do want it," she said quietly. "You see, it's the one challenge I haven't met—and I've won all my battles so far. I've even made you love me; you'll admit *that* took doing."

"Did you think I'd stand in the way?"

"I don't want a *career*, Paul; just to prove to Eric that I am an actress. Once that's behind me, I'll rest on my laurels. I could belong to you forever—if you still wanted me."

"I'll always want you, Kay—"

The argument (if she could call it that) had ended without words, as most of their discussions had ended, so far. Marriage was still unmentioned when he kissed her good-by that night and vaulted to the tail gate of a convoy truck going north. Kay had wept at their second parting—but not too bitterly. After all, she had just completed her plans for a tour of the front (though she had been careful to keep this surprise from Paul). The certainty that they would meet again blunted the pain of farewell.

Now that the fighting was in a genuine lull, the public-relations office at Seoul had been overjoyed at her offer to sing just behind the lines. For the next week she performed in mobile hospitals, in mountain caves made to serve as rest areas, in amphitheaters pocked by old shell holes. Dietz had been left in the Korean capital, since he was busy with a projected tour in Japan. When she told her current liaison officer (an apple-cheeked boy from GHQ) that she was eager to visit her old friend Chaplain O'Fallon, and hoped she could give her next song fest on Hill 1049, it had been quickly arranged.

That noon she had sung to wild applause at a regimental collecting station less than ten miles from the hill. An hour later, perched like a truant schoolboy on a box of supplies destined for Paul's surgery, with the pilot as her only companion, she was riding a helicopter to her destination.

vi

Her first view of the front was a pure anticlimax. She had seen foxholes before, and battery mounts; she had explored the strange burrows that passed for men's homes in this wilderness. So far, Korea had resembled the massif of the Sierra Madre behind the Sunset Strip in Hollywood: from the whirlybird, the resemblance seemed even more marked today—nor was the actual battle line (which the pilot sketched with a vague gesture) a jot different from the regimental base she had just quitted.

Then, as the helicopter settled upon its improvised field on the slope of Hill 1049, she saw that the earth here was more brown than green, that the battle scars were alarmingly fresh when contrasted with the grassy craters at the rear. The officer who greeted her when she stepped from the plane was a wizened, old-young lieutenant. His eyes were red from lack of sleep; his voice, at first, was peevish as his manner.

"Lieutenant Crosby, Miss Storey. Colonel's in the sack. As of now, we're badly understaffed: I'm all the welcome committee we could spare."

Paul's name was on her lips, but she suppressed it. She had told regimental headquarters that she wished to see the chaplain—and her reason was genuine.

"I'm sure I'm a nuisance, Lieutenant. But I flew in early to visit with Father O'Fallon before I perform."

"He's in the surgical bunker, ma'am." Crosby's peevishness had vanished, now that he had been granted a close look at the visitor. "Don't mind if I'm staring—but we seldom get entertainers this far north. Maybe never is the right word."

When she recalled it later, that conversation with Crosby seemed as inappropriate as her presence here. Her mind, like her nerve ends, felt strangely detached when she stepped over a sandbagged incline that tunneled down to Dr. Paul Scott's domain. She had pictured a clammy dugout, a welter of blood and groans: she had feared that she might surprise Paul in the midst of an operation. But this spacious cave resembled nothing more than a windowless bedroom in some university fraternity house—complete with neat cots, its walls thick with pinups. Only the sterilizer in the alcove, the precise geometry of a dozen field-instrument cases, and the bare operating table identified the bunker for what it really was.

Father Tim was seated in a corner, writing busily in a leather-bound book by the light of a portable gas lamp: he could not have seemed more at ease in his own rectory, nor did he notice her presence at once. Hesitating before she spoke, she marveled at the maturity that had settled on the young priest's shoulders—if *maturity* was the exact word for a change that seemed far more profound. There was a visible comfort in this man's presence, a strength that defied all labels. Even before she addressed him she was certain that he could explain the compulsion which had brought her here.

The priest lifted his eyes from his writing, and she saw that this was no philosopher in khaki, but a tired man who needed a definite effort to adjust to her presence. She drew back a little: she had not expected Father Tim to make her feel like an intruder.

"Call me any name you like," she said. "From *femme fatale* to plain busybody. I deserve them all."

"You do indeed, my dear," said Father Tim, rising to greet her with a warm smile that banished all her doubts. "But you're welcome just the same."

"I shouldn't have come, Padre. I knew as much when I stepped from that helicopter."

"I'm glad you did, Kay—really glad."

"At least it's a legitimate visit," she said lightly. "I'll be singing for the battalion later."

"Come into the light where I can see your face. It's wonderful how success has fulfilled you."

"I hope it hasn't spoiled me too."

"Nothing could spoil you, my dear."

"It was you I came to see, not Paul. Will you believe that?"

"Of course, Kay."

She had spoken in an outburst: it was much easier now to go on. "I came to tell you everything, Padre—about Paul and me. I want your advice for the future."

"Are you sure it's wise to ask me?"

"If I were of your faith, you'd take my confession."

"I hardly think you've anything serious to confess, my dear."

"What about the sin of pride, Father? Proving I can have anything I like these days—including this visit?"

The chaplain's smile forgave her in advance. "Now that you're here, let's make the best of it," he said quietly. "The enlisted technicians are checking supplies in headquarters. Paul's on the next hill for an emergency. So you chose a perfect time."

As though by common consent, they left the bunker to follow a path that snaked up the ravine to the distant spine of the hill. As they walked, Father Tim pointed out items of defense that Kay already knew by heart from similar tours: the machine-gun nests that flanked the headquarters bunker, the gun mounts on adjacent slopes that had held Hill 1049 against all comers, so far. She accepted the information gratefully, knowing that he was only talking thus to put her at her ease. . . . It pleased her to note that she had drawn few glances from the men who worked like patient, mud-brown moles along the slope. Thanks to her OD fatigues and the trench helmet that concealed her hair, she hoped that she was passing for the chaplain's assistant, absorbing a first lesson in salvation under enemy guns.

The actual enemy was nonexistent today. Even when they had climbed to the summit of the hill and entered an observation post that commanded the whole topsy-turvy landscape to the north, the mountains that faced them seemed empty of life.

"Why did you bring me up here, Father?"

"Two reasons, Kay. First, I wanted you to see the front as it really is: the whole sector is before you now."

"Don't tell me the North Korean Army is on that next ridge."

"A few weeks ago this post was in rifle range. Since then, we've pushed our outposts to the edge of the valley and forced their snipers to pull back—"

"You said we had *two* reasons for being here."

"The second is more important. Paul usually climbs to this spot for a breather at the day's end. I thought you might wish to meet him here—in a foxhole, between two hostile worlds. It would be something to tell your grandchildren."

"Will we have them, Padre? Grandchildren, I mean?"

"Isn't that the topic you came to discuss with me?"

She told him everything then—as calmly as though they were discussing the emotional impasse of a friend they both knew intimately. She described her night with Paul in Hollywood, the love that had crept in unheralded, to flower after his departure. She told of their reunion in Seoul and the communion it had brought them both. Finally she confessed to the folly of her front-line visit, the need for advice that was its only real justification.

Father Tim heard her in silence. When she had finished her recital he did not speak at once, though the pressure of his fingers on her arm told her that he understood her dilemma perfectly.

"What has the war done to Paul, Padre? Can you tell me?"

"Shall we say it has given him a reason for being—a reason he lacked before?"

"It's more than that."

"Call it a dedication, if you like, Kay. It's a word we all use: few of us could define it accurately. I think, however, that Paul's own case sums up for us both. After all, you and I are responsible for his success here."

Kay forced a smile. "Do you plead guilty too?"

"I wouldn't say this to another soul, my dear, but I'm sure I saved him from a suicide attempt back in San Pedro. It happened just before I introduced you at the canteen."

"Was Paul that desperate?"

"I'm afraid so—for that moment. Remember, it takes only a moment to snuff life out, and a whole lifetime to earn the right to call oneself a man."

"You saved him from dying?"

The priest nodded. "From a sickness of our times, Kay; from the despair we all feel when we discover that there is no security in our century, that our little world can crumble overnight. It was a small service and a negative one. *You* gave him the urge to fight back, when you gave him your love. I can guess how precious that gift has been."

"You don't blame me, then, for what happened in Hollywood?"

"As a man of the cloth, I must censure you most severely. If you were a Catholic, I'd prescribe the worst penance I could devise." The priest moved to the parapet of the observation post and stared down at the valley. "Not that it's my place to speak of atonement. God, in His wisdom, has already given you your special burden. I think you'll learn to bear it gallantly."

"Does that mean Paul can never belong to me?"

"No human being really belongs to another; the fact is more apparent when a man is truly dedicated. I'd say it was the first lesson Paul's wife must learn."

"I'm sure he wants to marry me, Father."

"There is nothing he wants more. As of now, he might even persuade himself to return to practice in Hollywood—while you have the success there that you so richly deserve. But I'm afraid he's outgrown that pattern, Kay: his destiny lies elsewhere now."

"Don't you feel that he should marry?"

"Of course he should."

"But I'm not the best wife he could choose?"

"Emotionally, you are perfectly suited. But it takes more than love to sustain a true marriage. One needs a shared achievement too."

"Surely 'The Girl Next Door' has her value."

"Her value is above rubies. She heals the wounds of the soul, no less surely than Paul heals the body. Perhaps she should continue doing that—even after the war; perhaps she has already found her destiny."

"Can't two destinies be combined?"

"I hope and pray they can; fond as I am of you both, I couldn't do less."

"What would you have Paul do if you had charge of his future?"

The priest smiled. "Now you're asking me to presume upon the rights of God. Only He can give orders to His army."

"You and Paul must have talked things over."

"We've talked more than once. I think he should go wherever man is oppressed by man. Only last night he was speaking of the miners in West Virginia, the miseries he

knows there at first hand. They could use a man like Dr.
Scott in those hills. Perhaps he'll settle there eventually
and open the clinic of tomorrow."

Kay suppressed a faint sense of loss as the priest's
quiet voice flowed on: already his wisdom had penetrated
to the roots of her being. What he had just told her was
unassailable: the true healer must dwell in a special world,
and the impulses that drive him are inviolate. Come what
may, she warned herself solemnly, I will never interfere. . . .

"The first lesson we must learn is the hardest, Kay. It
has nothing to do with you or Paul as people. We must see
this struggle in Korea for what it really is, in the frame-
work of a godless culture. Even the enemy has his place
in history when he is judged in perspective—"

"I thought you had no enemies, Father."

"The devil is my eternal enemy. If the Korean War
proves nothing else, it will go down in the books as a symbol. Here in these mountains the free world drew a line,
beyond which the devil could not pass. Not even when he
was wearing his most ancient disguise, the armor of Mars."

"Do you think we'll win here, Padre?"

"The fact that we made a stand is what really matters.
It will be remembered always—even if the present stalemate ends in a truce. Even if the truce is broken—"

"Why are you telling me this?"

"Because you must realize that we are all part of that
struggle. You with your music, Paul with his scalpel, and I
with the teachings of the Man I serve. If the naked force of
the enemy fails in Korea, it will be only our first victory.
The war with evil will go on. With other weapons on other
battlegrounds."

The priest stood with both hands spread on the sandbags of the parapet—as though the foxhole were his special
pulpit and Kay a congregation of one. Now he turned
and lifted her gently to his side. With that simple motion

he was Father Tim again, a rather tired Army chaplain in dirt-stained fatigues.

"Don't stop, Padre—"

"I've said all that matters, Kay. Enough to make you see that Paul and I are in *this* war for the duration, because this war is never-ending." Father Tim crossed the observation post and looked down the southern slope of Hill 1049. "The sermon is over just in time. Paul is coming up the ravine now, and I can see the men gathering at the headquarters bunker for your song fest. I'll go down and tell Corporal Jackson to tune his guitar."

vii

She had expected her performance (in a spacious, manmade cave beyond the headquarters bunker) to be something of an ordeal. Actually it was one of her greatest triumphs—thanks, in no small measure, to the easy authority of Jackson's guitar, which blended perfectly with her own ad-lib style. From his first lazy chords, she had sensed that the lanky corporal was a born musician. Once the jammed bunker had thundered into the chorus of "Oklahoma!", she felt she was among friends and enjoyed each note as thoroughly as her audience.

News had reached her, via field telephone, that her helicopter had suffered a breakdown on a nearby hill and would not be repaired before morning. She had taken the information without missing a beat, so complete was her identity with the singing voices that surrounded her. . . . At first, Colonel Hardin and his camarilla had been a puzzle: until the audience had warmed up, the antagonisms dividing the GIs and the battalion brass were as vivid as though a trench had bisected the cave where she was performing. But even that line had melted as song followed song. In the end the colonel was bellowing choruses as heartily as his newest replacement. Master

Sergeant Bates (a shifty-eyed regular Kay had disliked on sight) had straddled the line of demarcation, to lend a deceptively pure tenor to each song he knew. . . .

She had feared the moment when Paul faced her in the observation post. Fortunately he had been warned of her arrival. After their first wild embrace he had seemed almost calm while he explained the pattern of survival they followed here—and the tensions that had kept Hill 1049 in constant, undercover turmoil. She had led him on with further questions deliberately, if only to escape the scolding she knew she deserved.

"Why is it so different here, Paul? Why is it more dangerous? I've sung under the guns before."

"Not *these* guns, I'm afraid. Helicopters and parachutes are the only means of transport, for one thing. The main supply route is one long shell hole."

"Does that matter, if the front is quiet?"

"It's been quiet too long, Kay. That, in itself, could mean trouble—like living in Maine for ten days in January without a blizzard."

"Must you sound so ominous, darling?"

He grinned at that question, for the first time. "Sorry: I realize you're here to keep up morale—I mustn't break *yours* down. But I'll be happier when you've boarded the first 'copter that stops here tomorrow."

"Does that mean I get off without a scolding?"

"How can a mere battalion surgeon scold 'The Girl Next Door,' when she arrives through channels?"

"I meant to surprise you, Paul. I *hoped* you'd be pleased."

"Of course I'm pleased. Just promise not to surprise me this way again."

"I'll go quietly in the morning," she promised. "My mission's accomplished now."

After Paul's warning Kay had expected to find the whole battalion crawling with neuroses. When she was presented to Colonel Hardin (as solemnly as though they had never met in San Pedro) she had needed her self-control to avoid staring, to uncover the mad bull beneath the florid soldier's mask. . . . The colonel had been the soul of courtesy, so far as manners went. Only the puffs beneath his bloodshot eyes and his care with three-syllable words betrayed the fact that he was balanced on the fine edge of inebriation.

The single jarring note had come at the end of the song fest. She was still accepting the thunder of applause when a deeper thunder rumbled out of the night, somewhere beyond the blackout curtains. Even her untrained ears had recognized the *crump* of an artillery salvo—and it had pleased her mightily to find that she could hear that rumble without fear.

The second round of shells had dropped nearer, but she felt no threat in the sound: the fact that a dozen GIs had darted into the night without a word of command was part of the bizarre pattern of the evening. So, for that matter, was the greenish hue that invaded Colonel Hardin's cheeks and the muttered excuse that took him from the cave, on the double. Paul had prepared her for that withdrawal.

In a matter of minutes, it seemed, the song fest had dissolved. A noncom escorted her to the spot prepared for her night's rest—a storeroom deep in the headquarters bunker, complete with a folding cot and a hastily carpentered door. It was only when she had settled there that she remembered Paul had disappeared (no less hastily than Colonel Hardin), that Corporal Jackson, his guitar forgotten, had been on the battalion surgeon's heels. Later, of course, she would realize that both men had hurried to the aid station to prepare for expected casualties.

Exhausted as she was, she dropped into a deep and untroubled slumber. She wakened with a start, aware of the chink of daylight gleaming through a crack in that impro-

vised door. Until she could regain her senses she was positive that she had dropped off in a boiler factory.

Overhead, the air was a sheet of iron, shaken continually
in the hands of a maniac with designs on her own sanity.
The blanket on her cot was deep in silt that had fallen
from the beams above her, and her hair was thickly pow-
dered with the same brownish dirt as she shook the drowsi-
ness from her eyelids. . . . When she had scrambled from
the bed and donned her trench helmet the floor seemed
to tremble too—and, for the first time, she was aware of a
roaring quarrel in the orderly room outside.

The crack in the doorframe made an adequate peephole.
Paul and Hardin were pacing the floor just outside—she
had already identified the surgeon's voice, raised, for the
moment, above Hardin's taurine bellow. The third figure
in the churning group was strange at first—until the man
turned on his heel, and she recognized Lieutenant Crosby's hatchet-sharp profile.

The C.O.'s bellow, when it rose again, all but drowned
the artillery duel outside. "Damn it to *hell*, Scott! *I won't
have it!*"

"Sorry, sir. The deed's done."

"You've gone to division headquarters, over my head?
Yes or no?"

"It was imperative, sir. We needed helicopters on the
strip at dawn."

"Did you endorse the call, Crosby?"

"I did, sir." The lieutenant had managed to stand his
ground, though he had not met the blaze of hatred in the
colonel's eye.

"Why couldn't you waken me, man?"

"We tried, Colonel."

"We?"

"Chaplain O'Fallon and myself. You were—sleeping too
soundly."

Hardin whirled on Paul, with one trembling finger

extended. "Did you send that sky pilot to my quarters, Scott?"

"If you must put it that way, sir." To her amazement, Kay noticed that Paul had grown progressively calmer as the colonel's shouting increased in volume. "I wanted a witness when I reported you unfit for duty."

"Unfit for duty? *Me?*"

"For various reasons, Colonel. Shall I spell them out in my report?"

There was no time for more. A concussion that seemed to expand inside Kay's brain had sent every timber in the bunker into a crazy dance. While the blast endured she was certain that the walls had collapsed above their heads. Then, as the breath returned to her body, the dance of the timbers subsided: while the thunder died outside, she heard someone shouting for litter-bearers.

Colonel Hardin had pancaked to the floor with the first impact; now, on hands and knees, he scuttled for his quarters like a homing crab. Neither officer stirred until the door had slammed behind him. After the burst outside, the dugout was strangely quiet; when Paul spoke his voice was emotionless and a little tired.

"Easy does it, Crosby. We've been cut off before."

"Not with *this* fire power against us."

"We can handle things—if he'll stay under wraps."

"He always did when Major Prescott was here," said the lieutenant miserably. "The major could manage him—with help from Bates."

"From your last report I'd say the perimeter defense is still intact." Even in her bewilderment it seemed odd to Kay that the battalion surgeon, not the lieutenant, seemed to be issuing the orders. "If our lines hold until afternoon, the division can send an armored column through. That should peel them back—"

"It isn't a question of holding the perimeter, Doctor—it's the C.O. Remember how he screamed for a general retreat last time—until Prescott quieted him?" Crosby's face, at the moment, had a greenish tinge that recalled the complexion of his commander all too graphically. Yet Kay could sense that this terror, at least, was normal, the near-panic of a boy who had assumed a burden too big for his shoulders.

"I remember that last collapse all too well," said Paul. "This time, *you're* acting C.O. Try to behave like one."

Crosby's teeth closed on his upper lip. When he spoke, his tone was almost formal. "Just as you say, Doctor. Do I put Colonel Hardin on the morning report?"

"Sick in quarters," Paul ordered. "I'll sign it later." He stood back as Crosby half ran, half stumbled from the bunker in response to a shouted question outside. Then he turned to Kay's door and opened it. "I knew you were listening," he said quietly—and there was something in his voice that eased her thudding heart. "Apparently your tour of Hill 1049 is now complete."

"What happened, Paul?"

"With luck," he said, "we can still get you out."

"What *happened?*"

He took her hand and led her toward the bunker exit. "Tell you on the way," he said crisply. "Keep your head down. It's safe enough—for now. That last shell was looking for the ammo dump and fell short."

She permitted him to lead her up the bunker steps and into the glow of a flawless summer morning. Expecting death to menace her from every side, Kay was confused by the smiling face of nature. Paul's grip tightened on her hand as he noted her bewilderment.

"We'll make a run for it," he said. "Straight to the aid station. Up there you'll be nearer the landing strip."

"What *happened*, Paul?"

"The hill's surrounded. Run, Kay. Don't waste your breath."

Despite his warning, Paul himself continued to speak in snatches while they dashed up the ravine.

"Sorry, Kay, meant to come sooner. Couldn't. Been operating since midnight."

"You needn't explain, Paul—"

"Want you to know the worst. Better that way." He paused to gauge the approach of a shell. "We've had just one 'copter since dawn. Needed that for two shock cases—"

"I understand."

"This is the fourth time they've surrounded us. Each time we've smashed through from the division area and restored the supply route. We'll do it again if things don't get too hot—" He had held her against a solid outcrop of rock while he counted the shell bursts in the rear; now he flattened abruptly to earth, pulling her down beside him. The last shell from the distant enemy battery filled the air with a long, querulous whining as it passed overhead. The detonation, when it came, was too far off to seem real. Long before the sound could reach her, Paul had yanked Kay to her feet again and resumed their dash up the ravine.

"Taking no chances," he said. "Keep you under cover until things slacken off." They were on the last long slope now, with the haven of the surgical bunker just above them. Paul eased his pace for the first time and offered her the exhausted travesty of a smile. "'Copters will be coming in all morning, to take away casualties. They'll get you aboard somehow—" Again they flattened to the dirt while the shell whined in and struck, close enough to send a geyser of mud into the ravine.

"They fall short, now and then," he said, as though apologizing for the enemy gunners. "In you go, Kay. On the double!"

This time the battalion aid station was all she had imagined. Sergeant Furness and Corporal Jackson, stripped to the waist and glistening with sweat, were working quietly among the cots—and each cot groaned with its load of misery. A file of walking wounded awaited the surgeon in the sandbagged entrance; a windrow of litter cases had backed up outside during his brief absence. Some of the stretchers were already draped in blankets, grim evidence that these men, at least, were beyond help.

"Sit in the dispensary," Paul directed. "You won't be underfoot there." He had already turned to the operating table as the sergeant came up from the opposite side with an ampoule of pentothal. The case that awaited him, Kay saw, was a relatively minor one, the spraying type of wound that comes from a shrapnel burst. A quick debridement (she groped for the word in her R.N. lore and came up with it promptly) would take care of this one and make room for another.

Watching Paul work, she sensed the nicety of judgment that was essential here—and, in its way, as important as operative skill. Even at the height of the shelling a certain proportion of these cases would be ticketed for a base hospital and flown there: Paul's job was to decide who should go now and who could stay longer, to benefit from what surgery he could give under pressure. The routine crises were no less vital—the constant giving of plasma, the insertion of a tube in a shattered windpipe, a quick needle tap to relieve a collapsing lung. . . .

As the hours passed and the press of casualties continued, Kay grew tired of waiting in the dispensary. Long before the fury of the attack had eased outside the bunker, she found herself helping the hard-pressed medics—in small ways at first, then as a full-fledged partner. Once they saw that she was not afraid of the blood they accepted her gratefully. From that moment it was only a question of time before she was assisting the surgeon too.

Steadying the head of a brain-wound (Paul had paused over it just long enough to clear the approach and cover the wound itself with a dressing, before giving it top priority on the next helicopter), she knew he was aware of her presence, that he was grateful for another pair of hands that remembered their former skill.

He gave her no overt sign of recognition while he worked: this was a Paul she had never seen before, a technician whose concentration was absolute. Even when she had helped with several cases she did not cease to marvel at his easy competence, at the command decisions that made order of this blood-drenched chaos.

From her rough count Kay estimated that five of each six cases that reached the table had been selected for evacuation to MASH. Most of them would have a chance for survival, thanks to those tireless surgeons' hands and the roaring efficiency of the hospital 'copters on the strip outside. Working at top speed beside him, she had lost track of time—though she realized vaguely that it was already afternoon when he pushed back his mask at last and recognized her presence out of startled eyes.

"Why are you still here, Kay? Furness could have put you aboard a plane."

"He didn't dare," she said. "He needed me here too badly. So, I trust, did you."

"You're leaving the moment there's a place."

"If the place isn't needed." It was Kay's turn to look around her: she realized that the flow of new cases had stopped, though the din outside seemed more intense than ever. "Is every morning like this, Paul?"

"Only when the pressure's really on," he said. "We can all breathe for a moment now. I'll get coffee."

"That's *my* job, Doctor: I remember that much from my nursing."

She was still filling cups for the medics when Father Tim came down the bunker steps. The priest's slender body was sagging with weariness. He accepted the canvas chair that Kay offered, and the steaming cup, with a smile of gratitude: all that long morning they had worked side by side among the wounded—but there had been no chance to speak before.

"Will you tell Paul he mustn't have me on his conscience, Padre?" she said—as much for Paul's benefit as the chaplain's. Somewhat to her chagrin, she saw that the surgeon had already crossed to the far side of the bunker to check the evacuation-priority list with Sergeant Furness.

"I'm sorry you had to see this, Kay—"

"Believe me, Father Tim, I'm *glad* I stayed. I needed to watch Paul at work. It's helped me to see just what you meant yesterday."

The priest put down his cup and leaned back in the chair, pressing his fingers to his eyes. "Be that as it may, my dear, we'll breathe easier when you're back at the base."

"Are things really bad outside?"

"We're hard pressed, I'm afraid. It's never been quite like this."

"Isn't help on the way?"

"It may come—in time; we've always been reinforced before. The helicopters are doing a fine job in the meantime."

Kay lowered her voice. "Tell me about Colonel Hardin, Padre. Is he always drunk during an attack?"

The chaplain nodded soberly. "It's an open secret in the headquarters bunker. So far, he's brazened it out—and his staff has covered him. What the colonel can't endure is that Paul understands his fear and covers him too. He will this time, unless Hardin really goes berserk."

"If you've taught him to forgive Hardin, you've accomplished wonders."

"The forgiveness came from his own heart, Kay. He's a doctor first of all, and the colonel is a sick man."

"But should Hardin be in command?"

"Frankly, no—though it's something we'd never explain on the record. So far, he *has* held his position, and his tactics have been above reproach, to the outside world. Paul is hoping that he'll let himself be certified as unable to carry on for medical reasons—particularly after today's show. That's why he listed him on the morning report as sick in quarters: if it goes on long enough, he can certify him for evacuation too."

Lieutenant Crosby came into the bunker a bit later, mud-daubed to the eyes. A glance told Kay that the temporary commander was harried to the breaking point when he addressed Paul. Once again she was conscious of the strange reversal of their roles in the battalion: an outside observer, unaware of the two men's status, would have sworn that Crosby was reporting here for instructions.

Trying not to seem an eavesdropper, she heard their conversation only in snatches. Crosby was fresh from a tour of the command posts and brought back a tale of rising unrest among the men. Clearly he felt that Hill 1049 was already untenable—but the division commander had just telephoned an order to hold his position.

"The colonel would countermand that order if he was on his feet, Doctor."

"How is he now?"

"Sergeant Bates is working on him, with coffee and amphetamine. Can't you give him some kind of shot to bring him round?"

"A shot strong enough to bring the C.O. out of that bender would kill him."

"Suppose we *could* begin a general withdrawal, while it's still light?"

"You say you've lost contact with Hill 1056; it'd be suicide, without flank support."

"Not if we followed the ravines," said Crosby eagerly. "Easy Company brought in a gook weapons-carrier that ran out of gas. We could use that as cover—"

"Cover for whom—the headquarters command and a few wounded? It'd still be suicide for the men." Paul had spoken sharply: Kay realized that the whole bunker was listening now.

"But, Doctor—"

"Go back to headquarters, Lieutenant," said Paul, in a gentler tone. "Stay with your phones until the divisional commander changes our orders. It's all you can do."

Despite her best resolve, Kay could not keep herself from joining Paul after the lieutenant had made his unhappy exit. The surgeon was supervising the transfer of a splint-wound from table to helicopter: at his nod, she stayed beside the litter until the man was aboard the waiting plane.

"I wish we could send you out on this one, Kay. But it's been the same story since dawn."

"The wounded come first. We both know that."

Paul turned slowly and looked at her with admiration. "You're willing to stay—after what Crosby just said?"

"Will headquarters order a withdrawal?"

"Of course not. But it's beginning to look as though Crosby isn't experienced enough for his job."

Standing at Paul's side in the dugout entrance, she needed all her self-control to keep her fingers from closing on his hand. The pressure might have given him the answer he needed, the assurance that she refused to be afraid, so long as they could share the danger. They watched in silence while the medics transferred other cases to the helicopter. In another moment the ungainly craft had lifted from the slope, seeming to balance precariously between earth and heavy until it gained altitude and spun south toward the distant base.

"Don't be a heroine forever," he said. "It isn't healthy."

"I'm where I want to be, Paul. Won't you believe me now?"

ix

Within the next hour the last of the seriously wounded were evacuated, though there was still no room for Kay in the overloaded helicopters. In that interval there had been no fresh casualties and the throb of the guns had stilled somewhat, for no reason she could fathom. The answer came at dusk, when Sergeant Furness (who had been sent to headquarters bunker with a report on the wounded) came scrambling up the ravine, all but incoherent with news.

"Better see the colonel, sir. We're shipping out!"

Kay would always remember the babble of voices that followed, and the sudden, decisive motion of Paul's arm that froze the others into silence.

"Who gave the order—Lieutenant Crosby?"

"No, Cap'n. It was the C.O. himself."

"Is he on his feet?"

"Sergeant Bates finally brought him round."

"Did he contact division headquarters?"

"So they say. All companies are ready to move. They're loading the battalion records in the weapons-carrier. The C.O. wants us in the formation—pronto."

Paul addressed the four other occupants of the bunker. "It's suicide. The enemy's watching those southern ravines —*hoping* for a general withdrawal. It'll be far easier to cut the battalion down in the open than to root us out of these bunkers. The colonel *must* know that."

The words fell into a void of agreement, a silence which Kay broke when Paul moved toward the bunker steps.

"Can you stop them, Paul?"

"I certified Colonel Hardin as unfit for duty on the morning report." Again Paul seemed to address all of them. "This time he *stays* unfit, if I have to use handcuffs." He went up the bunker steps with the words, running with long, loping strides down the ravine. Ignoring Father Tim's warning, Kay ran out on his heels.

The path to the headquarters bunker, which had been so long that morning, seemed much shorter in that downhill rush. She made out the weapons-carrier in the thickening dusk—a monstrous shape with caterpillar treads and bulging armor. Dust roiled thickly at its flanks, and several gnomelike figures swarmed around it: even in the bad light she could recognize the members of Hardin's camarilla. It was only when she had tumbled down the last slope that she saw the platoons of the battalion, drawn up in close order and bristling with bayonets.

Each eye in that double column was fixed on the weapons-carrier. Kay could sense the uneasiness, the awareness that something had gone amiss at command level. Here, an almost indecent haste to cut and run was nakedly apparent. Sergeant Bates, popping from the bunker, seemed intent on no one's survival but his own. Lieutenant Crosby, already inside the carrier, was cursing frantically as he jabbed at the balky ignition.

Kay paused on the slope to watch Paul stride into the melee of crisscrossing orders. There was still no sign of Colonel Hardin: because of her vantage point, Kay was the first to observe his fuddled emergence from the bunker. The C.O. was in battle dress; he wore a heavy automatic strapped to one leg, and a crash helmet was pulled level with his eyes. At first glance he seemed furiously competent as he barked a command to close ranks and scrambled for a foothold on his transport.

Sergeant Bates, who had been busy elsewhere, hurried up a second too late: the colonel had already missed his footing and dropped to his knees in the dust. His crash helmet was knocked off in the fall. When he got to his feet again and faced Paul, his eyeballs were rolling wildly: without the master sergeant's support, he would have fallen a second time.

"What's this mean, Colonel?"

The C.O.'s voice, when it emerged, was oddly crisp—an incredible contrast to the sagging body that produced it. "Fall in, Captain Scott! You have your orders!"

"You're a sick man, sir. Go to your quarters."

"Fall in, I said!"

"Did HQ order a retreat, Colonel?"

"D'you question a direct command?"

"May I verify that order on the battalion phone?"

"Scott, are you calling me a liar?"

"With your permission, Colonel—"

The exchange in the shelter of the towering flank of the weapons-carrier had been short and venomous—with Kay and Master Sergeant Bates as the only witnesses. Now, as Paul turned on his heel, no other eyes saw Hardin's fist close on the pistol and lift it, butt-first, from its holster. Kay's cry of warning choked in her throat while the steel bludgeon descended in a vicious arc, to connect with the base of the surgeon's skull.

For a crazy instant she was back in time, moving too late to stop a similar blow delivered by the same hand in a San Pedro canteen. Watching Paul's knees buckle, she flung herself forward to save him from further harm—but the move was needless. Colonel Hardin, bellowing a final order, had already tumbled over the side of the unwieldy vehicle.

The command, repeated by a dozen voices, put the columns in motion before Kay could kneel beside Paul and cradle his head in her arms. Master Sergeant Bates, climbing into the carrier, gave her a brief, incurious glance before he, too, disappeared behind the armor plate.

In the cloud of dust set up by the caterpillar treads of the carrier and the fast-closing darkness, the marchers seemed oblivious of their surgeon's presence. Bemused as she was, Kay could not even summon a call for help. Instead, she continued to stare in silence while the battalion took the path to the southern ravines and fanned into open order. Here and there a splinter of dying sunlight picked out a bayonet before the last squad vanished in the murk.

Paul stirred in her arms and opened his eyes. "I should know by this time," he said. "Don't turn your back on a madman."

"Did he hurt you badly, darling?"

"Stunned me, that's all. I've a hard skull, as you should remember."

"I'll call the medics."

"Give me a minute longer to rest. After all, there's nothing we can do now. Hardin has resumed command." Paul's eyelids had dropped again, as though that flash of irony had exhausted him. "Call it a retreat against overwhelming force. It'll read that way in the records."

"Can't we *do* something?"

"Nothing but wait—and keep our heads."

Kay looked up as a step sounded in the loose rubble of the slope. In another moment Father Tim was kneeling beside them.

"Is he wounded, Kay?"

"I'm not hurt at all, Padre," said Paul—and proved it, after a fashion, by getting shakily to his feet, with the chaplain's aid. "Let's see if we can reach division headquarters by radio."

In the orderly room of the bunker the wall lamps burned brightly above a scene of the wildest disorder. The headquarters detail had emptied the battalion files helter-skelter, snatching what records they could carry in their dash for freedom. A glance at the radiophones told Kay that it was too late to report their plight. Someone (she could guess that it was Sergeant Bates) had smashed the tubes.

Paul sank to a stool and rocked his head in his hands. Without protest, he accepted a half tumbler of whiskey

Kay fetched from the colonel's quarters, and downed it in a swallow.

"At least Hardin left a bottle behind," he said. "It was more than I hoped for."

"Shall we try to overtake the column?"

"We'd only walk into enfilading fire. Any moment now, you'll hear them open up."

"Do you think he really called division headquarters, Paul?"

"He may have gone through the motions, to hoodwink Crosby."

A long roll of rifle fire swept up from the south, to be followed by a second fusillade and a third. Between the bursts, an angry chatter of M-1s responded as the 141st Battalion (discovering, too late, that it had blundered into enemy cross fire) did its frantic best to fight back. The protest, blotted out in a final, roaring volley, was short-lived—a spine-chilling demonstration of a basic fact of war. The battalion, its escape cut off, had evidently dispersed into the darkness in a last desperate scramble for survival.

Hysteria was building rapidly inside Kay's mind: she fought down that surge of panic with a great effort, grateful for the soothing pressure of Father Tim's hand on her arm. Paul's voice, when he spoke again, seemed very small in the quiet bunker.

"Who is left, Padre?"

"Just the five of us. You, Kay, the two medics, and myself."

"No walking wounded?"

"There were only a few," said the priest. "They got aboard the weapons-carrier before it moved out."

"You're sure that Furness and Jackson stayed?"

"Of course, Paul. They take orders from you."

"If Hardin had dug in until morning, we might have held our position." Paul's voice was a whisper: it was a statement of fact, made without bitterness. "Maybe the weapons-carrier got through the enfilade. If it did, they'll be lucky to lead a platoon to safety."

Already that quiet voice had done a great deal to restore Kay's courage. "Won't the colonel be court-martialed for leaving without orders?" she asked.

Paul shrugged. "He was in command when the withdrawal began—thanks to Bates and his amphetamine. He gave coherent orders to everyone—including me. It isn't his fault that I was the turncoat who refused to obey."

"*Turncoat*, Paul?"

"It's an insult he's flung at me before, when I've operated on North Korean prisoners. Give him time, Kay. If he gets through tonight he'll swear I deserted under fire."

"You've two witnesses who'll expose him."

"For what? A C.O. who pulled out to save his command? Battalion officers have a right to ignore divisional instructions when they consider a position untenable."

"Surely we'll get a chance to tell the truth?"

"Don't bank on it, Kay. Truth is the first casualty of war."

"Are we trapped, Paul? Tell me what you think: I can take it."

"There's no use pretending. By morning we'll either be dead or prisoners."

"We've still a chance," said Father Tim. "Don't forget our status under the Geneva Convention."

"So far, there's little evidence that the Chinese honor its provisions."

"All of us are noncombatants. There's a supply of brassards in the aid station and a few banners—white flags with a cross. They'll establish our status."

"Let us help you back to the surgery, Paul," said Kay. "We mustn't be captured here."

The mere acts of helping Paul climb the ravine, of rummaging in the medical stores, did much to improve Kay's morale. In the half hour following the retreat, each member of the oddly-assorted quintet had been provided with an arm band. Four of the square white banners (prominently displayed at each approach to the aid station) identified their haven beyond question. . . . Paul, resting on a cot while these precautions went forward, seemed himself again when Kay finally settled at his side, bearing a mug of coffee.

"What comes next, Paul?"

Her eyes followed his as he glanced around the surgery. The medics, their last chore behind them, had sprawled on a blanket for a game of acey-deucy, as calmly as though their world had not just collapsed outside. Father Tim had already taken his favorite perch on the dugout steps, where he could watch the slow wheeling of the stars. Paul's smile widened—and the grip of his fingers tightened.

"What comes next," he said, "is the greatest test of war— the waiting. At least I'm in good company."

x

Hours later, she roused from an uneasy doze in the first gray promise of dawn, aware that she had dropped off while she sat beside Paul's cot. A glance told her that he was relaxed in slumber, and she marveled again at the training that had permitted him a full night's rest, though death itself might prowl outside the bunker door.

Father Tim was dozing on the steps, his frail figure outlined clearly against the pale sky. There was no sign of the medics: when she joined the chaplain on the steps, Kay saw that they were scouting the ridge. The padre had a leather-bound book on his knee. She recognized the diary he had been writing in when they had met in the surgery— and put out her hand to close the book before it could slip to the ground. At that moment the priest opened his eyes:

with something that resembled a guilty start, he dropped the diary into the pocket of his trench coat.

"Forgive me, Kay," he said. "I'm seldom caught with my confession book open."

"Confession book, Father?"

"Since I've no confessional at the front, this diary takes its place. Eventually it will go back to my archbishop in San Francisco—as a record of my failure with Colonel Hardin."

"How did you fail with him?"

"At one time, I'm ashamed to admit, I hated him—almost as much as Paul did. Now, of course, we've both learned to accept his weakness. Still, I should have tried much harder to help him overcome it. His flight is proof of my failure."

"Some people are beyond redemption, Father Tim."

"No one is beyond redemption, my dear."

"The colonel is all evil. You couldn't have changed him in a thousand years."

"I would have been a better man for trying. More than once I've seen Paul operate on hopeless cases. Sometimes he saved them."

"Medicine is different. There's always an outside chance you'll succeed when you're dealing with something as complex as the human body."

"The soul is even more complex, Kay. I should have taken the outside chance." Father Tim touched the book in his pocket. "Pray God I'll be able to atone someday."

"Is that hope in your confession book, Padre?"

"Of course." The priest smiled gently, with his eyes on the hilltop and the two soldiers moving cautiously among the empty command posts. "It's a strange thing, Kay. Here we sit, facing possible death—or hardships that may make us cry out for the release that death brings. And yet, now it's morning and I've written down my shortcomings, I have no fear at all."

"How do you explain that, Padre?"

"I'm not sure, my dear. Perhaps confession is really good for the soul."

Kay moved softly into the dugout and stood above the cot where Paul was still relaxed in slumber. "You've watched him save lives here," she whispered. "Can he save *us* from the trap we're in now?"

"Paul—and God: don't forget they are both on our side. Perhaps we're more fortunate than we realize." The priest rose from his place in the shadow of the bunker entrance. With the morning light on his face, Kay could see the fatigue lines around his fine eyes. "Suppose we get some supplies together. Perhaps we'll be allowed to keep them later."

When they started rummaging in the dugout they found that the medics had anticipated them. Four packs were waiting in a corner, each containing a robust load of coffee, cigarettes, and canned ration.

"I'll make a pack for myself," said Kay. "They mustn't leave me out."

She was still working at this task, with the help of Father Tim, when Paul wakened and sat up with a long yawn. One glance at his face told her that the tensions of the night were left behind him—that he was ready (thanks to an alchemy she could only half understand) for whatever the day might bring.

"How's the head, darling?" She managed to keep her voice light and hoped that she had not betrayed the sick hopelessness that gripped her.

"Clear as a bell," he said cheerfully. "Apparently I've the sort of brain that thrives on hard knocks." He moved quickly to the dugout steps and studied the terrain beyond the ridge. "Did you notice that the firing has stopped?"

"I haven't heard a shot since midnight," said Father Tim.

Kay, strapping her impromptu food pack, managed to force a smile. "Could it be the war is over?"

Paul shook his head. "The enemy is waiting too—just as we've been doing here. Probably they can't believe that Hill 1049 is theirs at last."

The estimate was confirmed when the two enlisted men returned from their scout. "We worked down the ridge, sir," said Furness, "and we had a look in all the gullies. If I didn't know better I'd swear they'd gone home."

"Any sign of casualties to the south?"

Furness crossed himself before he spoke. "Counted a hundred dead on the first slope, sir. And the weapons-carrier was *kaput*."

So Hardin's dash for the rear had met its just reward. Kay could not keep down a savage thrill of pleasure at the news.

"Was he killed or captured?"

"Captured's my guess, ma'am," the sergeant said. "A line officer would be quite a prize."

Jackson, squatting on the bottom step of the dugout, straightened up with a bray of laughter. "No offense, Cap'n—but isn't it a victory for us—if the *gooks* have the colonel?"

"Don't sound off too soon, Harry," said the sergeant. "We may still meet in Pyongyang——"

The strained banter died as Kay gave a sharp gasp. *"Someone's outside, Paul!"*

Paul lifted his hand for silence as Jackson moved toward the door. "Shall I have a look, sir?"

"Keep your places—everyone. Remember, this is an aid station. It establishes our identity if we're found here as a group."

This time Kay discovered that emotion was stronger than self-control and gripped Paul's arm for assurance. In the silence that followed his order there was no mistaking the clatter of feet outside or the identity of the shadow that fell across the dugout door. Clinging to Paul with all her strength, Kay felt her heart skip a beat while the shadow changed into a man—a dwarf soldier in a blue-gray quilted uniform.

There was no need to translate the one-word command, barked in a strange tongue: like the burp gun on the man's arm, the meaning was unmistakable. Kay felt her grip on Paul relax. She raised her hands with the others in mute admission of her new status as a prisoner of war.

The Presidio

BEFORE they could leave Sausalito the bright promise of noon had blurred: fog warnings were lighted on the Golden Gate Bridge when the maroon convertible sped down the last ramp. Kay had passed the bridge entrance to the Presidio by instinct—turning instead to enter the bustle of downtown San Francisco. It had seemed only logical to grant Hi Saunders an extra quarter hour to state his case. Now, as the car sighed to a stop at a traffic light, she gave him a sidelong smile.

"Don't tell me I can still back out," she said. "We both know I'm in this for the duration."

"Bringing you in like this is a gamble, pure and simple," said the lawyer. "Have I made that clear?"

"Perfectly: you've said Paul can't win without me. What else matters?"

"Maybe nothing can save Paul. If this gamble fails, you may find yourself minus a career—and a reputation."

"Stop talking nonsense. Tell me what to do."

"I refuse to rehearse you, Kay. You're being smuggled into court today as a surprise package for MacArdle. We'd ruin the effect if we wrote the dialogue in advance."

"Suppose he asks questions I can't answer?"

"There's no question that can't be answered, once it gets past the presiding judge. That's the risk you'll be taking, Kay. Still game?"

The girl reached over to squeeze the lawyer's hand and jumped the car through the changing light. "I liked you better in Sausalito," she said. "When you were being completely ruthless. Can't you stay ruthless—for Paul's sake?"

"I guess that makes you our girl Friday," said Hi, much more cheerfully. "In fact, it was your final test."

"You'd put Father Tim on the stand if he were alive, wouldn't you?"

"Like a shot. This trial could use a saint or two."

"What about a sinner—if she has a good story to tell?"

"For the last time, Kay, we can't bring up Hill 1049. Sellers will only nail me for contempt."

"Surely there's some way to expose Hardin for what he is."

"When he's on the stand I'll get in every rabbit punch I can. With luck, a few of them may bruise him. But your story must begin with the meeting at Sinmak, when you were all P.O.W.s."

They fell silent on that gloomy note, while the car climbed the high ground to the Presidio. Kay spoke just once more, after Hi had shown his pass at the gate.

"Must I be in the same room with Hardin?"

"No, Kay—that's one thing you're spared in a court-martial. The witnesses come in separately. I'll closet you in a special room with Les Pearson. He's my junior partner —a Harvard man with a sense of humor and a sharp game of gin."

"You think of everything, don't you, Hi? Can I see Paul for a moment?"

"Better not—it might spoil everything."

ii

Paul was already waiting at the defendant's table when Hi entered the courtroom. A glance at the lawyer's bland countenance answered his question in advance.

"Enjoy your lunch at Tarrantino's?"

"Enormously," said Hi. "Did you take the rest I pre-scribed?"

Paul continued to study the lawyer narrowly. "You're go-ing to call Kay, aren't you?"

"Of course I am."

"Where is she now?"

"Down the hall, trimming my junior partner at gin rummy. What's more, you're to leave her strictly alone."

Paul subsided with a small groan that was not alto-gether despairing. Much as he feared the outcome of Hi's strategy, he could not keep down a feeling of release. With Kay outside the courtroom door he no longer felt alone.

"Will she go on the stand today?"

"Probably—if Hardin's been as well coached as Mac-Ardle's other boys. Once your old C.O. has recited, I'm sure the prosecution will rest its case. He's waiting to make his entrance: I saw him in the corridor just now, strutting for the photographers."

Lawyer and client rose while the court filed in to take its seats. Paul kept his eyes down when he heard Major MacArdle's crisp voice order a military policeman to bring in the next witness—but he was still amazed by the oblique glimpse of Colonel Jasper Hardin.

At Pyongyang the colonel had fared better than most—but he had resembled a scarecrow more than a line officer when he had led his troops from the compound for repa-triation. Today it was incredible that the bandbox officer in the witness chair and the prisoner Paul last remembered were one and the same. Hardin's manner was as sharp as the creases of his beautifully tailored uniform; even the snow-white hair and mustache added, in some queer fash-ion, to the impression of solidity. If those white hairs were dramatic proofs of the ordeal this man had suffered, the man himself had obviously emerged with colors flying.

The witness showed no awareness of Paul's presence at the defense table while he answered the first routine questions. His voice was both stern and relaxed: judging by the hush in the courtroom, he had made a good impression on his audience. At the press tables a score of pencils were dancing busily. Paul glanced at Larry Kirk—impassive as a totem in the midst of the fourth estate—and felt he could write the commentator's next broadcast in advance.

MacArdle asked his first significant question with deceptive gentleness. "Colonel, I believe you were the signer of the charges against Captain Scott?"

"I was."

"For your information, Specifications One and Two of Charge One have been withdrawn by ruling of the convening authority."

"I bow to orders, as always."

Paul, listening to every inflection, gave an inward sigh: Hardin, it seemed, was an actor of parts. Despite the correctness of his response, he had conveyed the impression that he disapproved thoroughly of the convening authority's action.

"Colonel, other witnesses have covered most of the period of your imprisonment. There has been testimony that you and Captain Scott did not get on well together. Can you tell us why?"

"Captain Scott was always resentful of military authority —particularly mine."

"Can you give some details?"

"He was lax in preparing his reports."

"Did you warn him of this specifically?"

"On several occasions. I explained, as kindly as I could, where he was in error. I gave him every chance to rectify his mistakes."

"Did he?"

"Eventually—and with obvious reluctance."

"Colonel Hardin, other witnesses have stated that there was a clash between you and Captain Scott near the Korean town of Sinmak shortly after your capture by the enemy."

"That is true."

"Can you recall the date?"

"My memory is hazy there. Scott's group and mine were taken separately. It happened the first moment we joined forces."

"Do you remember the cause?"

"Distinctly. According to military law I was in command of all personnel in the two merged groups, since I was the senior officer present. There was room for a few of us to sleep inside a covered area—I believe it was a cow shed. Captain Scott stated that he had already bribed the guards to open the shed. He used cigarettes from a pack of Army rations. As commanding officer, it was clearly my right to assign billets as I saw fit. When I attempted to do so Captain Scott was insolent and refused to let me make the assignments."

"Did he give a reason?"

"He said the cigarettes were his—and that the billets were already occupied by his own group."

"What did you do?"

Hardin shrugged—and the gesture was as tolerant as his voice. "I did not make an issue of it, though it was my clear duty to check the misuse of supplies by Army personnel."

"Colonel, was this your first major clash with Captain Scott?"

"Frankly I wouldn't call it a major clash. All of us were pretty tired: tempers are apt to flare at such a time."

"You say you were captured in two separate groups. How did that separation occur?"

Hardin hesitated so artfully that Paul could have sworn the reluctance was genuine. "When we withdrew from Hill 1049 Captain Scott refused to join us. He stayed in the first-aid bunker, and kept his detail with him."

"Did you order him to join the retreat?"

"I did."

"Wouldn't you say *that* was a major clash—if he refused to obey an order under fire?"

"It was a pretty tight corner for a civilian soldier. Perhaps he felt there was less risk in being captured than in joining a withdrawing action."

Paul leaned toward Hi across the defense table. "The court wouldn't let *us* cover what happened before the capture."

"Easy does it, boy—and don't ask me to object just yet. I'm giving them rope."

MacArdle fired the next question point-blank. "Why didn't you include this in the charges against Captain Scott?"

Again Hardin's slight hesitation could not have seemed more genuine. "The tension was great. I didn't wish to accuse a man of cowardice—"

"*Objection!*" barked Hi.

Sellers leaned down from the bench. "On what grounds?"

It was Hi's turn to rise and face the cameras—and the attentive courtroom. "I would much prefer to let this line of questioning continue," he said. "The court must realize that I was not allowed to question witnesses concerning events prior to Captain Scott's capture. Trial counsel has now introduced just such an incident. I must warn the court that the defense intends to probe this matter thoroughly during cross-questioning. If need be, we will recall all witnesses—until the true facts about the surrender of Hill 1049 are brought out."

For the first time Paul noted a spasm of uneasiness in the witness. Caught off balance, MacArdle did not counter Hi's statement at once, and it was necessary for Sellers to gavel the onlookers into silence before the trial counsel could speak.

"With the permission of the court," he said, "I move that

all questions and answers beginning with *You were captured in two separate groups. How did that separation occur?* be stricken from the record, and that the members of the court be instructed by the president to disregard them."

"Defense objects to this motion," said Hi. "It is designed to prevent defense from bringing out points favorable to the accused."

Again the president's gavel enforced quiet. "The motion is approved," he said. "The reporter will strike from the record all references to events before the capture." He leaned forward again—and this time his glare transfixed the unfortunate MacArdle. "Trial counsel is warned against further introduction of extraneous matter. You may proceed with the witness."

The prosecutor's voice had regained its timbre: only the receding flush at his collar line betrayed his awareness of a narrow escape. "Other witnesses, Colonel, have said they felt that Captain Scott was co-operating with the enemy when he was placed in charge of the prison hospital at Pyongyang. Was that your impression?"

"Not at the time."

Paul turned startled eyes on Hardin. Aware though he was of MacArdle's expert coaching, he had not expected this.

"When you began your prison term you had no doubts as to Captain Scott's loyalty?"

"None whatever. In fact it was I who recommended that he be put in charge of cleaning up the camp and improving conditions at the hospital."

"Why did you recommend him?"

"Dr. Scott was the best physician available; no one can deny that."

"Did later events justify the recommendation?"

"So far as the disease rate at camp was concerned. Both prisoners and guards were better for the change. But I can see now it was a serious error—so far as Captain Scott him-self was concerned."

"Why do you say that?"

"Well—by putting him in close contact with the Chi-nese, I'm afraid I made it easier for him to—"

"To collaborate?"

"Objection!" snapped Hi. "Trial counsel is coaching the witness."

"I will rephrase the query," said MacArdle. "Colonel, what evidence did you have of Captain Scott's alleged co-operation with the Chinese prison authorities?"

"First of all, there was the matter of the interroga-tions——"

"Interrogations?"

"All of us were badgered incessantly by the enemy se-curity officers. Some of us were tortured when we—refused to give the right answers." Hardin studied his beautifully-manicured nails. "Captain Scott was almost never ques-tioned, from the moment he took over the hospital."

"Was his lot made easier in other ways?"

"In many ways. For one thing, he used the hospital as a personal asylum—"

"More than his duties demanded?"

"In my opinion, much more."

"Was he quartered there?"

"He was not. I'd given orders that he should share a bar-racks with the other prisoners. I could hardly object to his spending time with the hospital personnel, and with Miss Storey."

"Was Miss Storey quartered in the hospital?"

"Permanently—after she volunteered to serve as a nurse."

"What were Captain Scott's relations with her?"

"They were very close."

"Closer than is usual with a doctor and his nurse?"

"I'd prefer not to answer that."

"I request that you answer, sir—however reluctant you may be to do so."

"Objection," said Hi. "Trial counsel is attempting to imply something improper in Miss Storey's relationship to Dr. Scott. It is no secret that they contemplated marriage at the time."

"Trial counsel will keep to the charges," said the president.

MacArdle bowed to the court. "It was your impression, Colonel, that Captain Scott was collaborating with the enemy. When did you become certain?"

"When he operated on Colonel Pak, the camp commandant."

"You were Captain Scott's commanding officer. Did he discuss the operation with you?"

"He did not. He knew I would object."

"On what grounds?"

"If Pak had died during the operation, there would have been reprisals against us all."

"Then, in your opinion, Captain Scott risked your lives by operating?"

"There's no question about it."

"Could not the opposite have been true, sir? Surely Captain Scott would have been punished had he refused to operate."

"He was the only competent doctor in the camp. Had he said it was not an operative case, none of his Chinese colleagues would have disputed the diagnosis."

"You believe, then, that Captain Scott seized this chance to ingratiate himself with the prison head—by making it appear that he had saved his life?"

"That is my opinion. It was shared by the whole camp. Scott was ostracized afterward."

"Let us proceed to the time of the armistice, Colonel. It has been stated that Captain Scott refused repatriation because he wished to remain with Chaplain O'Fallon. Defense counsel has alleged that the chaplain was desperately ill from a lung hemorrhage. To your knowledge, had Chaplain O'Fallon suffered this complication?"

"Not to my knowledge."

"Did Captain Scott, in your hearing, give this as a reason for his remaining behind?"

"No, he did not."

Paul could not trust himself to protest aloud. What Hardin had just said was outright perjury—yet an objection at this time would only have forced a question of credibility which could not possibly be resolved in his favor. Bottling his helpless anger, he contented himself with a glance at Hi—whose shrug told him that the lawyer was also aware of the impasse.

MacArdle, pretending to consult his assistant, had given Hardin's last reply a good ten seconds to register. Subsiding in his chair, Paul admitted that the prosecutor's timing had been perfect. The faces of the seven officers on the bench, which had seemed calmly judicial when the afternoon session began, now loomed above him like avenging Fates.

"What reason, if any, did Captain Scott give for remaining at Pyongyang?"

"He gave none in my presence."

"Did he request that you notify the American truce authorities?"

"I had no such request," said Hardin.

"Why, in your opinion, did he choose to remain?"

"I judged that he had chosen to cast his lot with the enemy."

"Did you attempt to dissuade him, Colonel?"

"No. I felt that it was quite useless. We had been over two years at Pyongyang. For most of that time I had observed his leanings toward Communism—"

"Objection," said Hi. "No such leanings have been proved."

"Denied," snapped the president. "Subject to objection by any member of the court."

So far, this coda to the president's ruling had been a mere formality. This time, however, Major Duggan leaned forward. "I object to this denial," he said quietly. "I request a vote by the court on the question."

For the first time in the trial the judges did not rise to discuss the point at issue—and this reluctance to leave the courtroom was, in itself, an ominous portent. After a moment of whispers and note taking, Duggan leaned back in his chair with a chastened look.

"Objection is overruled by vote of the court," said Colonel Sellers. "Proceed, Major MacArdle."

"You may complete your answer, Colonel."

"I had seen Captain Scott leaning toward Communism for a long time. I was hardly surprised at his decision to remain behind and felt it would be pointless to discuss the matter further."

"Did you make any comment on his decision?"

"I may have."

"Your sergeant major has testified that you said *I don't care if the son-of-a-bitch never goes back home—except to face a court-martial*. Did you make such a statement?"

"I believe it was to that effect."

MacArdle turned to the prosecutor's table and returned with a much-creased sheet of paper. "I now introduce this paper as evidence," he said solemnly. "I request that the reporter mark it exhibit for identification."

The paper went from hand to hand and was duly recorded.

"Have you seen this paper before, Colonel?"

"I have. It is a copy of a confession made by Captain Scott at Pyongyang."

"Objection," said Hi. "It has not been proved that such a confession was ever made."

"The prosecution is in the process of proving that very thing."

"Objection overruled," said Colonel Sellers, "subject to objection by any member of the court." He glanced at Duggan, but the major's face was a stone mask.

"When did you first see the paper you now hold in your hand, Colonel?"

"Last fall at Pyongyang. It was one of two copies."

"Were the copies identical?"

"They were."

"Who asked you to examine them?"

"Colonel Pak."

"Were both copies signed?"

"Yes—by Captain Scott."

"Did you recognize his signature?"

"I did."

"Would you certify that this is one of the originals?"

"I would. In fact I have done so on this sheet."

"Please read the entire document, Colonel."

Hardin opened the paper on his knee and read slowly and deliberately—a schoolboy rendition by a man unused to reading aloud. For that very reason the impact of the words were even more damning:

> "I, Captain Paul R. Scott, a medical officer in the United States Army, make this confession of my own free will and without torture or coercion.
>
> "I confess that I helped to prepare bombs containing bacteria and other disease-producing agents, to be dropped on defenseless towns and cities of North Korea.
>
> "I have been shown one of these bombs that was dropped on the city of Pyongyang, and I have identified it as being

```
exactly similar to bombs which I myself
helped to load.

    "I make this confession so that the
world may know how I and my fellow Ameri-
cans have used inhuman methods of warfare
against the North Korean people and the
Volunteers from the Chinese People's
Republic.

    "I am sorry for my part in this in-
human action and state that the punish-
ment I have received is a just one for my
crimes.

                    Signed, Paul R. Scott.
                    Captain, Medical Corps.
                    United States Army."
```

There was a long moment of silence in the court when the reading finished, which the prosecutor made no effort to break. When he spoke he did not lift his voice above a whisper.

"No further questions at this time."

iii

Hi Saunders got to his feet. Before he began his cross-examination he stared hard at the witness. "That was a most effective reading," he said. "Obviously you are quite familiar with this document."

"Naturally I am. I brought it from Korea."

"For the express purpose of persecuting Captain Scott?"

"Objection," said MacArdle: he had not troubled to raise his voice—and barely smiled when the court sustained him.

"Colonel, why were you so careful to bring this document from Korea?"

"I felt the authorities should see it without delay."

"You have testified that this was one of two original copies—both of them signed by Captain Scott. How did you manage to obtain it?"

"Colonel Pak gave it to me the day it was signed," said Hardin. "I felt it should be preserved as part of the camp records."

"The newspapers have stated that other prisoners made similar confessions in that same compound. Did you also preserve copies of their confessions?"

"They were not given to me by the Chinese."

"But the document you are holding was?"

The witness passed the paper to the court reporter. With the gesture, he seemed to wash his hands of a distasteful contact. "I have so stated."

"Colonel, doesn't it seem strange that only this alleged confession was handed to you—out of several others broadcast by the Chinese?"

"Not at all. Colonel Pak valued it more highly than the others."

"Isn't it true, Colonel, that you *asked* for this original document so that reproductions could be made?"

"It is not."

"How do you account for the fact that the whole camp was flooded with copies?"

"I can't account for it."

"Weren't they mimeographed and distributed by members of your staff?"

"Not on my order."

"Very well, Colonel. You have testified that, as ranking officer in the compound, you were in charge of prisoners?"

"I was—subject to the authority of the Chinese commander."

"Did you know that Chaplain O'Fallon and Miss Storey were placed in solitary confinement?"

"I had heard that they were."

"Did Captain Scott tell you that they had become dangerously ill?"

"He did."

"What action did you take—if any?"

"I spoke to Colonel Pak; he refused to release them."

"You're positive you intervened, Colonel? You did not refuse aid and order Captain Scott from your quarters?"

"I did not."

"And you did not realize, months later, that Captain Scott signed what he knew was a bogus confession—in order to save Miss Storey and Chaplain O'Fallon from dying?"

"I realized no such thing."

"Very well, Colonel. Let us now proceed to the operation on Colonel Pak. You have said that you think Captain Scott endangered the safety of the prisoners by rushing the operation?"

"That is correct."

"You have also stated, I believe, that Captain Scott is a competent surgeon."

"I said he was the best available."

"Would you expect a competent surgeon to let a man die—after he had diagnosed a condition which surgery could cure?"

"Perhaps not—if he had the patient in a modern hospital. With the equipment in the prison, a major operation was obviously hazardous."

"More hazardous, for example, than one performed in a front-line surgical bunker?"

"Circumstances alter cases."

"Do they? For your information Captain Scott operated on me in the front lines when the whole salient was under heavy enemy pressure. The operation he performed on me was an intestinal resection—far more dangerous than Colonel Pak's. Yet, had he not taken that risk I would be dead today—and so would Pak. Do you still feel that he should have let the patient die?"

"I think he should not have operated," said Hardin firmly. "Whether or not Pak would have died is a question I cannot decide."

"Colonel Hardin, have you ever heard of medical ethics?"

"Of course."

"Didn't Dr. Scott's code force him to operate if he thought there was a chance of saving a life? Isn't it immaterial if the patient was friend or enemy?"

"Perhaps. But I repeat that his decision was influenced by his desire to curry favor with the Chinese. It is my opinion that he needlessly risked the lives of others in the camp by aiding the enemy."

Hi faced the television cameras for a moment of thought. "Let us proceed to another topic," he said. "Other witnesses have testified that you operated a special prison mess for your headquarters. Will you tell the court whether or not your staff had better food than the other prisoners?"

"We may have. The Geneva Convention says that differences in treatment among prisoners is lawful and is based on rank."

"Did Captain Scott receive preferential treatment?"

"He spent much time at the hospital, as I've already said. Food was better there."

"Is it your belief he ate at the hospital?"

Hardin shrugged and glanced at the court. "It was his own fault if he didn't."

"Then it is your opinion that if Captain Scott did not get enough to eat, it was his own fault?"

"Something like that. Prison conditions at Pyongyang were unspeakably bad."

"Were they hard for you, Colonel?"

"Extremely. I was very low for the first fortnight of my imprisonment—"

"May I ask the nature of your illness?"

"It wasn't an illness. It was exhaustion, following the march to Pyongyang."

"Who made that diagnosis?"

"Dr. Scott."

"Did he treat you thereafter?"

"I recovered on my own. All I really needed was rest and nourishment—such as it was."

"But Dr. Scott prescribed a regimen that hastened your recovery?"

"Not as I recall—beyond standard medication."

"Colonel Hardin, isn't it true that you were suffering from the aftereffects of alcoholism?"

Major MacArdle was on his feet with an instant shout of fury. "Counsel for the defense is trying to blacken the witness' character, for obvious motives." He was still sputtering when Colonel Sellers' gavel fell.

"Court desires to address the witness," he said. "Colonel Hardin, you need not answer the last question—"

"I've no objection," said Hardin. "The answer is no."

"If the court please," said Hi, "we are prepared to prove the contrary."

"How?"

"By the testimony of two witnesses—Miss Storey and the accused."

"Do you have medical records to back this assertion?"

"No, sir. No records were brought from the prison camp at Pyongyang other than Colonel Hardin's file."

"Objection sustained," said Colonel Sellers. "The honor of an American officer is involved here, Mr. Saunders. Further questions in this vein may force me to lodge a contempt charge against you."

Hi stood with bowed head while the whispers died in the courtroom.

"Disregarding the nature of your indisposition, Colonel," Hi said, "did you recover promptly?"

"In about two weeks—yes." During the exchange, Hardin's plumage had remained unruffled. He seemed to preen himself now as he pulled down the waistband of his perfectly cut tunic, the left breast heavy with its sunburst of campaign ribbons.

"Colonel, I have here two reports of physical examinations that I am about to introduce into the record. I will read paragraphs from each report, describing the general condition of the person examined—"

The president frowned down from the bench while the court reporter was tagging the exhibits for the defense. "Mr. Saunders, can any possible purpose be served by this expenditure of time?"

"The court has my assurance that a considerable purpose will be served."

"You may proceed."

"Colonel Hardin, here is a general description of one prisoner returned after the armistice; he was examined by Major Strauss of the Army Medical Department at the exchange point in Korea. I will read from the record, as signed by Major Strauss."

> This officer is markedly emaciated. Practically all the subcutaneous fat is absent. Lips and mucous membranes quite pale, indicating advanced secondary anemia. Moderate night blindness. Advanced skin irritation of the pellagric type. Exquisite tenderness along the peripheral nerves. Marked inflammation of the gums suggestive of scurvy. Whole picture indicates chronic advanced starvation and vitamin lack. Hospitalization was suggested but refused by the patient.

Hi put down the first sheet of the exhibit and picked up the second. "Now, Colonel, I'll read from an examination made by the same medical officer on another returning prisoner:

> This officer's skin is tanned and smooth. Color
> of lips and mucous membranes good. Some evi-
> dence of loss of weight, but general state of nutri-
> tion excellent. Reflexes normal. No tenderness along
> the peripheral nerves. State of teeth and gums
> sound. No disturbance of vision to gross tests.

The defense lawyer returned both sheets to the reporter.
"I don't think one needs to be a physician to see a marked
difference between these two prisoners—do you, Colonel?"

"Obviously not."

"The first officer has certainly suffered a starvation regimen—as did most of the inmates at the camp in Pyongyang?"

"It seems logical from the evidence," said Hardin.

"I read these reports into the record, Colonel, because
the first describes the condition of Captain Paul Scott on
his repatriation. The second report is your own. No further
questions."

No one stirred in the court when Hi returned to his table; even MacArdle (whose mouth had opened to shout an
objection) had restrained the impulse in time and sat with
sagging jaw. It was only when Sellers glanced in his direction that he rose for his rebuttal.

"He'll make this short," Hi whispered to Paul. "That *was*
a rabbit punch—and I intended it to be."

The prosecutor had accepted a glass of water from his
assistant before he snatched up his notes. He seemed to
address his first question to the court rather than Hardin—
who was staring glassily into space out of a face that had
turned into a turkey-red mask.

"Colonel Hardin, did you at any time ask for special
favors from the Chinese commander at the Pyongyang
prison camp?"

"Never."

"So if your treatment *was* better than others, it was
through no request of yours?"

"It was not."

"No further questions. The prosecution rests."

iv

There was no visible reaction from the spectators while Hardin passed down the aisle, walking with his familiar marionette strut. Only the slight sag between his shoulder blades told Paul that he had felt Hi's last blow: the military mold had weathered the impact, no matter how the man within might be cringing.

When Kay entered the courtroom behind the sergeant at arms her color was high: Paul surmised uneasily that her path had crossed Hardin's in the anteroom. Hoping that she would offer him a passing glance, he knew that she would be too wise to risk it. This, after all, was an ordeal she had sought against his pleading.

Hi took his time in the preliminary questioning, building the background picture with a few strokes, and permitting Kay to tell her story in her own words. This testimony included her arrival in Korea and the impulse that had brought her to Hill 1049.

"Will you describe your capture, Miss Storey?"

"The five of us were alone in the bunker when the firing stopped. All at once there was a Chinese soldier in the doorway. Then a half dozen. Then a swarm—"

"Were you harmed in any way?"

"No, Mr. Saunders. We were—herded with other prisoners and marched to the rear—"

Hearing the clear, quiet voice go on, Paul remembered his own astonishment at that matter-of-fact capture. Somehow the ordeal would have been less dreadful had there been overt abuse—but their captors had simply taken them for granted. Accustomed as they were to bagging prisoners in wholesale lots, they had handled that day's batch like cattle—feeding them enough to keep their feet in mo-

tion, letting them pant a few moments at the roadside when
exhaustion overtook them. . . .

"Let us proceed to your reunion with Colonel Hardin's
group, Miss Storey. How long had you been marching
when you reached Sinmak?"

"I'm not sure. I'm afraid I'd lost track of time."

Time had really stood still that day, thought Paul—time
had become a waking dream with no visible boundaries,
broken only by those halts in the open field, the occasional
feedings. But he could remember the farmyard outside Sinmak clearly—the whitewashed command post that dominated the crossroads, the guards with fixed bayonets and
identical stares, the sudden, grateful pelting of the rain on
his dust-caked body. When they had tumbled into the
straw of the cow shed that formed one wall of the farmyard they had been too exhausted to think. No one had
troubled to ask why this small group of five had been detached from the marching column. . . .

"Did your captors explain the reason for the halt at Sinmak, Miss Storey?"

"Not at the time. We learned the reason later. They'd
found our records on Hill 1049. Enough, at any rate, to
learn that we were a medical unit attached to the 141st
Battalion."

The mills of the law grind slowly, thought Paul: he
could truly admire Kay's poise and the precision of her answers. The fact that Colonel Jasper Hardin and the members of his staff had been held captive in a compound
nearby to await their arrival here was only a coincidence
of war. The fact that a truck had rolled into their bivouac
that night, dumping Hardin into the courtyard before it
rumbled on, seemed a grotesque joke—though all of them
were too tired for laughter. . . .

"Can you recall when your two groups made contact,
Miss Storey?"

"Perhaps a half hour after sunset."

"You had already taken possession of the cow shed?"

"Only Captain Scott and I were awake. The others had collapsed in the straw."

"And the newcomers?"

"None of the guards spoke English. They simply pushed Hardin and his group into the courtyard and locked the gates."

"Leaving them to shift for themselves?"

"You might put it that way, Mr. Saunders."

"Were you carrying rations at the time?"

"All of us had packs."

"Did you offer to share them with the others?"

"Yes, we did. One of the men had been slightly wounded. Captain Scott put on a new dressing with my help and gave him some tablets."

"When and how did the clash between Captain Scott and Colonel Hardin occur?"

"When they began searching for billets and found we'd taken the shed."

"Why, in your opinion, did Captain Scott refuse to surrender his shelter?"

"We'd been marching for days; they had ridden all that afternoon by truck. Captain Scott felt we should keep up our strength. Besides, Chaplain O'Fallon was suffering from a persistent cough. Both of us refused to waken him. When Colonel Hardin attempted to force an entrance, we barred the door. Unfortunately we forgot to close the hay chute as well—"

"Why do you say unfortunately?"

"Sometime that night an attempt was made on Captain Scott's life—"

"By whom, Miss Storey?"

"We'll never be sure now. But I think it was Colonel Hardin."

This time the surge of voices in the courtroom went unrebuked, while Sellers glared down at the witness as though he could not quite believe his ears.

"Mr. Saunders, I've already warned you—"

Hi stood his ground and his voice was as harsh as the president's. "If it please the court, Miss Storey's opinions are her own."

"The court will question the witness."

Silence clamped down on the room as the president fixed his eye on Kay. "Miss Storey, the insinuation you are making is of the utmost seriousness. Think well before you answer. Why did you mention Colonel Hardin's name?"

"For two reasons." Kay's voice was clear and cold. "Father O'Fallon was a light sleeper. He wakened around midnight and saw the colonel's face at the hay chute. Captain Scott himself wakened later and heard an intruder moving about the shed. They wrestled for a moment. Then the—visitor left the way he had entered—"

"By the hay chute?"

"Yes. This time Captain Scott closed the trap door and slept until morning. That's when he discovered the weapon."

"What weapon?"

"A *sake* bottle. Or rather the neck, and a broken edge."

"What does this have to do with Colonel Hardin?"

"The night before, he was drunk when he got down from the truck. Drunk on *sake*—we smelled it on his breath."

"Miss Storey, did you see this bottle with your own eyes?"

"I saw it in the morning."

"Did *you* see anyone enter the cow shed?"

"I'm afraid I slept through it all."

"Are you aware that hearsay is not evidence in a court of law?"

"Mr. Saunders said I could express an opinion. Someone tried to take Captain Scott's life that night—"

"Your opinion cannot be accepted," said the president.

"Not without eyewitness proof. The reporter will strike this whole interchange from the record." Sellers turned back to Hi. "Defense counsel is excused in this instance—the witness is obviously unrehearsed. But a similar allegation, if unsupported by prima-facie evidence, will earn a citation for contempt. This is your final warning."

Hi acknowledged the rebuke with a curt nod. "With all due respect to the court," he said, "I must point out that a threat upon the life of the accused is most pertinent."

"Miss Storey was asleep. So, it seems, were Sergeant Furness and Corporal Jackson. Father O'Fallon is in the grave. Produce an eyewitness, Mr. Saunders, or take another line."

Hi turned back to Kay. "Let us move on, Miss Storey. You say that Colonel Hardin and his group arrived by truck. Did they use the same means of departure?"

"They left by truck early the next morning."

"Did the colonel offer you transport?"

"He did, but I refused—after he said he couldn't take Chaplain O'Fallon as well."

"How did Colonel Hardin react to your refusal?"

"He told me that on second thought there was no room for either of us in the truck."

"Was it then that Lieutenant Crosby volunteered to walk with your group—so that the chaplain could ride?"

"It was. Even then the colonel was reluctant to take Father Tim."

"Can you give any valid reason?"

"There were two: the chaplain and Captain Scott were good friends."

"And the other?"

"Am I forbidden to say that the colonel was suffering from hangover and had run out of *sake?*"

Hi turned to Sellers with a wordless apology, while the president gaveled for silence.

"In your judgment, Miss Storey, was there room in the truck for both you and Chaplain O'Fallon?"

"There was room for us all."

"Let us move on to the prison camp at Pyongyang. When did you reach it?"

"About two weeks after Colonel Hardin."

"Did you march the whole distance?"

"We marched as long as we could. Eventually we collapsed by the roadside. We were taken the rest of the way in carts."

"How do you account for your assignment to the prison hospital as a nurse?"

"It was Captain Scott's suggestion. He knew I'd had nursing training and felt I'd recover my strength there."

"Was your recovery complete?"

"Yes—except for an attack of amebiasis. I was in good health until I was placed in solitary confinement."

"When was that?"

"In the spring of 1952. Solitary was a special discipline at the camp, to punish prisoners who wouldn't co-operate. We were put on a starvation diet—"

At the defense table Paul closed his eyes as the voice went on. He could still remember the skeleton-thin body that had emerged from the detention pen: had Kay been the phantom she resembled, she would have seemed heavier in his arms. . . . Somehow, he told himself, her story *must* reach the hearts of the court. But there was no change in those seven masks as the recital went on.

"Toward the last," said Kay, "I was too delirious to remember what really happened—until I wakened in a hospital bed."

"Did anyone explain why you were confined?"

"They wanted to make Captain Scott sign the confession."

"Did you expect him to sign it?"

"I prayed that he wouldn't."

"Even if it meant your death?"

"I knew that Colonel Hardin would use the confession to wreck Paul's career."

"You loved Captain Scott enough to die rather than let that happen?"

"I hoped I'd have the courage to endure. When I was out of my head I was afraid I'd send for him. But I didn't. I'm sure of that much."

"We now come to the repatriation of the prisoners, Miss Storey. Did Captain Scott tell you why he stayed behind?"

"He did. Chaplain O'Fallon had suffered a severe hemorrhage after his own confinement in solitary. He would have died if Captain Scott hadn't given him a transfusion. When the exchange of prisoners was arranged the chaplain was too weak to move: Captain Scott was almost sure he'd die eventually—but he felt he should remain."

"Did he tell anyone else of his decision?"

"He informed Colonel Pak—in Colonel Hardin's hearing."

Paul saw that the president had glanced up sharply at this contradiction of Hardin's testimony. The look he fastened on Kay was far from benign.

"The court will question the witness, Mr. Saunders. Remember, Miss Storey, you are under oath. Were you present at the meeting you describe?"

"I was not: I was ill myself at the time. Captain Scott told me about it later."

"The reporter will strike the witness' last reply from the record as hearsay. Proceed, Mr. Saunders—and try to keep to your point."

"Did Captain Scott send any message to the United States Army authorities?"

"Yes—via Colonel Hardin."

Again the court cut in sharply, forcing Kay to admit that this, too, was hearsay—and again the reply was erased.

"Did you also wish to remain and nurse the chaplain?" asked Hi, with weary patience.

"Very much—but I was too ill. Captain Scott insisted I leave at once so that I could be flown to Japan."

"Were you surprised when you learned that Colonel Hardin had accused Captain Scott of collaboration?"

"I was more shocked than surprised. I knew it was inevitable."

"No further questions."

v

MacArdle came forward with a cat-and-canary smile.

"Miss Storey, what is your profession?"

"I am an actress."

"Am I correct in assuming that you plan to star in a forthcoming motion picture—based on your experiences in the Korean War?"

"Such a picture is in preparation. So far, no contracts have been signed."

"It is true that you attained wide popularity among the enlisted men in an act called *The Girl Next Door?*"

"It was a song fest in which the men participated—not an act."

"Did you also entertain the prison inmates?"

"Yes, on the few occasions the Chinese allowed us to sing."

"Now, Miss Storey, a statement has been made in court —by the defense, I believe—that you and the accused were very close during your imprisonment. Is it not true that there has been intimacy between you?"

"At one time we planned to marry—"

"Answer my question, Miss Storey. Have you ever had intimate relations with Captain Scott?"

Hi was already roaring toward the bench. "You need not answer, Miss Storey—"

The president's gavel banged. "The court will rule on all answers, Mr. Saunders."

"Colonel Sellers, I must object, in the strongest terms. This line of questioning is beneath the dignity of the uniform the trial counsel wears. It is an insult to the witness and to the court."

"This witness," MacArdle countered, "has practically accused Colonel Hardin of perjury and of assault with intent to murder. In the face of such monstrous charges, it is my right to attack her credibility."

"Objection denied," rapped out Sellers, "subject to objection by any member of the court."

Major Duggan leaned forward, thought better of the interruption, and settled in his seat again. MacArdle's eyes swiveled to each face on the seven-man court: apparently he liked what he read there. "The reporter will read the question," he said quietly.

The corporal at the stenotype read tonelessly: *Answer my question, Miss Storey. Have you ever had intimate relations with Captain Scott?*

Kay did not speak at once; the flush that had stained her cheeks was gone now. "Yes—I have."

There was a scramble at the press table as reporters for afternoon papers dove for the hallway and the phones. Glancing at MacArdle, Paul guessed that he had been prepared for a negative response, which he would have been forced to twist to create the effect he desired. For once, he seemed at a loss for words.

"I—appreciate your frankness, Miss Storey," he said at last. "Let us go on to the encounter in the farmyard outside Sinmak. You have already told the court that you did not see Captain Scott's alleged attacker—"

"I know he was attacked."

"How can you know?"

"I believe what Captain Scott told me."

"Naturally, considering the intimacy between you."

"Objection!"

"Sustained," barked Sellers—and glared down the

bench, as though daring anyone to dispute the ruling.
"Clerk will strike the prosecutor's statement from the record as immaterial."

MacArdle rolled easily with the punch. "Now, Miss
Storey, about your hospital work. Didn't you fare better
there than you would have in barracks?"

"Yes, I did. It was something I worked for."

"That I can believe," said MacArdle.

"Proceed, Major," said the president. "We'll dispense
with dramatic asides."

"Miss Storey, were you permitted to live in the hospital
because Captain Scott specially recommended you?"

"I wasn't specially recommended. Captain Scott said
only that I was a former nurse—and that I might be useful.
There were no women's barracks: it solved the problem of
my billeting."

"After you'd established yourself at the hospital, Miss
Storey, did Captain Scott put in a good word for you
then?"

"I am sure he did not."

"On what grounds?"

"He said often that he could never bring himself to ask
for favors—either for himself or for me."

"But he did intervene to obtain your release from solitary?"

"Only because he knew both Chaplain O'Fallon and I
were dying there."

"We come now to the time of your repatriation. Did you
see Chaplain O'Fallon after his alleged hemorrhage?"

"He was under treatment at the hospital. No visitors
were allowed."

"So you have no personal knowledge that a hemorrhage
occurred?"

"Captain Scott told—"

"To your own knowledge?"

"No."

"So this illness of the chaplain's *could* have been used by Captain Scott as an excuse to refuse repatriation?"

"That is impossible."

"How do you know?"

"I know Captain Scott."

"I am nearly finished, Miss Storey: forgive me if this has proved trying. On your journey to Panmunjom and after-ward—how did Colonel Hardin treat you?"

"With courtesy."

"Did he not insist upon hospitalization in Tokyo and arrange plane priority?"

"He did—because Captain Scott asked him."

"Not because he, too, was genuinely concerned?"

"I thought so at the time. Now I see he was anxious to get me in a hospital bed before I could be interviewed."

"Why, Miss Storey?"

"Because he feared that I might refute the charges he intended to make against Captain Scott."

"If you felt this so strongly, why didn't you deny his statements at once?"

"I was desperately ill for weeks and didn't see a news-paper. When I did the damage was done. I made denials then, but it was too late—"

"That is all, Miss Storey."

MacArdle settled in his chair with the air of a school principal dismissing an unruly sophomore. Sellers glanced at Hi, who got to his feet.

"The defense has no further questions."

"Does any member of the court?"

When there was no answer the president rose and bowed to the witness with an odd old-world courtesy. It was, Paul felt sure, the salute of one fighter to another, the acknowledgment of a lost cause that had been contested gallantly.

"The court stands adjourned until ten tomorrow. You may step down, Miss Storey."

vi

Kay walked out of the courtroom with her eyes straight ahead. Though she did not risk a glance at the defense table she knew that Hi had laid a restraining hand on Paul's arm, lest he rush out after her. Despite the tumult in her brain, she could be grateful for that small mercy. Convinced, as she was, that she had just dealt Paul his death-blow, she could not face him now.

At the press table the staring moonface of Larry Kirk loomed up at her briefly: she could have sworn that he had nodded before he plunged into his notes. Then she was in the open air, blinking down the tears—and fighting the photographers.

"Just one more, Miss Storey!"

"Got a statement?"

"Will you marry him?"

"Still making that movie for Lindman?"

She got through, in time, with an assist from the MPs. When the gate of the parking lot clanged shut on the wolf pack, she knew privacy of a sort. It was a heaven-sent relief to be alone, to fumble at details—the car ticket in her purse, the ignition key that unlocked the door of her convertible. In a moment more she was roaring out of the Presidio. Through the racing motor she heard someone call her name and feared that it was Paul. She knew better than to look back.

Kay remembered little of the long, careening drive through the afternoon traffic. The room clerk at the Mark Hopkins brought her back to reality when she asked for the keys to her suite.

"Mr. Lindman took them, Miss Storey. He's been waiting for you since noon."

At least she was prepared for Eric: she was even grateful that he had come in person to release her from her agreement with the studio. At her foyer door she drew a deep breath before she tiptoed into the suite. Eric (magnificent in a white linen suit and a Liberty silk neckcloth) was stretched on a divan before the dead TV. A telephone was cradled on his shoulder; evidently he was in the midst of a long-distance call—a standard activity for the wonder boy, who was always giving his opinions to people at the ends of the earth. . . . This time, Kay gathered, long-distance was no farther than Hollywood, and the recipient of Eric's lecture was his studio head. What was really astounding was the fact that Barney Gould had been charmed into silence.

"I've told you this once, Barney," said Eric, "and I'll tell you again. Not even *I* can guess which way the public will jump. . . . All right! Eighty-one per cent of the messages came from women. Who else sets the fashion at the box office? . . . *Of course* you did right to tune in, Barney—you never did a smarter thing. . . . Yep, the press release is out: I phoned it in myself. . . . It'll hit the street in the late editions—"

Listening to the confident cadences of Eric's voice, Kay told herself that he might have spared her this—even though he could hardly know that she was an unwilling eavesdropper. A moment later, when he had replaced the phone, she squared her shoulders and made a brisk second entrance.

"*Eric!* I thought you were in Hollywood."

"I was, darling," said the wonder boy. "Until I heard you meant to testify. You've cost the studio a pretty penny in plane fares."

"You didn't have to fly back."

"I figured you'd need me afterward. Now I can see how right I was."

Kay stripped off her gloves, and flung her hat aside. "The picture's dead, Eric. You've already said as much."

"On the contrary. The picture was never more alive."

Kay settled in the nearest armchair—just before she felt

her knees give way. "Wasn't that Barney Gould on the phone?"

"It was Barney."

"Does he *still* want to sign me?"

"I've already initialed the contract in your name."

"But you *said* I'd dig my own grave if I testified—"

"Sometimes I'm appalled by my own ignorance." The wonder boy rose from his chair, circled the television warily, then gave it a punishing blow with one fist. "I've always insisted that this squawk box would ruin Hollywood—but it does have its uses."

"It does indeed," said Kay bitterly. "Today it helped to drive the last nail in Paul Scott's coffin."

"It also gave us the last big scene for *The Girl Next Door*. The *scène à faire*, as the French say—"

"Will you make sense, Eric?"

"Wake up, darling. Forty million females were glued to that box today, watching you go to bat for your man. And there's nothing the average female loves more than sacrifice."

"*Will you make sense?*"

"The moment you left the witness stand the studio was jammed with calls demanding that you get the part. It's been the same at the network. Your public has spoken, Kay —you can't ignore its voice."

Her first impulse was to knock the highball from Eric's hand, if only to crack that smiling mask. And then, as the import of his words reached her mind, Kay realized that he, too, was applauding her courage in his own strange fashion. Incredible as it might seem, Eric Lindman could be human at times. . . . If he had prolonged the suspense deliberately, it was only to drive his message home.

"Don't tell me the public is backing Paul?"

"On the contrary. So far, they've voted him guilty as charged. Those who were intelligent enough to express an opinion think that you were tragically misled—and they're cheering you all the more for it. In case you've forgotten, it's an old American custom to stand by the man you love. Never mind if he's hero or villain."

Kay covered her eyes with her hands. Her temples were throbbing madly: she needed all her strength to keep down a shout of idiot laughter. "So the picture goes before the cameras—if I still want the part?"

"You can't refuse it, Kay. I've just phoned your acceptance to the afternoon papers: it'll make the late editions."

"Eric, do you enjoy the role of *deus ex machina?*"

"As I've said, my part in this business has been anything but intelligent. I'm doing my best to make amends."

"Suppose I do say yes—will you promise me one thing?"

"Anything at all, darling. Even if it isn't in reason."

"Don't let me see Paul again until the trial's over. I've harmed him enough."

vii

Paul, pacing his room at the BOQ, looked up for the tenth time at the step in the hall. Some of his tension vanished when Hi Saunders came in briskly, an evening paper folded under his arm.

"Did you find her?"

"I got Lindman on the phone. Kay refuses to see you—or anyone." Hi slapped the newspaper face down on the table. "Don't look so blank, pal. What else did you expect?"

"She must have realized that I'd want to talk to her."

"With or without reporters?"

"Don't make jokes, Hi. I *had* to tell her—"

"What? That we're sorry Kay behaved like Kay on the witness stand? We both know she did her damnedest to clear you: it isn't her fault she failed. MacArdle just happens to be a smarter lawyer than I figured—and a good deal less of a gentleman."

"Did you expect her to perjure herself—like Hardin?"

"Not for a minute, and I still say we were smart to put her on." Hi turned the paper over so that Paul could see the headlines. "This front page bears me out. Never mind what cynics like Lindman are saying—"

Paul stared down at the fresh-faced likeness of Kay Storey that smiled up at him from the paper, in the glossy perfection of a USO release. "So she's making her picture, regardless."

"By public demand," said Hi. "Any good lawyer could have told Lindman that."

"Thank God we didn't spoil her career, Hi. She'll have that now—no matter what becomes of me."

"Don't let that headline throw you," said Hi. "It's true a few million readers think you're guilty. So will your judge, I'm afraid—if we can't rip Hardin open and show what makes him tick. Just the same, your girl stood up for you in court. Win or lose, you've a potential movie star on your side. It'll help when the chips are down."

"Isn't there some way I can see her?"

"You've nothing to say to each other now," said Hi. "Meanwhile, you take the stand tomorrow. The final witness in the case of Paul Scott versus American public opinion. Any notion of what you're going to say?"

"Must we go over *that* again?"

Hi glanced at his watch—and the night that had begun to invade the immaculate green parade outside. "It's the last toss of the dice, boy. This time we've got to roll a seven."

"We can't hit Hardin—and we can't change my story."

"Brood on it awhile: I'll come back after dinner for a real huddle. Maybe there's still a gimmick we can use."

"What if there isn't?"

"Face it, Paul. So far, Sellers and company assume we've been shadowboxing to cover you. If you repeat the same story on the stand, they'll think you're lying to save yourself. We need a new angle or we're sunk."

"Isn't the truth enough?"

"It isn't that simple, Paul. The law aims at certainty: it must test one witness against another. So far, in this case I've been a bricklayer without straw."

"Don't blame yourself, Hi. No one could have fought harder."

"I'm blaming no one," said Hi. "Not even the climate of suspicion we live in today. Don't start me on *that*, or I'll begin preaching a sermon—and I must let you collect your thoughts." He turned to the door and paused with one hand on the knob. "Have a tray sent up—and this time, try to rest afterward. I'll be back around nine for your final briefing."

When Hi had gone Paul saw that his first problem was to stay clear of the phone. Three times in the next quarter hour of pacing he yielded to its magnet and lifted the receiver to dial the Mark Hopkins. Each time he replaced the receiver at the first ring, knowing that only Lindman would answer. He could be thankful, in a way, that the Army had confined him to the Presidio. Otherwise he might have roamed Nob Hill until morning, hoping that he might catch a glimpse of Kay. . . .

Instead, he told himself, you must marshal your strength for the final duel with MacArdle; you must rehearse your story from beginning to end. You must keep to the truth —only the truth will make you free.

Where did his story really begin—and how (if he meant to save his good name) could he end it? *Keep to the truth, for the truth will make you free.* Had that ancient maxim outlived its usefulness? Had the Hardins of his century, riding down all men who opposed them, changed truth into falsehood, good into evil?

Thanks to MacArdle's smoke screen, he could not begin at the beginning. The truth about Hill 1049 would never emerge at this court-martial. Nor would the truth about the events at Sinmak—Hardin's insane assault in the cow shed, with intent to kill, the brutal refusal to share his transport on that hell-march to Pyongyang. Perhaps, if he insisted, the court would permit him to speak of the incredible hardships of that two-week trek. From the court's viewpoint it would seem only an exercise in self-pity.

Could he describe his first glimpse of the prison compound? Merely by closing his eyes he could bring back that thirty acres of sun-cracked earth again—the barricades at the gate (as real as the mouth of hell made visible), the tar-paper barracks, the walking cadavers that dwelt there. It was a picture he could never share—unless the listener had endured the same trial and learned to rise above it. . . .

The misery in which so much of the world dwelt today (he repeated the conviction with a sinking heart) was actual only to the dwellers. Here at home, sufferings in far places had been overdramatized in a hundred books, overpreached by a thousand do-gooders—until they had become a crashing bore. Once again he would only be accused of bidding for the court's pity.

Of course, he might use Pyongyang as a point of departure for his own achievement. He could tell how he had fought with Colonel Pak to obtain proper rations, heat for the shacks in their first winter, elementary relief from the filth and vermin that had claimed lives by the score. He could describe the horror of the meningitis epidemic that had killed Lieutenant Crosby, and the steps he had followed to conquer it. . . . But even here, he would only be laboring a point that MacArdle had conceded at the beginning—the fact that he was a dedicated doctor, willing to heal friend and foe alike.

What of Hardin—a sodden wreck when he had finally reached Pyongyang, a near-maniac trembling on the brink of delirium tremens, now that even the solace of *sake* was denied him? Would it help his chances if he told how he had pulled the colonel back from madness—or would he be accused once again of lying? Knowing that answer in advance, Paul let his mind slide over the long first year of his imprisonment, without a pause. After all, it was the *second* year that mattered, the time when the deep comradeship he had shared with his fellow inmates had changed to black hatred—the months of compromise for the sake of those he loved, of betrayal and forgiveness.

Forgiveness? He weighed the word and knew it was well chosen. He *could* forgive Hardin, now that he saw the man's pitiable weakness clearly. Still, he could not go down before Hardin's savage onslaught without a fight—however feeble the weapons he might summon in his defense.

Take it from there, he told his rebellious memory. Tell a straight story tomorrow. Make it sound real, no matter how incredible it seems in retrospect. . . . Probably they won't believe a word. Men who have lived on the earth's abundance have a way of closing their ears to harsh reality. . . . Yet you must tell the story of that second year at Pyongyang if only to convince yourself that you did right.

Once he had made that decision, he could feel his mind settle painlessly into the groove of memory. Kay, at least, had been rewarded for her unselfishness: no matter what the court's verdict, her career was safe. . . . As for Captain Paul Scott, he would face the future without fear. Father Tim had endorsed his conduct at the prison camp. He would endorse it tonight, were he still among the living.

Pyongyang

THE SNOW nightmare had come again, just before dawn. Now, sitting bolt upright on his pallet in Barracks Number Four, Paul blinked for a long and frightening moment before his eyes could focus clearly on the summer light outside the lattice. It was a comfort of sorts to note that the day promised to be fair and warm: for a time, at least, the horror of window-high drifts outside was only a visitation from the past.

He was glad that he had wakened ahead of the others. As doctor to the whole prison camp, he was entitled to leave the barracks when he wished. Since he had put down the meningitis epidemic, he had found it simpler to shun his fellow inmates whenever he could do so naturally. . . . He glanced at the boy who lay curled in slumber on the next pallet: a new prisoner, he thought dully, is a novelty here. Now that Colonel Pak had stepped up the food ration at his urging (enough, at any rate, to hold death by starvation to a minimum), there had been no vacancies for over a month.

The newcomer was an Air Force navigator, picked up from the wreck of an American bomber: his gray-green battle uniform was still spotless, a glaring contrast to the ragged sleepers beyond. It was significant, thought Paul, that the navigator should have taken the pallet next to his own—unaware that the others now slept apart from him, so far as these cramped quarters permitted.

Wondering what would be said when his back was

turned, Paul put the question aside. It was enough to know in his own heart that he had acted for the general good when he had treated guards and prisoners alike in that last-ditch fight to stop a deadly epidemic. He could hardly blame the camp for calling it his first long step down the road to collaboration. How could they think differently—when his hospital duties claimed him from dawn to dark? How could he convince them that his endless meetings with Colonel Pak were all that had ransomed many of them from the grave?

ii

In the doorway he returned the salute of the guard and paused to stare back at the fetid rookery he was quitting after a few hours of exhausted stupor.

The hundred-odd prisoners who shared Barracks Four were still deep in oblivion. In repose they seemed oddly defenseless and heartbreakingly young. True, there were exceptions—Dalton, the squadron leader who was rounding out his second year as a prisoner (and resembled a gnome from some nameless inferno), and Pierce, the grizzled sergeant who had been shot down in the same strike. Both of these men were moaning in their sleep as they continued to battle their own special demons: both would require forcible detention in the near future. . . . For the rest, he thought, there was still hope of salvage—if Pak kept his promise and held the rations to the minimum necessary to sustain life.

Since there were less than fifty pallets, the sleepers took turns on the bare floor: save for the inevitable rice bowls along one wall, there was no other furniture whatever. The garb of each prisoner was identical—OD blouses in various stages of ruin, and nankeen pantaloons thrust into laceless boondockers (a bootlace made an excellent garote if a man planned to strangle a guard or take his own life).

Thanks to the guards' habit of boarding up each window, the air above the pallets seemed almost too heavy to breathe. The only light fell in chinks through the lattice of the single doorway: it was easy to imagine phantoms from the past, stirring restlessly in this mongrel time between night and day. . . . Last winter (when the snow nightmare had been all too real) a dozen men had died of the numbing cold; three others had gone via the suicide route, before the guards had stripped them of their last means of self-destruction. Others had died—just as deliberately—in a crazy rush for the gateway after the third day without food, a punishment for some breach of discipline Paul had long since forgotten.

Their first year of prison, he reflected, had separated the weak from the strong. Today the survivors of Barracks Four were united in a common will to endure—and a common hatred for their captors that passed the bounds of reason. Naturally the fact that he served as prison doctor (and stood with a foot in both camps) had made him suspect. Even Furness and Jackson, who had once given him unquestioning loyalty, had begun to whisper with the others, to turn their backs when he risked a greeting in the compound. . . . He shook off the impasse with a sigh of pure frustration and stepped into the clean morning air.

Seen in the light of the September dawn, the camp was even more forlorn than usual. For a reason that Paul could not define, he had always found the huddle of tar-paper shacks more bearable in bad weather. Pressed down in the midst of a treeless plain, this huddle of roofs seemed more deserted than usual today, a ghost town forgotten in the glow of the flawless sunrise. For the hundredth time he thought how much his prison resembled the set for a third-rate Western, months after the last cowboy had moved on to another acting chore. . . . Only the ditch beyond the barbed wire and the floodlights on the four watchtowers brought the picture into focus. It would be real enough in the next half hour when the prisoners had turned out for morning roll call and the dismal routines of the day began.

The hospital stood on a low rise, between the commandant's quarters and the cabin that had been assigned to Colonel Jasper Hardin. Following the path to the dispensary, Paul forced his eyes to dwell for a moment on the colonel's billet and the plume of smoke that rose from its special cookshack. Master Sergeant Bates, busily dismembering a chicken on the chopping block outside, waved a greeting which Paul ignored: he had been long aware of Bates' campaign to discredit him in his barracks, and the man's hypocrisy today was more than he could endure.

As senior officer in the compound it was logical that Hardin should have separate quarters. By the same token he had the right to his own rations: no one knew what skulduggery Bates used to obtain such unheard-of items as fresh poultry. . . . At least Hardin had been deprived of his bottle for almost a year: Paul had seen to that, just as he had supervised the colonel's drying-out. Now that the C.O.'s abstinence was a *fait accompli,* his delirium tremens was only an ironic note in the hospital log.

Bates had been Paul's wholehearted ally in that drying-out: the little weasel was shrewd enough to see that Hardin must be deprived of alcohol during his imprisonment, or go screaming mad. . . . The shutters that still masked the cabin windows were a reminder of the measures they had taken to keep his condition under wraps. Later (after Hardin had ceased his doglike baying for *sake*) Bates had treated the episode as a figment of Paul's imagination. When the colonel was well enough to resume his daily musters, the sergeant major had simply donned his armor of insolence again.

Paul had expected no gratitude from Hardin himself: if anything, the C.O.'s hatred had been strengthened by the therapies which had saved him. More surprising (because of the Spartan regime of the camp and the food that Bates procured in such quantities), he seemed healthier than he had been in years—but this, too, was a fact for which Hardin assumed sole credit. The near-fatal thirst of yester-year, like the cowardice that had driven him from Hill 1049, had suffered the same blackout.

Putting the colonel and his psychosis firmly out of mind, Paul crossed the hospital porch and entered the sanctuary of his own domain. Part of the building had once been a Buddhist shrine, in the days before Marxism had invaded North Korea: the gilded statue of the god looked down at Paul from a lacquered niche. (Each morning he found solace in the inscrutable smile, pitiless though it seemed to Western eyes.) With the acceptance of the night charts from the Chinese orderly in the foyer, he began his day as camp surgeon.

Because of Paul's insistence on a better diet for the prisoners (even though that diet was at the rice-and-vege-table level, for the most part), the disease rate in the camp had dropped sharply during the spring. In the summer months fevers had once more plagued the inmates; after a recent reduction in the shipment of vitamins and other essential drugs the wards had begun to fill again. Today he needed a full two hours to make his rounds: faint though he was from hunger, he did not dare to pause, for fear he would be unable to continue. . . . Food that could keep an idle prisoner almost healthy was not sufficient for this exacting routine—yet he had consistently refused to sup-plement the barracks rations from the hospital larder. Even at the best, there was little enough to divide among those crowded beds.

He had long since learned that it was essential to check each case. Dr. Chang, the ex-intern who had been in charge here before his arrival, could follow direct instructions (though he was apt to fly into a hissing torrent of excuses if confronted with something really serious). The four male nurses who served the ward were competent enough in their sullen fashion—and Kay had been a tower of strength from the start. Paul still found it impossible to leave the hospital with a clear conscience until he had visited every bed and verified each notation on the charts.

When his morning inspection was behind him he managed to steal a few moments' rest in the doubtful privacy of the consulting room he had set up just off the surgery. There was a splinter of mirror on the wall: he glanced at his image before he settled in the single broken-back chair and closed his eyes. His face, like the body beneath the tattered uniform blouse, was skeleton-thin: the cords of his neck seemed taut as violin strings tuned beyond their pitch. Obviously, he told himself, you can't go on like this forever. . . .

Hardin had recommended him for this post because he had had no choice. Once Paul had proved his worth, the C.O. had been prudent enough to keep clear of all hospital matters—and contented himself with an occasional dressing down, for which Paul could have supplied the words in advance. Recently the colonel's attack had been mounted on another front—the whispering campaign that had begun to fasten the dread label of "progressive" on the camp doctor. So far, with the solid achievement of the hospital to sustain him, Paul had managed to endure the goading.

Resting his head on a desk top for a stolen nap, he remembered last night's emergency operation, the elevation of a skull fracture. He had managed it with Chang's inexpert help: Sergeant Furness had been the unwilling anesthetist, and Kay had served as instrument passer. The patient had been one of the guards, the wound an aftermath of a break from Barracks Two, which had resulted in the merciless machine-gunning of seven prisoners. He had performed the same operation often: the present case was a routine one. But this time it was an enemy's life he had salvaged: once the story had spread through the camp, the gulf that divided him from the others would be even wider than before.

At the moment, however, it was not his ostracism that bemused him. He was remembering an ominous incident while the operation was at its most ticklish stage. For a second of animal terror, he was positive that the lights above the table had dimmed to mere coals. His hand (fastened on the Hudson burr he had been using for his trephine) had trembled so violently he had needed all his will power to hold his ground. The attack had passed and he had finished the operation. But his emotional exhaustion had been complete when he groped his way into the consulting room.

Kay, following him at once, had knelt by his side and put her arms around him. It was one of the few moments of tenderness they had allowed themselves here.

"What happened, Paul? I was sure you'd faint at the table."

"I'm afraid it was night blindness."

"Doesn't that mean a lack of vitamin A?"

"That's the usual cause."

"We have some vitamins here. Why haven't you been taking them?"

"For the same reason I eat barracks food and sleep there with the others. Just because they're sure I have special privileges here, I feel I must refuse them."

"You've the right to a few tablets, darling."

"The supply is limited. We'll need all we have for our pellagra patients—and the beriberi cases."

"Paul, how can you call yourself a doctor—and be such a stubborn fool? Suppose *you* come down with pellagra—or have another blackout?"

He had yielded then and obediently swallowed several of the precious tablets, which Kay brought from the padlocked medicine chest. "Keep this our secret," he warned.

"Otherwise, they'll be calling me a progressive to my face."

"They won't dare. Not after you've saved them all, ten times over."

"All I've really done here is hold a few bodies and souls together."

"If you'd *explain* why you acted as you did in the epidemic—"

"They'll never forgive me for treating the guards, too. You see, Kay, hate's about the only luxury a prisoner of war can afford. They wanted to see a few Chinese die in agony—the way poor Crosby died."

"All right, darling. We'll admit that this existence brings out the worst in some of us. Father Tim knows you did right—and so do I. Is that a large enough jury for now?"

He took her in his arms then—and kissed her for the first time in months. Her lips were warm and alive as she clung to him fiercely. In her embrace, the wretched world about them had seemed to dissolve, to lose its meaning.

iii

Paul lifted his head from the desk and shook off his treacherous brooding. Reverie of this kind was a thing he could afford only in snatches; with a great effort he forced himself to return to the foyer and the makeshift admissions desk he had placed there. No new cases had been recorded in the daybook. He was almost sorry to find himself faced with an hour of idleness; at the moment he would have welcomed some task to blunt the sharp edge of his thoughts.

Kay would still be sleeping after last night's emergency duty. He decided to look in on Father Tim—who had recently (and much against his will) been admitted here as a patient. He needed such a pause to collect himself before he faced the compound again, swarming with life at

the moment, while a thousand prisoners shuffled through
the dusty routine of noonday exercise.

The chaplain's cot had been placed in a special cubicle,
apart from the crowded ward: Father Tim was deep in
slumber when Paul picked up his chart. Thirteen months
behind barbed wire had taken their toll of his vitality: on
his admission to the hospital he had been cadaverous rather
than merely thin, and the racking cough that had troubled
him on the march to Sinmak had returned, despite the fine
weather. Even more disturbed by the red stain in the
priest's cheeks, Paul had insisted on a week of bed rest.

Father Tim had been entered in the admission book with
a diagnosis of acute bronchitis and dysentery—a disease
that was all but universal in the compound. Later, Paul
had X-rayed his chest, using the inferior equipment at his
disposal, which did little more than distinguish the lungs
from the rib cage. There had been no evidence of the thing
he feared—a budding case of tuberculosis. In the past few
days Father Tim's rapid improvement had done much to
dissipate his fears.

Now, as he looked down at the slender figure in the cot,
Paul could not help reflecting that the priest's appearance
had become more saintlike with each passing day. The
prisoner's beard helped, of course (it was strange that it
should be so luxuriant a red). So did the faint nimbus of
sunlight that fell through a skylight overhead. Yet there
was something in the padre's appearance that brought its
own aura of peace, a strength that transcended the frail
body. Even in this short, wordless communion with the
sleeping man, Paul had discovered the refreshment he
sought. . . .

He found that he stood in need of refreshment when he
stepped out to the hospital porch and met Sergeant Luppino, one of the less offensive members of Hardin's
camarilla.

"C.O. wants you at headquarters pronto, Cap'n."

"We've nothing else but time here, Sergeant. Why must it always be pronto?"

"Search me, sir. Guess the old man figures it's important to keep up our morale."

"Apparently it suits you, Angelo," said Paul: he was already following Luppino's cocky progress through the compound. In a suit of freshly washed suntans, with his cap at a rakish angle, the sergeant might have stepped from a regimental PX: his boots shone like chestnuts, and even the cigarette between his lips was tailor-made. The stare he bestowed on the ragged hulks he shouldered from his path was the hallmark of Hardin's staff: Luppino (whom Paul remembered as a thoroughly decent noncom) had finally assumed the protective coloration of his group.

For all its ramshackle exterior, the C.O.'s quarters were comfortable enough—a fact that Hardin was careful to keep guarded. Colonel Pak had long since granted him virtual autonomy in his sphere, and Hardin had taken full advantage of that privilege. To say that the compound was run with all the efficiency of a marine boot camp (as Hardin boasted) was highly inaccurate—most of the prisoners were too feeble for that. Yet the C.O. was a stern moral policeman, insisting on daily formations, rigorous barrack policing, and more saluting than seemed humanly possible under such conditions.

From the start Hardin had exacted fines for the smallest lapse—and the noncoms were merciless in their enforcement. True, there was little to fine these days: the usual routine was to farm out offenders for road mending and the repair of bomb damage in Pyongyang. This strictly illegal labor was dispatched through Colonel Pak's office, and his guards herded the prisoners to and from their tasks. But Paul had long since guessed that Hardin was paid for their work—usually in food, soap, and other items beyond price here. It helped to explain the glow of health that

filled the cabin, as tangible as the odor of roasting chicken
that still hung in the shuttered air. . . .

Hardin, as was his invariable custom, kept the camp
doctor waiting a quarter hour before he strode in porten-
tously from the kitchen. He was wolfing the last of a drumstick and ignored his visitor completely while he settled at
his improvised desk. Glancing at this crude worktable,
Paul saw that the documents the C.O. was fingering were
copies of his own medical reports, run off on the mimeo-
graphing machine which Bates had recently procured in
Pyongyang. It was not the first time that Hardin had prepared his sermon beforehand, complete with notes.

"Why is this sick list padded, Scott?"

The question, spat out with the drumstick, stabbed at
Paul's mind with a familiar, dull pain. As always in
Hardin's presence, he had the sensation of a noose tighten-
ing, though the rope was still invisible.

"I'd call it only normal, sir—for a bad week." He had
long since abandoned hope of a *modus vivendi* with the
colonel. At Sinmak he had wrestled with the man when
Hardin was too drunk to stand, and knocked a potential
murder weapon from his fist; in this same room he had seen
him roll on the floor like a sick animal and beg for a drink
with tear-filled eyes. . . . The fact that he had pardoned
the C.O. for an attempt on his life (and rescued him from
the alcoholism that had nearly destroyed him) was something Hardin would never forget—or forgive.

"What d'you mean, a *bad* week? One's as bad as another
in this hogpen."

"We've managed to survive, sir—thanks to the deal I
made with Colonel Pak." Paul regretted the words instantly—knowing that Master Sergeant Bates was behind
the door with a notebook. "I promised to keep his guard
room well if he'd do as much for us."

"It isn't your province to make agreements here, Scott.
You take orders from me."

"Granted, sir. I was only trying to get what food and medication I could—for the whole camp."

"It seems your deal miscarried. Your ward is filled to the last bed."

"I've admitted only the worst cases of malnutrition and avitaminosis."

"Skip the medical jargon, man. Explain this deal with the commandant."

"The details are common knowledge, sir."

"So they are, Captain. And what I hear is hardly to your credit."

Paul stood his ground patiently. "Am I accused of collaboration, Colonel? If so, I'd like to face my accusers."

"No accusations have been made—so far. I'm still wondering why you spend so much time in Colonel Pak's office."

"I've reported those meetings, sir, as fast as they occurred. So far, they've been standard interrogations—"

"Until you made your deal?"

"It was the commandant's suggestion, not mine. He was impressed by the lives we saved during the meningitis epidemic."

"There were still twenty deaths, as I recall." Hardin glanced meaningly at a paper on the desk. "Four of them were barracks officers. The epidemic raged through the whole camp, but not a single guard was taken sick. How d'you explain that?"

"The disease began in Barracks Two, when Lieutenant Crosby died there. Others were infected before I was allowed to begin treatment with sulfadiazine. Naturally Colonel Pak insisted that his own personnel receive treatment first—"

"Excuses of that sort will get you nowhere, Scott."

"The facts will stand, sir, before any medical board: so will my agreement with Colonel Pak. I've promised to do my utmost to keep his guards in health. In return, he's granted a ration for each prisoner sufficient to sustain life. Vitamins to cover all normal breakdowns—" Paul could hear his voice trail off in the face of Hardin's apathetic stare: he had seen the colonel's eyes glaze over before, in these meaningless interviews.

"So *that's* your reason for filling your hospital with gold-brickers?"

"These men are badly ill, sir. Despite the improved diet, most of them were too weak to stand when I admitted them—"

"This is a prison camp, and I'm responsible for its discipline. I can't maintain morale if you turn your ward into a rest home."

For an instant only, as he faced that sneering, too-healthy stare, Paul let his resentment rip to the surface. It was sheer luxury to snatch the paper from Hardin's hand and circle a single item. "Speaking of rest homes, will you match the calorie count in your kitchen with my own figures for the barracks diet list?"

The shot rang a bell. For an instant Hardin's full-fleshed visage went white to the eyes. "Is that a threat, Scott?" he roared.

"I'm only reminding you that not a man on your staff has appeared on sick call since the epidemic. Your own health has been excellent since you recovered from your—battle fatigue." Paul stressed the word lightly, feeling an unholy joy as Hardin's eyes dropped. "As I say, I'd like to know your secret. Since you won't share it, I must keep down our disease rate as best as I can."

But Hardin had already recovered his aplomb. "You're here to answer questions, Captain, not to ask them. I won't remind you that rank has its privileges. Even you must realize that elementary fact—"

While Hardin launched into a long and rambling diatribe against what he termed the coddling of hospital patients, Paul listened without really hearing. Already he regretted his jab at the older man's pride. At the moment Hardin's number-one project was, obviously, the destruction of his battalion surgeon. He was shrewd enough to realize that Paul had saved the camp from wholesale decimation—and thus had a certain value. But this was only a temporary protection for the victim. When the war ended and the prison gates opened at last, Hardin would be sure to strike—and the blow would be a crippling one.

"These cases you call avitaminosis, Scott. I say these men are only in the hospital to get extra food, which means there'll be less for the others—"

"Believe me, sir, there was no other way to save them." Since the interview began, Paul had stood rigidly at attention: he could feel the ache of his resentment seep into his bones. *You* haven't missed night latrine because you were half blind and afraid of falling in the ditch, he added silently. You wouldn't know how it feels to rot with scurvy or wake up howling with the pain of beriberi. . . .

"I see you've got Chaplain O'Fallon on the sick list. Is *he* turning gold-brick too?"

"The chaplain is under observation for tuberculosis of the lungs."

"Have you made such a diagnosis?"

"Not definitely, so far. The X-ray was inconclusive."

"Then why keep him on bed rest?"

"He was badly run down, sir. No one in this camp has lived on less—or given more."

"That's a matter of opinion," Hardin snapped. "I want O'Fallon discharged the moment he's fit—along with the others you've been mollycoddling. There will be no special cases, Captain, and no favoritism. Is that clear?"

"Quite, sir."

"That will be all—except for this. In the past year, you've done an adequate job of organizing our sanitation. Because of it, you've been given a certain freedom. But no one is indispensable. Now that your work has been done, others

can carry on. Keep this in mind before you make your next
deal with Pak."

iv

Once he stood in the noon sunshine again, Paul felt his
head clear. As ordeals went, his collision with Hardin had
been standard brand. He could spell out his daily interview
with Colonel Pak just as accurately and he was overdue
for that appointment now. Squaring his shoulders (and
ignoring the scornful stares of the prisoners he encountered
en route), he forced himself to march briskly across the
compound of the high-stilted office that housed the prison
commandant.

Pak's quarters had been strategically placed, a wide-
windowed room that commanded a panorama of the entire
camp. Beside it, across a boarded passageway, was a
matching building that served the needs of the Security
Police. A boarded passageway between the two (known
among the barracks as "pneumonia alley") was also used
for interrogations. In the winter months prisoners were
stripped to the skin there and forced to stand at attention
by the hour, while questions were dinned into both ears
with the persistence of a trip hammer. . . . So far, for reasons he could not fathom, Paul had not been questioned
in either of these star chambers, save for an occasional short
workout: that task had been assumed by the commandant
himself.

Today, when the camp doctor paused in the doorway,
Colonel Pak was seated alone at his worktable, examining
what appeared to be a fragment of shell casing. His smile
could not have been friendlier had they been brother officers sharing the comforts of the same club.

"Sit down, Doctor. Tell me what you make of this
souvenir."

Save for a sibilant or two, the commandant's English was

perfect. Paul settled unwillingly in the comfortable visitor's chair. No one, he reflected, could look less the tyrant than Colonel Pak—or more the humorous philosopher. Even the colonel's appearance belied his calling: he was far taller than most members of his race and a good deal plumper. His full-lipped moonface would not have disgraced one of these United Nations posters that insist all men are brothers.

One needed a second, wiser look to realize that the man was neither as robust nor as relaxed as he seemed. The bottle of anti-acid pills on the table (which Paul had prescribed for a persistent stomach ailment) were proof enough that the Chinese suffered from a peptic ulcer. The febrile dart of his hands, as he continued to fondle the shell casing, was a further reminder that he had not been given this sensitive post by accident. Colonel Pak (and Paul had sensed it from their first encounter) was an efficient instrument of propaganda, eager for victims.

"Surely, Captain Scott, you recognize the unpleasant object in my hands?"

"I'm a doctor, Colonel, not an artilleryman."

"It was dropped on a suburb of Pyongyang," said Pak. "You might even have helped load it."

"Battalion surgeons in America do not load shells, Colonel. The armies of the United Nations are not that short-handed." Paul spoke the conventional rebuttal a little wearily. Knowing what was coming, he had made the counter as automatically as a chess player responding to an opening gambit.

"This weapon was not prepared by ordnance, Doctor. It contained a far deadlier charge—bacteria."

"It looks like an ordinary bomb to me."

"I wish I could agree. For sometime now, we've been trying to obtain one of your germ-warfare bombs intact. Fortunately we've been able to reconstruct the apparatus from fragments such as this." Pak put the shell casing aside and picked up a blueprint. "Here is a scale model which should convince you that our engineering experts are as alert as yours. As we understand it, the device is simple enough—a light bomb of the incendiary type, with just enough war head to fragment the casing and spray the contents widely."

Paul took the blueprint and studied it carefully. The drawing was flamboyant, with a flourish that bespoke the Oriental artist with more imagination than background. It was in two parts—the first showing the bomb in flight, the second after its impact. The winged menaces released by the explosion suggested the opening of a Pandora's box.

"Is the re-creation accurate, Dr. Scott?"

"In my country, Colonel," said Paul, "a high-school student could have made this drawing in an hour. You'll have to do better if you expect to convince anyone but your own people."

"We have already convinced them, Doctor—but not with this evidence alone. We have a number of statements from your fellow prisoners as to how the bombs are handled—"

"I know," Paul said grimly. "I've helped to doctor them after their interviews."

"Let us not confuse the issue with details: a confession obtained by any means is still valid, in our eyes. At present we need only a statement as to how the bomb is loaded, and with what bacteria, to make our proof complete."

"Are you suggesting I supply that misinformation?"

The commandant looked up sharply: it was evident that he had not expected this riposte. "Surely you can see the wisdom of doing so."

"We both know that this is an absurd fake. Can you ask me to perpetrate a lie?"

"Captain Scott. We have been at great pains to assemble this bomb; as you already know, I regard you as a man of intelligence. Surely you'd oblige me in this matter to save your own life."

"If I were concerned with my own welfare," said Paul wearily, "I'd have come to you long ago."

"I must say I expected that answer. Despite your intelligence, you are also a born romantic."

"Put that another way: I'll have myself to live with when I get out of here."

"If you get out, you mean."

"*Touché*, Colonel. The fact remains."

"Surely there must be a way to persuade you. Proof that you Americans originated germ warfare is vital to us. We will go to any lengths to obtain it."

"Including the abandonment of all principles of civilized warfare?"

"War has never been civilized. And you mustn't accuse me of lack of principles, Dr. Scott. I have extremely strong principles—though they happen to be the reverse of yours."

"I can believe that, Colonel."

"One of them is that the end always justifies the means. Perhaps we will not win a clear-cut decision on our present try in Korea. The thrust may be made elsewhere. Or we may choose the same battleground later, with a force that is really invincible. Meanwhile, we're determined to convince Asia that the United States is not the great white hope of mankind—"

"Aren't you having delusions of grandeur, Colonel?"

"By no means. Once we accomplish this end, we will have neutralized your influence on this continent. Make no mistake, it is in Asia—and in Africa—that we must prove our philosophy will rule the world."

"Even if you won such a victory—could you take pride in it?"

"Dr. Scott, let us not waste time on trifles. I intend to persuade you to sign a confession stating that you helped to load bacterial bombs. Since you are a medical officer, such a statement will carry great weight. It will also contribute to my pride in my own dialectic."

Paul drew a deep breath as the Chinese pushed the shell casing aside, opened a desk drawer, and tossed two typewritten sheets on the blotter. So the test has come at last, he thought. He forced himself to answer calmly.

"I'll never sign such a document, Colonel."

"Never is an ambitious word, and one that idealists use at their peril. It is my unpleasant duty to tell you that Major Sung of our Security Police is waiting now in the room across the way. I promised him that this confession would be signed on his next visit. You'll find him a far less gentle persuader than I."

The commandant touched a buzzer on his desk: two guards appeared instantly in the doorway. Paul was seized by the elbows and hustled from the office with no need of a formal command. Pneumonia alley, even in summer, had a special chill of its own. Before the guards could thrust him into the interrogation room beyond, he could feel goose flesh prick his skin and knew that his heart was pounding.

He had stood in the star chamber for routine inquiries, so he was prepared for the lights that glared down from the ceiling, the folding table and its facing stools that were the only furniture the windowless room boasted. The man seated at the table was a slender North Korean officer with the lidless stare of a dacoit thug. His uniform, with the green tabs of the Security Police at the shoulders, was faultlessly tailored. His cold glance bored into Paul before he spoke. The eyes were large and seemed unpigmented as the eyes of a fish.

"I am Major Sung," he said, in a voice that was so high as to seem almost feminine. "You will face me, please."

Paul glanced at the second stool: a prod from the guard's rifle brought him to attention. Apparently the purpose of that other seat would be explained later.

"Your name, rank, and serial number?"

"Paul R. Scott, Captain Medical Corps, United States Army Reserve; serial number 0-270106."

"Organization?"

"We are not required to give that information under the rules of warfare."

The security officer stared at him haughtily. Why did the man remind him of Hardin? Was it because each word he had spoken today seemed part of the same futile pattern?

"I have been warned that you might prove uncooperative, Doctor. It will be better if you cause no trouble for yourself."

So far, the probing had been standard. "The United Nations forces are instructed to give their name, rank, and serial number when captured," said Paul. "I am only obeying orders."

"I give orders here, Captain. What is your organization?"

"I am not at liberty to say."

The interrogator snapped an order to the guard, who gave Paul a backhanded slap that sent him sprawling. As he got to his feet (and braced for the next blow) Paul told himself that this was only the beginning.

"*Attention!*"

Once again Paul squared his aching shoulders, his torso rigid, his hands at his trouser seams. It was a perfect brace, and he took a certain perverse pride in it. Somehow it lessened the sting of the guard's blow, though his head ached from the impact.

"That is better, Doctor. For a medical officer, you are well trained. Now tell me what organization you served before your capture."

"I am not at liberty to say."

This time the guard used his fist to tumble Paul to the floor; since his body had been rigid, he could not roll with the punch. For an instant he lay there, too stunned to move: a second command brought both guards to his side.

He was kicked without mercy—just hard enough to drive
the breath from his body, without cracking the rib cage.

"Get up, Doctor. You may be seated."

He did not quite remember how he reached the stool,
though he feared it was on hands and knees. His pride returned, after a fashion, and he snapped again to attention
as he sat facing Major Sung, with only the field table between them.

The interrogator smiled affably: Paul had long since
noted the same change of front in Colonel Pak. Apparently
it was part of the oriental technique of questioning—a crude
assault to stir anger, then a sudden show of sympathy to
catch the prisoner off guard.

"You can see how useless it is to oppose us, Captain Scott.
Naturally I have your organization in my notes—the 141st
Battalion."

"Why ask me then?"

"To see for myself if you were as stubborn as your reputation. Tell me, where do you get the bacteria that your
airplanes drop on innocent North Korean civilians?"

"We dropped no bacteria."

"What about flies, mosquitoes, and the mites that cause
fever?"

"We dropped no insects. It would have been like carrying coals to Newcastle."

The major's smile vanished instantly, in favor of a sus-
picious frown. "What are coals to Newcastle?"

"With the flies and mosquitoes you now have, a few more
would make little difference."

"Then you admit your planes did drop them?"

"I admit nothing. The rules of war require me to give
you my name, rank, and serial number. You have that—so
you'll get nothing else from me."

"Have you observed our methods of torture, Doctor?"

"Only the end product, in my hospital."

"As a scientist, you will be interested in our techniques.

Permit me to offer an elementary demonstration. Will you give me your hand?"

The major took a small case from his pocket. Grasping Paul's wrist firmly, he opened the case and extracted a sliver of bamboo no larger than a toothpick. His free fingers had the tensile strength of steel as he anchored Paul's thumb to the desk and began to work the sliver through the nail bed, between it and the nail itself. The insertion was accomplished with great skill, as though Sung had performed the act many times before. A tongue of flame lanced at the nerves in Paul's forearm: he drew back instinctively, but his hand and wrist were solidly anchored.

"Are you beginning to see, Doctor, why it is simpler to confess your misdeeds and those of your comrades?"

The bamboo sliver was now deeply embedded: Paul felt the sweat pearl his forehead and wondered how long he could endure that lance of pain without screaming. Major Sung, he gathered, had barely started. He braced himself as the interrogator extracted a tiny mallet from the case and began to tap gently at the end of the bamboo, driving it still deeper.

Each tap was deliberate, as though Sung was husbanding the torture he could inflict. Meeting the man's unwinking stare, forcing himself to keep from flinching, Paul could feel his stomach knot under the agony. And yet, despite the pain, there was a strange comfort in the discovery that fear had left him. Now that the enemy's method was nakedly apparent, he could put his strength into a wordless defiance—and pray that that strength would endure.

"Of course this is just a sample, Doctor. Sometimes we set fire to the bamboo. You've no idea how long these slivers will continue to smolder before they burn out beneath your nail. I'm told the sensation is exquisite—"

Was he swooning at last, or had his brain moved into an area beyond pain? Paul's face was drenched with sweat, but there was no coolness there: rather, each rivulet felt

like a stream of fire upon his skin. Yet he knew that he
would not yield so long as he could keep that strange gulf
between mind and flesh. It was as though an unseen hand
had cut the current that pulsed normally from finger end
to skull—permitting him to watch his torturer from a distance.

"Why did you load bombs with bacteria, Doctor? Why
did your planes drop them."

"We dropped no germs—"

The interrogator plucked the bloody splinter from the
nail and ground it under his heel. Despite the strange
emancipation of his brain, Paul could feel his nerve ends
respond to that unexpected relief so violently that he just
escaped tumbling to the floor.

A double buffet from the guards' gun butts restored him
to the stool, and he understood why Sung had abandoned
the torment. This was a surgeon's hand—and as such it
could hardly be mutilated beyond repair. After all, those
fingers had saved a guard's life in the surgery last midnight.

"We have other tortures, Doctor. I will describe them for
you."

Paul listened with that same fixed smile as the major's
toneless voice recited the litany of man's barbarities to
man, a list of torments as old as the Neanderthals and as
new as a haunted tomorrow. He did not flinch when the
guards' fists belabored him, though he was now bruised
from head to toe. Nor did he cry out when he was restored
to the stool and Sung repeated the bamboo torture on the
opposite thumbnail.

By then he had lost track of time: when his tired body
slumped on the stool, a jab of the guards' rifles restored him
to a rigid attention, until the flesh of his legs and thighs
seemed inert as frozen jelly and just as helpless under the
next rain of blows. But he knew that his victory was certain, the sundering of mind and body complete. What was
better, he saw that Sung knew it too, and continued his

techniques more from desperation than any hope of success.

Twice in the next few hours he must have fainted briefly, for he felt the sting of water on his face as the guards worked to revive him. Finally, with no real sense of shock, he could feel himself lifted from the floor and realized that he was being carried into the commandant's office and placed on a cot. A rolled coat was thrust beneath his head and water was dashed into his face before the guards withdrew. Half blinded as he was by exhaustion, he could still glimpse Pak's silhouette, relaxed in a chair nearby.

"I warned you, Colonel—" It was an effort to speak, but he forced out the words. "You are wasting your time."

"So it seems, Dr. Scott." Pak poured a stiff shot of brandy and held it to the camp doctor's lips: the gesture seemed part of the cat-and-mouse battle from which he had just emerged. "Of course I suspected as much from the start— but Major Sung was most insistent. It is usually wise to let the Security Police have their way."

"Will you tell him his methods are useless?"

"At the moment that is impossible. Your interrogation has prostrated him: he will sleep until morning, at least."

Paul managed a glance at the wall clock. The torture had lasted a little over six hours. It had seemed far longer.

"Wouldn't it be simpler, Colonel, if you killed me out of hand?"

"Don't talk nonsense, Doctor. You're too valuable a man to lose."

"I'll die before I sign your confession."

"Don't say that, please. I have other means of persuading you."

"What are they?"

"Today, you gave us ample proof that you do not fear death—for yourself. But what if death should threaten those you love? The chaplain, say—or Miss Storey? Or both?"

v

Colonel Pak did not speak again, and Paul could find no answer in his whirling brain. When he dared to glance toward the chair that stood across the room, it was vacant. Perhaps he had dreamed the last words, he thought drowsily, from the black pit where he lay. Perhaps, if he closed his eyes again, the commandant's phantom would give him peace. . . .

When he wakened bright sunlight glowed at the wide office windows. He was still sprawled on the cot. A glance at his battered body told him that someone had dressed his wounded hands and poulticed the worst of his bruises. Dr. Chang, he thought sleepily: Pak would never admit Kay to his office. . . . The thought of Kay brought back the commandant's threat. He got shakily to his feet just as the door opened and Pak strolled in—debonair as ever in a fresh uniform. The commandant was polishing his glasses on a snow-white handkerchief: save for the military dress, he could have passed for a benign exchange professor, fresh from a summer-school forum and still relishing the meeting of minds.

"Where are they?"

The commandant shook off Paul's hands with his familiar, urbane smile: the gesture was almost gentle. "If you are referring to your friends, Dr. Scott—I sent them to solitary confinement yesterday."

So the threat had been real; the shock was no less intense as the man's words fell into the stillness. Paul sank into the nearest chair and groaned aloud. The pain of Major Sung's torture was as nothing when measured against this discovery.

"Somehow, Colonel," he said, "I didn't think you'd dare go that far."

The commandant's eyebrows lifted. *"Dare,* my dear

Captain, is a strong expression for a man in your present plight."

"This is a fight between you and me. The chaplain and Miss Storey have no part of it."

"If they can bring you to your senses they have a vital part."

Paul continued to rock his head between his hands: the full import of the news had penetrated slowly. "You put them in solitary *yesterday?*"

"Yes, Dr. Scott. While you were still defying the Security Police."

"Have I been dead to the world since then?"

"Major Sung put a severe strain on your constitution. I'm afraid he was carried away by his zeal. I had Dr. Chang give you an opiate by injection."

"What happens to my friends—if I won't play your game?"

"Nothing, really."

"*Nothing?*"

"They'll gradually be forgotten, Doctor. You've seen it happen to other prisoners."

Paul needed no blueprint to complete the enemy strategy. More than once he had been granted permission to enter the building that housed the solitary cells, to give the wretched inmates what aid he could. For the most part the cells were used to discipline recent arrivals at the camp, usually with the hope of extracting military information. The building itself was a converted storage barn on the edge of the compound. Most of it (as was usual in Korea) had been sunk below ground level. Here, with an ingenuity typical of his calling, the commandant had built a series of minuscule cells that were, in reality, no more than pens. Some of these individual jails were mere up-ended coffins, just large enough for a man to stand upright or crouch in twisted slumber. Others resembled Pullman berths cast in concrete. . . . The camp doctor had seen many prisoners enter that converted storage barn. A few had emerged in time, ready to babble the information Pak sought. Other more stubborn inmates had gone straight to the camp cemetery, with no detour to the hospital.

"Well, Captain Scott? Need I tell you more?"

He came back to the commandant's office, and Pak's ever-tranquil smile. A single blow of his fist would spoil that feline grin beyond repair: he resisted the impulse in time. "You've said quite enough, Colonel."

"At last we understand each other. I have played my trump card, Doctor. As you can see, it takes the trick."

"May I see my friends?"

"Of course—if you feel up to it. Believe me, I'm trying to be reasonable."

In the compound the prisoners were clustered thickly around the barracks. Paul caught the knowing glances of his own group and realized that they had drawn the worst conclusions from his long sojourn in the commandant's quarters. Reason told him to approach his former friends and exhibit his wounds. A perverse impulse made him thrust both hands into his pockets and continue in silence to the warehouse as though he were bound on a routine medical check.

As always, two guards stood at the doorway. The manner in which they saluted, before they stepped back to admit him, struck a jarring note: had he worn the enemy uniform, the two blue-quilted marionettes could not have seemed more deferential. Paul closed his ears to the hostile murmur in the compound and plunged down the stairway leading to the detention cells.

A turnkey with a bull's-eye lantern beside him had been dozing on a stool at the near end of the slimy corridor; he sprang instantly to his feet, another indication that Pak had already set the stage for his visit. Paul followed the man in silence as the bobbing lantern led the way through utter blackness; there was a low, constant moaning that was almost but not quite human, a stench that seemed older than the Stone Age. . . . Kay's cell was at the far end of the corridor, a box bare of furniture save for a little straw, lightless and without ventilation. There was a grating flush with the low ceiling.

The turnkey put the lantern into Paul's hand and drew back a deferential pace. A full half minute elapsed before he could force himself to lift the bull's-eye and peer inside.

It was hard to believe that the figure in dungarees, hunched between the stone walls like a broken jack-in-the-box, was Kay Storey. She did not lift her eyes at once, though the lantern was trained directly upon her bowed head. This in itself was chilling evidence that she had been under constant scrutiny since the steel door had clanged shut.

"It's Paul, Kay."

"*Paul?*"

He had spoken in a husky whisper, half afraid to disturb her numb repose when he had no solace to offer. Her reply was dreamlike, almost inaudible. The sudden, incredulous widening of her eyes when she lifted her head at last stabbed him to the heart.

"I thought you'd never come," she said quietly. It was a simple statement, with no hint of reproach.

"Pak only told me a moment ago—"

"What have I done, darling?"

"Nothing, Kay. Nothing at all—"

"Then why would he put me here? He knows I have no military information."

Paul glanced at the guard, who stood above him with folded arms and the familiar, unblinking stare that seemed an extension of his uniform. Uncertain of the man's English, he wondered if he could risk the truth. It was surely a needless cruelty to hold back the reason for Kay's confinement in this modern oubliette. Anything was better than the nameless terrors that surrounded her.

"Have you seen Father Tim?" he asked—if only to gain time.

"We were brought here together. Does *he* know why?"

"I haven't talked to him," Paul admitted. "I'm not even sure I can tell you—"

"Then it *is* something we've done?"

"No, darling. Pak is using you both—in a game he's playing with me." Once the basic fact was out, he found he could tell her everything, omitting only the worst details of his treatment in the hands of Major Sung.

Kay heard him out in silence—with only a gasp of pity at his mention of Sung. Watching her chin lift at the end, he saw that she had taken the news with far more courage than he had mustered. "Now that I'm here," she said slowly, "I wonder why he didn't think of it sooner."

"Strange as it sounds, Pak is something of a scholar. He believes the doctrine he preaches—and he takes pride in his skill as a debater. I think he hopes to win me over— even now."

"Are you sure they won't torture you again?"

"Reasonably. As a doctor, I'm too valuable to damage."

"Then don't worry a moment about *us*. Pak won't let us die. If he did, he'd lose the only weapon he has."

"Just because I've refused to give in so far, I can't let you and the padre suffer. I'm going back now—and tell Pak he's won."

"But you can't, darling. I won't let you."

He could not help smiling, despite the pity that twisted his heart. "How can you stop me?"

"You'll stop yourself, Paul—when you think it over. Pak hasn't won. He couldn't break you with torture. Why should we break, just because we're locked up underground?"

"It's worse than that. You've seen what a few weeks in these cells can do to a man."

"You mean the ones that gave in—and the punishment

cases? The Chinese didn't care if they lived or died. Father Tim and I are here for another reason. Pak's counting on you to give in right away. When he sees you won't he'll probably release us."

He hated to argue with her, to drive home the hopeless truth that Pak would stop at nothing. "You could be right," he said. "I doubt it."

"Talk to the padre. I'm sure he'll say the same."

He had known she would answer thus, from the moment he peered into the cell: he had come down the corridor determined to counter all her arguments, to insist on saving her. He had not expected that her own strength would weaken his decision.

"You'd endure this for my sake, Kay?"

"For all our sakes. Prison life hasn't been too hard on me, so far. I can thank you for that, Paul. I'll feel that I've paid you back if I can keep you from signing that confession. Besides, the armistice may come at any moment—"

"We've lived on that hope for a year."

"Let's live with it a bit longer. Promise you won't give in, darling?"

"I'll promise—for now."

He left her on that, with only a whispered endearment. The turnkey took the lantern and led the way down a second corridor to the chaplain's cell.

This detention pen, by way of contrast, was one of the horizontal type, a concrete shelf with bars down its length: there was just room enough for the occupant to turn from side to side. Father Tim lay there serenely with his hands crossed upon his breast. It was an attitude of repose suggesting (all too graphically) the effigy of a crusader on some medieval tomb. But the priest's smile of recognition was both warm and untroubled when Paul thrust an arm through the gratings and pressed the thin hand.

"It was good of you to come, Paul."

"I'd have come sooner—if they'd let me."

The chaplain nodded. "You needn't explain: I've learned a good deal of Chinese this past year. Apparently you made Major Sung lose face: the guards are betting he'll be transferred."

"I'm afraid my refusal to give in has helped nobody, Father. It's the reason you and Kay are here."

"I know that, Paul. And I know you won't change your mind."

"Frankly I came here to tell you I'd already changed it."

"Until you talked to Kay?"

Paul glanced sharply at the priest, but Father Tim's expression of serene acceptance was unchanged: it was not the first time he had anticipated a thought. "I'm not sure, Padre. Tell me what to do."

"Leave us."

"*Here?*"

"Don't deprive us of our little moment of resistance. We'll not yield to the godless the first time we're tested."

"Maybe that's what I'm afraid of. That you'll never ask for mercy until it's too late."

"Did you ask the commandant for mercy, Paul? Or Major Sung?"

"Pak has a dozen germ-warfare confessions. Can one more make that much difference?"

"It must, Paul. Remember, the best brains in Asia will ask for real evidence before they'll accept so monstrous a charge."

"Padre, the girl I love is being left to die in darkness. How can I condemn her to that?"

"The girl you love will be the first to cheer when you stand up to Pak." A spasm of coughing shook the priest's frail body, and he turned his head away. "You'd better go, Paul. Seeing us like this has only distressed you needlessly."

"How long will *you* last here—with that cough?"

The coughing had subsided and the chaplain could speak again. "I've given no thought to dying, Paul. And I have refused to let myself suffer. The mind can rise above most pain, if the heart has faith. It's a lesson you'll learn in time."

"Perhaps I'm learning it now," said Paul slowly. He was remembering the agony of the bamboo torture—and the strange release that had lifted him, however briefly, above the anguish of his body. It was only natural that the cough-racked figure before him should recall that experience and its aftermath. At this moment—when the priest seemed to totter on the edge of extinction and could still ignore the void—he felt the stirring of their greatest kinship.

"Go back to the compound," said Father Tim. "Take up your duties again as though nothing had happened. To-night, before you sleep, say a prayer—for all of us. You'll find the strength to go on tomorrow. I'd stake my life on that."

"You already have, Padre."

The priest smiled. "Only faith is eternal, Paul. And even that can get a bit tarnished if it isn't reaffirmed."

vi

A few moments later, when he knocked on Colonel Hardin's door, Paul knew it was the counsel of desperation that brought him there. He had spoken his last coherent word to Hardin months ago (so far as the colonel himself was concerned). The present visit was solely for the record.

To his surprise, the C.O. received him at once. His manner was nearly affable as he accepted Paul's stiff-armed salute and waved him to a chair.

"You may sit down, Captain Scott. I gather you're some-what done in."

"I'm afraid I am, Colonel," Paul said grimly. "Until an hour ago I was unable to walk."

"Did you spend the last day in Pak's office?"

"When I wasn't in the interrogation room. Dr. Chang gave me an injection of morphine after that was over." Hardin's apparent solicitude had already thrown Paul off balance. Knowing the C.O.'s power, he was positive that the man had reconstructed his acts to the last detail. Nevertheless, as a junior officer it was necessary that he make his report. He told his story from the beginning with no special pleading—including his visit to solitary.

"So you couldn't wait to see how the chaplain and Miss Storey had fared."

"I hope I did right, sir." Paul continued to watch Hardin warily—wondering when this teasing technique would end.

"Your courage does you credit," Hardin admitted. "So does your concern for your friends. Unfortunately your fellow prisoners won't understand too well."

"Nobody could believe I *enjoyed* a night in Pak's office?"

"I've heard a dozen accounts of that stay, Captain. The least damaging rumor states that you were drinking with the commandant and trying to curry favor by losing to him at chess."

"Do *you* think I'm a progressive, Colonel?"

"At the moment," said Hardin, "I'm not sure what to think. It might help if you'd explain the next deal you have in mind."

"Isn't the next move yours, sir? Obviously I've done all I can."

"So far—if your story is true—you've done nothing."

"Colonel, will you intercede?"

"As a protest for your treatment?"

"Never mind me. For the chaplain—and Miss Storey."

"How can I intercede in a matter outside my province?"

"You have influence with the commandant, sir: he's put

you in charge of all prisoners. With armistice talks pro-
ceeding, you can say he's committed a grave error—"

"How has he erred? By sending two prisoners to solitary,
as a disciplinary measure?"

"I've explained what's behind the move."

"Suppose your story is true, Scott—in every particular.
The threat is to you, not to the camp as a whole."

"Does that mean you'll do nothing?"

"I am responsible only for the administration of the
barracks. This is a propaganda matter instigated by the
Security Police. How can I interfere?"

"Surely you could go to Colonel Pak. As a matter of
common humanity—"

"Since when has a gook been human?"

Paul tried one more time, though he was all but choking
with rage and despair. "Chaplain O'Fallon and Miss Storey
are the two best-loved people in the compound. When the
news gets out that they're in solitary—"

"A few of the prisoners will be distressed, of course. But
at times like these the average soldier thinks only of himself. Things would be worse if I meddled. It could have
repercussions on *everyone's* welfare."

Paul bowed his head in silent admission of defeat: he
got up slowly, feeling the pain of last night's beatings run
down his legs in a rocket burst of nerves. "As you wish,
sir. If you'll excuse me—"

"A moment, Captain. You aren't dismissed."

"I'm sorry, sir. After last night—"

"Come to attention, dammit!"

Paul clenched his teeth and flung his body into the
straining brace the order demanded. It was sheer torment
to hold the pose: as a matter of pride he knew that he
would not budge until Hardin gave his dismissal—and that
his level eyes would force the other to turn aside.

"Yes, Colonel?"

"As I said, the next deal is yours, not mine. I'll wait for you to show your hand."

"Are you suggesting I sign that confession?"

"Far from it; in your place I'd know my duty to my country. However the whole camp is convinced you've some kind of understanding with the Chinese. Where there's smoke there must be fire."

"Will that be all, Colonel?"

"Go, by all means. I see you're about to commune with your conscience. Far be it from me to interfere."

"I'll ask one question first," said Paul. "Outside of your own group, just three people know the true story of Hill 1049—and are prepared to tell it after the armistice. Are you planning to destroy two of them here? And if you succeed, how will you dispose of me?"

Hardin's grin widened as he jerked a thumb toward the door. "Don't put ideas in my head, Scott. It could be dangerous."

Stumbling down the path to the hospital, Paul found it necessary to pause for a few long breaths before his sick frustration could spend itself. When he had assumed his daytime mask again he strode into the hospital without returning the curious glances that followed him.

Let them think the worst, he told himself, let them take Hardin's story as gospel. At least there would be work piled up in the wards. He would need the numbing pressure of that work to ease the battle he would now be fighting alone.

vii

In the weeks that followed, Paul could almost welcome a series of epidemics that raged through the barracks in defiance of all medical logic.

The first was a mysterious pyrexia that menaced prisoners and guards alike, which he finally diagnosed as acute hemorrhagic fever spread by mites. A thorough dusting with DDT powder stopped that menace before it could take a single life. Next came a bout with the scourge of all concentration camps—dysentery in its most virulent form. This time the ancient plague swept to the door of Hardin's own quarters, killing Sergeant Luppino and driving the C.O. into a state of complete isolation. Last and most vexing was a prolonged bout of virus hepatitis that he could only let burn itself out for lack of any specific treatment.

Weeks grew into months, another savage winter smote the camp—and Paul was, quite literally, too busy to think beyond the problems of the moment. Each night, as Father Tim had directed, he prayed for the chaplain and for Kay—and, by some alchemy he dared not explore, the prayer sustained him through the morrow. . . . Again and again, when he could spare a little time from his duties, he made desperate attempts to penetrate the catacombs of solitary, but on each occasion entry was barred.

Bribery of a guard whose ills Paul had treated produced bits of meager information. At least he could tell himself that Kay and the padre were alive and in reasonable health. Fighting a rear-guard action with his deepest instincts, insisting that he must find the strength to reject Pak's bargain, he made no attempt to seek another interview with the commandant. . . . He was hardly surprised when a message reached him one icy December evening, stating that Pak had just been admitted to the hospital and required his services immediately. The new patient's ulcer had kicked up before: Paul had always realized that someday more than anti-acid pills would be needed to control it.

When he entered the emergency room of the hospital he found Pak stretched on the couch, his face drawn with pain. Dr. Chang, in the act of releasing a syringe of morphine in the commandant's arm, drew back to allow an examination. Between them they had diagnosed the na-

ture of Pak's ailment long ago: both had agreed that the
appearance of real complications was only a matter of time.

A quick check of the patient's abdominal muscles (rigid
as boards and exquisitely tender to pressure), was all the
confirmation Paul needed. He had already sent for Sergeant Furness when Chang returned with the X-ray plate.
As they had expected, the film showed a bubble inside the
peritoneal cavity, beneath the diaphragm. It was proof
positive of an opening in the stomach or duodenum from
which air had escaped, along with the scalding acid contents of those organs.

The sergeant was in the operating room when Paul appeared there to check on the preparations Dr. Chang had
made. Sometime in the past month (time had a way of
blurring, these days) Corporal Jackson had left his hospital duties entirely and moved into Hardin's quarters after
a long and adroit wooing by Master Sergeant Bates. In the
interval the sergeant had developed into an adequate
anesthetist. Now, as the two men moved about their task
of readying the instruments, Paul could sense a reluctance
in Furness' movements—a slowdown that had grown familiar of late when they aided camp personnel.

"Aren't you well, Sergeant?"

"I'm fine, Doc."

Paul gave his anesthetist a covert glance. Over the past
week—as he was too well aware—Furness had been dropping into Hardin's cabin for an occasional meal: he could
guess that the sergeant had dined there tonight, if only
from the air of well-being that surrounded him.

"What's with Mr. Big, sir?"

"Mr. Big?"

"The gook in the consulting room."

"My diagnosis is perforated duodenal ulcer."

"You mean you're goin' to *operate?*"

"Of course."

"Cap'n, d'you mind if I bow out?"

"Of course I mind. Who else is competent to give the anesthetic?"

"What about Chang?"

"Dr. Chang will pass instruments. I'm afraid that's all he's good for."

"I'd still like to bow out, sir."

"You'll stay where you are, Sergeant. That's a direct order."

For an instant doctor and medic matched glares across the sterile gleam of the operating table. Watching Furness' eyes go blank with fury, Paul braced himself for the sergeant's departure: Hardin, he was sure, would sustain any act of insubordination. Then, with a profound sense of relief, he watched discipline reassert itself.

"Very good, sir."

"You can get ready, Sergeant. I'll have another look at the patient."

In the emergency room he found the commandant relaxed under the opiate and talking in whispers with the Chinese intern. There was no fear in Pak's eyes as he bent above the couch.

"Chang has prepared me for the worst, Dr. Scott," he said. "Am I about to die?"

"Not at all. An operation of this kind is simple if it's performed by a capable surgeon. I need hardly add that there is only one surgeon in this camp—myself."

Pak waved Dr. Chang from the room. "Is this by any chance an attempt to bargain?"

"Precisely. Your life—for two others."

"So the chaplain and Miss Storey have been on your mind of late. I was beginning to fear you had spurned my offer."

"I'm not interested in your offer. For once, Colonel, *I* hold the trump card. You are in no real danger at the moment, thanks to our prompt diagnosis. But you will probably die by morning if I don't correct your condition."

"Chang has explained that much, Dr. Scott. The question is—will you really refuse to operate, if I do not free Miss Storey and the chaplain?"

"You'd refuse in my place, wouldn't you?"

"I am not in your place, Captain Scott. And you are not Colonel Pak. If you were, life might be simpler for us both."

Paul did not speak for a long moment. The Chinese, of course, had put his finger on the single weakness in an otherwise perfect plan. "Are you sure you know me that well, Colonel?" he finally asked.

"Well enough, certainly, to put my life in your hands."

"You must realize there is a point beyond which you cannot push the strongest man."

Pak smiled cryptically, out of the relaxation of the morphia. "Eventually I'm sure that even you will reach that point," he said. "Tonight you are still an American surgeon and a Christian. As such, you can never bargain with lives."

Paul turned on his enemy with a curse on his lips—but the commandant had already drifted into limbo with the same relaxed smile. Shouting for Chang to prepare the patient, he went to his consulting room and buried his face in his hands: tonight, the tears that filled his eyelids rose from a well of pure despair. . . .

As he had expected, the operation was a textbook affair: there was no real element of danger, once he had subjected Sergeant Furness to a narrow-eyed check and assured himself that the anesthesia was flowing smoothly. Chang, as usual, was a bungler with the instruments—but the surgery was elementary, and Paul had long since learned to manage his own retractors. A suction pump cleared the area in short order, once the incision was established: the perforation was a classic one, in the duodenum, just beyond its juncture with the stomach wall.

The perforation—it was in the duodenum, and easily accessible—was no larger than a match head. Paul closed it with a catgut suture. Then, reaching for a tab of omentum (the fatty sheet that draped the abdominal organs like an apron), he secured a small patch of this tissue over the area for re-enforcement. When he had closed the incision he gave the patient an injection from the small store of penicillin that remained in the medicine chest and made his entry in the record. The job had been done in a trifle over twenty minutes. Par for the course, he thought grimly, and stood back to permit two male nurses to wheel out the patient.

Five minutes later, when he returned from the scrub room, he saw that Sergeant Furness had thrown his mask and gown on the floor and departed without a word of good night.

viii

Colonel Pak's convalescence was a prolonged one. Because of the severe winter weather (which twined icy fingers through the whole camp, including the jerry-built hospital), the patient was threatened for a time with pneumonia, and special drugs were flown from Mukden to assure his recovery. It was not until the first signs of spring were apparent beyond the barbed wire that the commandant was able to transfer to his regular quarters again and resume his work—after a fashion—from an easy chair.

Once his patient was off the critical list, Paul had held aloof, permitting Chang to handle the medications. Three days after Pak's departure from the hospital he received the expected summons to his office.

In a dressing gown and mandarin cap the Chinese looked oddly unmilitary—and resigned as a philosopher who has put most earthly lures behind him. The hands that rested on the arms of the chair trembled just a little, belying the man's air of repose; the eyes he fixed on the camp doctor had all their remembered fire.

"I've wanted to thank you for some time, Dr. Scott," he said in a tired voice. "You'll forgive me if my gratitude is expressed so tardily?"

"You've no reason for thanks, Colonel Pak. I did no more than my duty; as I told you, the operation was a simple one."

"Be that as it may, I feel a great obligation toward you. Will you accept living quarters here in the future?"

"My accommodations are adequate now."

"A pallet in a barracks where you've been ostracized for months?"

Paul shrugged. It was true that he had been shunned by the entire camp since the operation, but no one could change that. "You know I've just one thing to ask of you," he said. "Release the chaplain and Miss Storey."

"Sorry—my price for their release is unchanged." Pak turned the chair toward the desk and took two sheets of paper from a drawer. "Here is your confession, Captain—typed in duplicate. You need only sign both copies—and your friends will be under your care at once."

"You must realize they both advised me to resist you to the end."

The commandant's eyebrows lifted. "Captain Scott, the *end,* as you call it, may be nearer than you think."

Paul felt his heart constrict. From the start, he'd had reports from the guards assuring him that both captives were surviving their ordeal. Still, in the hell of that underground dungeon, death could strike quickly.

"Are you telling me they're dead, Colonel?"

Pak shook his head. "Not yet, Doctor. But I'm afraid that things went somewhat further than I intended, due to my own long illness." He held up a detaining hand as the camp doctor turned instinctively toward the door. "Patience—you may see them both in a moment. There is still time if you'll co-operate—"

"*What have you done to them?*"

"Not I, Captain Scott—solitary confinement. Dr. Chang tells me that Miss Storey is suffering again from a condition which you treated last year."

"Amebiasis?"

"That is the word. I understand that it can be dangerous unless treated properly."

"And Father O'Fallon?"

"He has a definite tuberculosis of the lungs, with small hemorrhages." The commandant was speaking calmly, in a dry-as-dust tone, as though he were disposing of a boring detail of camp routine. "I am surprised by your astonishment, Captain. You must have realized that their health would break in time, if not their spirits. After all, that was the reason I confined them."

Paul could not trust himself to speak again. While he fought for control he deliberately reviewed the illness for which he had treated Kay almost a year ago. The amebic infection had been mild then, but he could well imagine the ravages of a relapse that had gone unchecked. In Father Tim's case, he was not surprised. He had expected something like this for months—and the time spent on that damp stone shelf had merely hastened the crisis.

"Why did you wait so long to tell me?" It was an effort to force out the question, but his voice was steady now.

"My illness confused the timetable, Doctor. If you'll permit me, I'm prepared to atone for the lapse."

"How can you?"

"Would you care to examine the patients—here and now?"

"*Here?*"

The commandant tapped a bell on his desk. "I took the liberty of having them brought over. Time, as you will see, is now of the essence."

The outer door had already swung open to admit four litter-bearers and their dreadful burdens. Paul could not quite choke down the cry of revulsion that rose in his

throat at the first sight of Kay. Emaciated as she was, he
would hardly have known her had he discovered her in an
anonymous hospital bed. There was no recognition in the
fever-hot eyes that brushed him, then closed again in
sockets that were no more than skin-covered bone. Only
his medical training saved him from a complete breakdown as he knelt by the litter to examine her.

Desperate though her condition was, he saw at once that
she was not in the last extremity. The pulse, for all its
galloping rhythm, was still strong—and the skin (burning
and loose from the dehydration that was a symptom of her
illness) retained some of its former resilience. But Pak was
right: his timetable of destruction had gone awry. Had Kay
been left in solitary a few more days, it would have been
too late.

"I'll save you, darling. With God's help, I'll save you."
Paul had addressed the promise to no one in particular.
Certainly there was no way of reaching the wasted human
being on the litter; Kay had long since fallen into delirium
too deeply to react to speech.

"Don't sign the confession, Paul!"

The voice startled him, and he turned—with a guilty
flush—to Father Tim. At first glance Paul had the bizarre
certainty that time was a dream: the priest seemed exactly
as he remembered him from his visit to solitary. Even the
air of repose was identical—the hands crossed on the
breast, the prophet's beard like a flaming banner above
them. . . . Once again, the compulsion of his call saved
Paul from tumbling into madness. It took an effort to leave
Kay's side even for a moment, but he forced himself to
move to the second litter. The color burning in the padre's
cheeks was ominous confirmation of Chang's report; so was
the familiar cough that seized him when he tried to speak
again.

"Not another word, Father. You're in your doctor's
hands now."

"*Don't sign, Paul!*"

"I'm afraid I've no choice."

"*Don't yield to the godless!*" This time the effort proved too much, and the spasm of coughing seemed never-ending. The padre closed his eyes as he fought for breath: he made no further objection when Paul signaled to the bearers to lift the stretcher.

"Will you send them to the hospital, Colonel?"

"Of course, Doctor."

Paul did not meet the commandant's eyes as he snatched up the two sheets of paper that lay on the desk, and forced his mind to take in the neatly typed words:

> I, Captain Paul Scott, a medical officer
> in the United States Army, make this con-
> fession of my own free will and without
> torture . . .

There was more, but he did not read further before he slashed a signature across both copies, flung the sheets at Pak, and hurried out on the trail of the stretcher-bearers.

The Presidio

COLONEL SELLERS' gavel, breaking Paul's recital, seemed unusually loud in the quiet of the courtroom. Meeting the president's cold but impartial stare, Paul was grateful for the interruption. The wall clock announced that he had been only an hour on the stand—but he felt he had been talking forever.

"The court will question the witness, Mr. Saunders."

Watching Hi step back, Paul saw that his relief was shared. The defense lawyer had permitted his client to use his own words, with a minimum of direct questions: from Hi's viewpoint the intervention of the court might be a hopeful sign. . . . One of the most ominous aspects of Paul's testimony had been the aloofness of both bench and prosecution. Throughout, MacArdle had doodled on a scratch-pad without a single objection. Sellers' own withdrawal had seemed just as definite.

"You say that Miss Storey's recovery was a *miracle*, Captain?"

"There's no other word to describe it."

"What of your own skills as a doctor? Weren't they of help too?"

"I'd reached the limit of my skill. And she was still sinking."

It was true enough, Paul thought—with a familiar ache at the memory. Even after the chloroquine phosphate and the plasma units had done their work, the fever had continued to rage in Kay's blood stream. Indeed (as is so often the case with a patient whose condition is desperately poor), the treatment itself had seemed to cause an actual flare-up of the infection. For two long days he had done his poor best to save her. During that time he had stayed at her bedside, holding her in his arms when she cried out in her delirium—hoping, at least, that she would realize he was there while the flame of her life force wavered.

"When the crisis came," he said, "I could do nothing else but pray."

It had happened as simply as that, and as incredibly. Since it was so incredible, how could he make Sellers accept it?

After two days of alternate chills and fever Kay's body had seemed frail as a feather, the lips and ear lobes blue from deadly oxygen lack. It was then that the prayer had come unbidden to his lips. The words had poured out in a torrent—not for himself, this time, not for any desire of his own, but for this woman he loved so greatly. . . . When had the voice answered him, assuring him that his terrors were groundless? When had he found his own strength again, in the knowledge that Kay would live?

"On the dawn of the third day," he said, "her fever broke. After that I was sure of her recovery. But it wasn't *my* doing."

The president of the court continued to stare down from the dais. "You may resume examination, Mr. Saunders," he said at last. The small shrug that accompanied the words was more emphatic than any formal dismissal.

Paul closed his eyes as Hi took up his questioning: he could feel his voice droop with defeat as he made the first mechanical response. Miracles, it seemed, are not the stuff on which court-martials are won: he was positive that his whole story had fallen on deaf ears.

Nonetheless he forced himself to tell that story to the end. His hopeless struggle to save Father Tim. Kay's long but steady convalescence. His insistence that she leave with Colonel Hardin's group when the armistice was a reality. . . . Finally he told of the padre's need of his presence, the fact that he had informed Hardin that he must remain, his belief that Hardin would take the truth to Panmunjom. He spoke briefly of Father Tim's death, of his own repatriation, and of the salvo of flash bulbs that had greeted him when he crossed the truce line.

Waiting for MacArdle to assemble his notes, he was glad that he had done no more than mention Father Tim's last hours on earth. Like Kay's return from death, that was sacred ground. Why, when the court had refused to accept a miracle, would they believe the priest could die with a smile on his lips and his faith unshaken?

The soul of Father Timothy O'Fallon (Paul told himself solemnly) had been at peace when he wrote the last entry in his confession book. His mind (divorced from the ills of the flesh) had remained sunny to the end. But he could never put that resignation into words. It was enough to know that Father Tim had absolved him of all guilt when he closed his eyes. Whatever the verdict of this court, he would treasure that absolution always.

ii

Major James MacArdle approached the stand with his notes neatly folded, his expression almost benign. "Captain Scott, you are aware that you're under oath?"

"I am."

The prosecutor launched his attack on Paul's testimony with quiet good humor; by his very underplaying, he suggested that he was performing an elementary task, with all the dispatch at his command. He covered Paul's defiance of Hardin at Sinmak, his appointment as medical officer at the prison camp, his operation on Colonel Pak. The duplicate of the confession was brought to the box and offered to the witness.

"Do you acknowledge that this is your signature, Captain?"

"I do."

"You persist in the statement that you signed this document to save Miss Storey and Chaplain O'Fallon?"

"That was my only reason."

"You did not sign to obtain favors for yourself? Or to help the cause of Communism?"

"I signed to preserve two lives."

"Aren't you ascribing a great deal to yourself, Captain? First, you assert that you saved the whole prison camp in a meningitis epidemic. Next, you magnanimously save the life of the prison commandant. Now you tell me that you saved the lives of Miss Storey and Chaplain O'Fallon."

"Not Chaplain O'Fallon. In my own opinion I was the cause of his death."

"Then you're not infallible after all, Captain?"

"I have never claimed to be. Chaplain O'Fallon died because I originally withheld my signature—after months of pressure."

"You still maintain, in the face of Colonel Hardin's statements, that you signed only to save two people from death?"

"I do."

"Let us move up to the time of repatriation, Captain. You have heard Colonel Hardin say that he knew nothing of the chaplain's alleged hemorrhage. Do you still assert that such a thing did happen?"

"It happened as I have described it."

"Isn't it true that both you and the chaplain preferred to remain with the Communists?"

MacArdle's expression of patient industry remained unchanged when the court had sustained Hi's instant objection. "Captain, you have testified that you notified both the prison commandant and Colonel Hardin of your intention to remain."

"I did so notify them both."

"You didn't, by any chance, invent this story to protect yourself—*after* you decided to renounce Communism?"

"The facts are as I have stated."

The prosecutor tossed up his hands. "Since you persist in evading the truth, there is little point in my detaining you. No further questions at this time."

Hi Saunders came forward to re-examine. "Captain, I wish to establish one point with the court. When you decided to remain with the chaplain did you know of any authority that justified your action?"

"Yes—Article Fourteen of Title Three in the provisions of the Geneva Convention."

MacArdle sat up in his chair for the first time that day: Paul noted the hard worry wrinkle that had suddenly defaced his forehead. At the defense table Hi had already opened the book that lay there.

"I will read Article Fourteen into the record: *It shall be lawful for belligerents reciprocally to authorize, by means of private arrangements, the retention in the camp of physicians and attendants to care for prisoners of their own country.* The defense contends that Captain Scott, through his notifications—to both the prison commandant and to Colonel Hardin, his own commanding officer—has completely fulfilled this provision. Therefore the defense moves at this time that, as to Specifications Three and Four of Charge One, a finding of not guilty be entered on the grounds that they have not been proven."

The courtroom stirred before the president's gavel fell. "You may state your reasons for this motion, Mr. Saunders."

"First, on the matter of Specification Three. It alleges that Captain Scott signed a confession for the purpose of obtaining preferential treatment. Testimony has shown that the defendant branded the so-called confession as a lie at the time of signing, and that the signing itself was a formality, performed to save lives. Specification Four alleges that Captain Scott refused repatriation for personal reasons. He has just testified that he remained at Pyongyang to care for another prisoner of war, who was too ill to travel, and such conduct is justified by the Geneva Convention."

MacArdle was on his feet. "This is a preposterous request," he said—he was really shouting now, his pose of tolerance forgotten. "No such thing has been proved. Colonel Hardin's testimony is in direct contradiction to that of Captain Scott's."

"The court is aware of that fact, Major MacArdle," said the president drily. "Mr. Saunders, is it your intention to imply that Colonel Hardin's testimony regarding these specifications of Charge One constitutes perjury?"

"The defense so contends," said Hi. "Were it not for the court's ruling—which prohibits testimony on events occurring before the capture of Hill 1049—the reason for this perjury could be shown clearly."

"This is a grave charge, Mr. Saunders."

"So are the charges against the accused, sir."

"Do you wish to re-examine the witness further?"

"Not at this time."

"You may step down, Captain Scott. The court will withdraw to consider defense counsel's motion."

Paul resumed his seat at the defendant's table. "What are we shooting for, Hi?"

"The moon. It seemed worth the try."

"Will they sustain your motion?"

"It's our final test. Your case will stand or fall, depending on whether they believe you or Hardin. I'm trying to dramatize that issue—simply by reminding Sellers that the colonel has a reason for lying. One we haven't been permitted to reveal."

"Will it register?"

"Perhaps not. It's a stab in the dark—but it's now or never.

At least the motion's on the record. I'm positive it will help in the Court of Military Appeals."

"Is that our next port of call?"

"Let's face it, Paul. I rocked Hardin with a few punches, but he made a fine showing in his league. Whether they'll admit it or not, the court's prejudiced in his favor." Hi glanced up sharply as a door opened and the spectators got to their feet. "Here comes your answer—I'm afraid it isn't favorable."

Watching Colonel Sellers take his chair, Paul knew that his lawyer was right. The man's whole face, from the flaring nostrils to the black-browed stare, breathed doom.

"The court has deliberated upon the last motion of defense counsel," he intoned—and his voice was an oddly gentle contrast to his manner. "The motion is denied."

Hi spoke in the barest of whispers. "There goes our ball game, pal."

"All of it?"

"I'll try for an extra inning."

Sellers was frowning at the colloquy. "Does defense counsel have additional witnesses?"

"Not at this time, sir. May I request an adjournment until tomorrow?"

"Approved—subject to objection by any member of the court. May we expect closing arguments at that time, gentlemen?"

"The prosecution has already rested," said MacArdle smugly. "It considers a closing argument superfluous."

"The defense will state its intention in the morning, sir." Hi had begun to strap his brief case with the words. "Chin up, boy," he said in a taut whisper to Paul. "We mustn't look like dead pigeons—even if we are."

At the Mark Hopkins Kay crossed the parlor of her suite and switched off Larry Kirk's television broadcast.

Once again the famous commentator had prejudged Paul with all the techniques in his arsenal—dismissing today's testimony as so much moonshine and calling the defense counsel's request for an adjournment a last desperate fumble for time. . . . All the long day while she watched the telecast of the trial itself, Kay had been dreading this improvised verdict. Now that it had been spoken, she was drained of all feeling.

Eric Lindman, sprawled in picturesque repose on the divan, rose from a brown study of his own to mix two highballs. She managed to contain her resentment until he handed her a glass.

"Did you ever hear anything more unfair?"

"You won't believe this," said Eric. "But Larry was doing his best to be objective."

"By judging Paul ahead of the court?"

"Forty million vidiots expect it, darling. So, I daresay, does his sponsor. Remember, as Kirk goes so goes the nation."

"I still insist that Kirk should be drawn and quartered."

"Try to get out of yourself for a moment," said Eric. "Judge this case on the testimony, as Larry is forced to do. Would *you* believe that any mere mortal could be as selfless as Scott? Or that Hardin wasn't acting for the good of the Army when he made his report? Or that it wasn't a heaping dose of chloroquine phosphate that snatched you back from death, instead of the hand of God?"

"If you were Paul, would you have testified differently?"

"Naturally. For one thing I'd have found some way to peel off Hardin's hide and nail it to the barn door for the world to see."

"Hi Saunders tried that. The court refused to play."

"We'll do it better in the script, darling. You can be sure of that."

Despite her aching brain, Kay found that she could laugh at Eric after all: it was quite like the wonder boy to complain because reality was not always so neatly packaged as his own make-believe. She was still laughing (and there was a note of hysteria in her mirth) when the hall buzzer sounded. She opened the door cautiously—though she knew that Paul could not leave the Presidio. It was not the man she loved, but the note that was handed her was inscribed by his hand.

Eric, at ease again on the divan, watched her narrowly while she read it through.

"What does he say?"

"Who told you it was from *him?*"

"Your face, Kay."

"He's positive they'll convict him tomorrow. He—wants me to go back to Hollywood, and forget him."

"His advice is excellent. Are you going to follow it?"

"I've decided to make one picture for you," she said. "Maybe more. Enough to finance an appeal—and maybe a free clinic that was one of our dreams in Pyongyang."

"You can't build clinics at Leavenworth."

"Maybe he won't go to Leavenworth. In any case I'm meeting him outside the courtroom tomorrow."

"Don't put *that* in writing."

"I already have," she said defiantly. "He has my letter now. It must have crossed his."

Eric stared down at his drink for a moment of unaccustomed silence. "We do *lots* better in the script," he said.

"Perhaps you should mail a copy to Colonel Sellers," said Kay bitterly. "It might change his verdict."

"This is no time for irony, darling. Think hard: isn't there a witness *somewhere* who can expose Hardin? Who can tell the truth and not make it sound like special pleading?"

"You should know better than to ask."

"We find a witness in the script," said Eric. "On the last day of the trial. Are you positive that Father Tim died in Korea?"

"Paul read the burial service at his grave. Will you stop talking like a fool?"

"It's different in the script," said Eric patiently. "In the last sequence you get amnesia—a damned bad case. You aren't yourself again for *weeks*—"

"It was amebiasis—and it's far worse than amnesia."

"Don't interrupt, darling. In the script, you only *hear* that your witness is dead. Then he walks into court and saves the day—"

Kay found that she was staring at the wonder boy with wide, round eyes, as a great rocket burst of inspiration exploded in her brain. For the moment she stood motionless at the hearth, oblivious of the highball that had just slipped from her hand and shattered there.

"Eric—d'you realize what you just said?"

"Of course. Pictures are better than life. That's why we'll always have an audience."

"You'll have an audience for this one, all right. *And* a witness."

"For *The Girl Next Door?*"

"No, you fool! For Paul's court-martial."

"Are you out of your mind?"

"I almost was. Thanks to you, I've recovered my sanity. To say nothing of my memory."

"You'd better lie down awhile, Kay. Offhand, you look as though you'd just seen a ghost."

"Maybe I have, Eric."

"What's his name?"

"Will you stop asking silly questions and phone Hi Saunders?"

Paul, entering the courtroom the next morning between
two MPs, was mildly startled by the projector and portable
screen that stood before the bench—and the thick air of
mystery that pressed down on the defense table. Hi, scribbling in his usual ambush of lawbooks, gave him no more
than an owlish nod of greeting.

"Aren't there enough gadgets in this chamber now?"

"Easy does it," said Hi. "Sit down quietly. Try to look
omniscient. Can't you see that projector is worrying Mac-
Ardle?"

"It's worrying me too. What's up?"

"When I took this case, Paul, you gave me carte blanche.
Remember?"

"All too well."

"This morning I'm taking a real flyer. If I explained it
in advance, you'd only make trouble. *Now* you're just a
captive audience. I'm asking you to keep a straight face
today—and, above all, not to intervene."

When the court took its places it was obvious that Colonel Sellers resented the new equipment in his courtroom.
For a moment he seemed about to bark a query as he
wrestled with a mass of papers on his desk. The question,
when it finally emerged, was mild enough: it seemed to
take in both lawyers at once.

"Word has just reached me that a new witness is to be
called," he said. "Will someone enlighten me?"

"Prosecution has no new witnesses, sir," said MacArdle
promptly.

"Defense has one, sir," said Hi, without glancing up from
his scribbling. "Two, if need be. They are waiting now."

"No other witnesses for the defense are listed on the
charge sheet," said MacArdle. The worry wrinkle was
etched deep in his forehead.

"If the court please," said Hi, "the fact that this witness

could give evidence of vital importance to Captain Scott became known only a few hours ago. There was no time to send a formal notification."

"Defense has every right to introduce new evidence as it develops," said Sellers. "Have your man sworn, Mr. Saunders."

"The sergeant at arms will call His Excellency, Archbishop Steifel," said Hi.

A buzz of interest ran through the court when the prelate marched in behind the sergeant at arms. The Roman Catholic Archbishop of San Francisco was a man of commanding presence: the shoulders in the long-skirted clerical coat were massive as a fullback's. The head, for all its close-cropped white hair, seemed oddly youthful; only the eyes, as they swept the crowded room, betrayed the man's calling. It was a glance of almost evangelical fervor, a look that seemed to understand every ill of the world and to pardon most of them in advance.

Watching the archbishop take the stand—and the oath— Paul could see that he had won his audience even before he revealed the purpose of his visit. It was only when the prelate settled in the witness chair and arranged the folds of his coat that Paul noticed the book he was carrying. Even at a distance, it seemed familiar.

Hi moved quietly to the witness box. "Your Excellency, will you show the court the book you are holding and identify it?"

The archbishop lifted the book for all the room to see. "I am holding the diary—called by him a confession book —of Chaplain Timothy O'Fallon, now deceased."

Paul drew in his breath—an audible sigh of understanding that was almost a gasp. MacArdle, he observed, had also pounced on Hi's intent: he bounced to his feet in a fury—and his objection was almost a bellow. Sellers' own voice, louder than it had been during the whole trial, brought order to the court.

"If you'll try to be coherent, Major MacArdle?"

"The prosecution objects—in the strongest terms—to this last-minute showmanship by the defense."

Hi cut in swiftly. "Is trial counsel accusing an archbishop of the Roman Catholic Church of participating in a hoax while under oath?"

MacArdle was in control now. "By no means. But I am demanding an explanation."

"Archbishop Steifel is about to explain in his own words—"

The president leaned down from the bench as MacArdle settled in his place again. "The court will question the witness. Your Excellency, you have called this volume a confession book. If you are using that expression in its commonly accepted meaning, how can you divulge its contents?"

The prelate, who had already opened the diary on one knee, looked straight into Sellers' eyes: when he spoke his voice had the resonance of a man accustomed to addressing a multitude. "I, too, was troubled by that question," he said. "However, when Mr. Saunders requested it, I read through the book again last night. Father O'Fallon was a very devout man. At times, I'm afraid, he was too conscious of his unworthiness. Large portions of this book are indeed a confession—which he made while on duty in the front lines. He chose this method of unburdening his sins, as he called them. I was thus his ultimate confessor."

"Surely this is no concern of the court."

"Nothing would induce me to make those particular pages public, sir. I have told Mr. Saunders that I would read only the portions which concern day-to-day occurrences—while Father O'Fallon was a prisoner of war in Korea."

"How did you obtain this diary, Your Excellency?"

"It was handed to me a few weeks ago by Miss Katherine Storey. She told me that it had been given to her by Captain Scott—who took it from Father O'Fallon's hands at his sickbed. The exchange occurred when Miss Storey left the prison camp for her repatriation."

MacArdle spoke without rising from his seat: his voice, though it was irascible as ever, had somehow lost its cutting edge. "How can the court be sure this diary is genuine?"

"The book has been in Archbishop Steifel's possession since it was brought to San Francisco," said Hi. "Captain Scott and Miss Storey will testify as to its transmittal."

"It may still be a forgery."

Hi addressed the court. "Defense has anticipated this objection. May I call my second witness?"

"You may, Mr. Saunders."

"The sergeant at arms will call Mr. Gregory Fontana."

The rising murmur among the spectators told Paul that the compact man in the rumpled seersucker who hurried to the stand was well known. He understood why when Mr. Fontana was sworn and identified himself as a handwriting specialist employed by the San Francisco police. When MacArdle had grudgingly accepted his qualifications, Hi introduced a letter in evidence—a report addressed by Father Tim to the bishop, shortly after the former's induction. While this missive was being labeled, two court attendants adjusted projector and screen. The shades were drawn, and a sample page of the diary was flashed on the screen, side-by-side with the letter. Fontana called them identical after a careful study. So did every pair of eyes in the courtroom.

"Archbishop Steifel has selected certain passages of this diary, upon which he will testify," said Hi. "If the court wishes, each page can be projected upon the screen to prove the authenticity of separate entries. Or, if the court prefers, Mr. Fontana is ready to examine each page and give us his opinion as to whether they were written by Father O'Fallon."

"The court sees no necessity for so exhaustive a procedure," said Sellers, with a testy glance at MacArdle. "Does trial counsel desire an exception?"

The prosecutor spoke through taut lips. "No exception, sir."

The handwriting expert was excused and Archbishop Steifel resumed the stand. Once again Paul found the massive, black-clad figure a magnet from which he could not withdraw his eyes: the man's manner, like his physical bulk, was a living monument of integrity.

"Your Excellency," said Hi, "can you recall just when this diary came into your possession?"

"It was given to me in my study by Miss Storey. The moment she arrived in San Francisco she telephoned me and insisted on putting it into my hands. I noted the date in my own diary: it was October tenth last."

"Did Miss Storey request that notation?"

"She did not."

"Did she ask for a receipt?"

"No, Mr. Saunders. Her only concern was that I receive the diary in good condition—since that was Chaplain O'Fallon's dying wish."

"Your Excellency, in your opinion, did Father O'Fallon have more than one reason for sending you his confession book?"

"I did not think so at the time. As I said, he was a very devout man."

"Did you read the confession book at once?"

The prelate smiled faintly. "I had many other matters on my mind this October. I'm afraid I put the book aside with only a cursory look—promising myself, of course, that I'd return to it later."

"When did you give it a rereading?"

"Last midnight, Mr. Saunders. At your special request."

Hi let his eyes go to the courtroom and the TV cameras. "Your Excellency, did you uncover another reason last midnight?"

"A compelling reason."

"Will you explain to the court, in your own words?"

v

The prelate's hesitation, though prolonged, was entirely natural. When he spoke, it was with honest diffidence. Here (and the listeners felt it) was no posturing witness, counting six beats to a well-rehearsed cue. This was a man of God, choosing his first words with care.

"I think I should begin with Father O'Fallon's last entry," he said. "It is dated August 3, 1953. May I read direct from the confession book?"

"Of course, Your Excellency." It was Colonel Sellers, ruling from the bench. The fact that he had ignored both lawyers in that pronouncement was evidence enough that the witness had his audience in hand.

When he began reading the archbishop's voice was soft, almost diffident. And yet, once he had caught the rhythm of the words, Paul found himself listening as avidly as any spectator.

> "*I am going to die* [Father O'Fallon wrote].
> *There is no doubt in my mind. The last hemorrhage
> was by far the worst. The transfusion that Paul gave
> me last week has spared me for a while. But the
> next hemorrhage will mean the end. It will find me
> quite resigned.*
>
> "*This is the day of Kay Storey's repatriation.
> Since she herself is still very ill, Paul feels that we
> should not meet to say good-by—but he will put this
> book in her hands when I have made the final entry.
> Somehow, it must find its way to Archbishop Johann
> Steifel in San Francisco, a man who has been both
> my friend and confessor from seminary years.*
>
> "*Paul has insisted on staying here with me—so
> the others will go south to the exchange point with-*

> *out him. He knows that I could never survive the*
> *journey—and assures me that Colonel Hardin will*
> *tell the American authorities just why we must re-*
> *main. But I am still afraid for Paul, since Colonel*
> *Hardin hates him so bitterly. Once he has crossed*
> *the truce line, I feel sure that he will do his best to*
> *injure Paul.*
>
> *"If wrong is done to Paul because of his devo-*
> *tion to me, I pray that my archbishop—or whoever*
> *receives this confession book—will use it to right that*
> *wrong."*

The prelate looked up from the diary. For an instant his
eyes rested on MacArdle. "This entry alone," he said,
"would justify reading relevant passages from Father
O'Fallon's diary in open court. Shall I continue, Mr. Saunders?"

"I'll add one footnote," said Hi. "Only so much of this
confession book will be read as is sufficient to satisfy the
court concerning Captain Scott's actions—which are the
subject of the charges. I am well aware that he does not
wish to compromise those who have testified against him."

The president spoke curtly, with his eyes on the church-
man. "Your forbearance is a matter of record, Mr. Saunders.
You may proceed with your witness."

"I will ask Archbishop Steifel to read the entries describing the rescue of the chaplain from solitary confinement."

The archbishop was already leafing through the diary,
working backward from his first reading. "There is a lapse
of several weeks at that point," he said. "Father O'Fallon,
I gather, was too weak to write for a long time after his
release.

> *"It is like heaven to lie in a hospital bed again.*
> *"I have yet to see Kay. Paul tells me that she*
> *was far closer to death than I, though she is out of*

*danger now. He feels that it was God who saved
her life: I have told him that it was the same Power,
working through his hands and skill. Each day I
thank the Almighty for the dedication and devo-
tion of Paul Scott. Without it, the whole compound
would have long since succumbed.*

*"Corporal Harold Jackson visited me today. He
brought with him a copy of the 'confession' which
Paul signed in order to secure my release and Kay's.
The corporal was on our side before he defected to
Colonel Hardin's group. I did my utmost to explain
Paul's true reason for signing but I'm afraid my
words fell on barren ground.*

*"It is sweet to live. I reproach myself for the joy
I take from breathing clean air again, from resting in
a bed. In my heart I know that Paul should have
left both Kay and myself to our fate; instead, he has
placed himself in the power of two evil geniuses—
the prison commandant and Colonel Hardin. I have
tried to forgive Hardin—but after what has happened I can see that he and Pak are but two faces
to the same coin.*

*"Neither Kay nor I could have lasted much
longer in that dungeon. Dr. Chang showed me the
latest X-ray of my lungs and chest: even to the layman's eye, the inroads of tuberculosis are all too
clear. Paul assures me that a technique known as
pneumothorax will close the cavity—but this time
my wisdom goes deeper than my doctor's. I feel sure
that I am not long for this world: I can only hope
that I will be spared to testify in Paul's behalf when
the time of reckoning comes.*

*"Each day I pray that God will soften Colonel
Hardin's core of hate (it is a hate that takes in all
the world, but Paul is the chief target). Yet he seems
beyond my prayers. He and those who share his
cabin have lived well from the start, when men*

were starving in the barracks, yet he did nothing to
better conditions until Paul came.

"When Kay and I were put in solitary he made
no move to intervene, though Paul begged him to
do so. I cannot escape the conviction that he wanted
us to die there, so that his revenge on Paul could be
complete."

The archbishop turned several pages rapidly—as though
he was reminding himself, just in time, that he had read
beyond a danger point. "Here is another entry that seems
pertinent," he said. "It was made shortly after the one I
just read: it refers to matters that had already occurred. I
ask the court to remember that Chaplain O'Fallon was
desperately ill—and made some of these notations after the
event.

"I have only just learned that Sergeant Furness,
like Corporal Jackson, went over to the enemy long
ago. If I write enemy when I should say Hardin I
can only ask the indulgence of my confessor.

"With both his medics gone, Paul is now with-
out expert help in the hospital. Dr. Chang tells me
that Paul pulled Kay through her almost fatal illness
singlehanded. Now, it seems, he is undertaking a
similar task with me, despite the pressure of his
other duties. I cannot find the courage to tell him
that it will be fruitless.

"I tell myself that Furness and Jackson are not
to blame for their desertion. It is hard to go on
starving when it is possible to eat well in Colonel
Hardin's cabin. But the bitter fact remains: out of
those who were captured in the aid station on Hill
1049, only Paul, Kay, and I remain united. Who
else will dare to tell what really happened there?"

Again the archbishop turned several pages of the confession book before he addressed the court. "Mindful of Mr. Saunders' warning," he said, "I am reading as little as possible. What's done is done—tragedies of yesterday cannot be mended by unearthing the details. But I know that Father O'Fallon would have wanted that one fact brought out."

"There is another point that needs clarifying," said Hi. "At your natural insistence, Your Excellency, I have not seen the padre's confession book myself. Is there any reference to the operation performed on Colonel Pak?"

"I am coming to that entry now," said the prelate. "It was obviously made some weeks after the operation occurred.

> *"Paul has been savagely criticized throughout the camp for saving the commandant's life on the operating table. I have spoken to many of the prisoners on this matter when they came to the hospital to visit me. Not one of them so far can rightly argue that Paul could have acted differently.*
>
> *"Here, once again, is the age-old dilemma of man's inhumanity to man—and, by contrast, the example of the healer who remained steadfast to the precept which Christ has expressed so beautifully in the fable of the Good Samaritan. By his action, Paul Scott reaffirmed a credo that cannot be stated too often, if our faith is to endure.*
>
> *"No man has the right to let another man die when it is in his power to save him—even if the dying man is an enemy. Had Paul followed another course, he would have placed himself on a level with the Communists. No true Christian will ever fight evil with evil."*

The archbishop glanced at Hi, then turned to the bench. "With the court's permission," he said, "I will read just one more entry. I think it will complete the story that Father O'Fallon desired to tell the world."

"Does it concern events prior to the chaplain's capture?"
asked Hi. "The court has forbidden testimony on all that
happened before."

"No, Mr. Saunders. There is a great deal in this confession book concerning prior events—and much of it seems
pertinent. However, since it is the court's wish, these pages
will remain unread. The incident described here occurred
while Captain Scott and his party were en route to Pyongyang as prisoners of war."

> "*Today I arrived at our destination, the prison
> compound near Pyongyang. I made this journey by
> truck, with Colonel Hardin and his group—other-
> wise I could not have come this far alive. This has
> been my first chance to write in almost two days.*
>
> "*Again and again my mind returns to the farm-
> yard at Sinmak where the truck stopped to collect
> prisoners. This is where Lieutenant Crosby gave up
> his place that I might ride. There was ample space
> for us all—but Colonel Hardin refused to merge
> Paul's group with his own. Had not Crosby dropped
> off at the last moment, he would have denied me a
> place as well.*
>
> "*Everyone knew that Hardin was drunk on
> sake, the night before we left Sinmak. But only a
> few of us knew of the attempt made on Paul's life
> that night.*"

Archbishop Steifel paused deliberately in his reading
and let his eyes rove to the bench, as though asking for a
possible objection. When none came he turned even more
deliberately to the prosecutor's table, where MacArdle sat,
his face inert as his own death mask. Then he turned toward Paul: it was a compassionate glance that conveyed a
special message. Like the silence in the courtroom, it told
the accused that truth, at long last, was in the open.

"*The attempt was made while we slept in a cow shed that was part of the farmyard.*

"*Paul himself did not see the intruder's face: it was pitch dark inside the shed, and they struggled but briefly before he took to his heels, via the hay chute. But three facts must be set down here. Fact one: when I wakened that same night, I saw Colonel Hardin's face clearly, peering through the hay chute from ground level. Fact two: Lieutenant Crosby informed me the next morning that he, too, had wakened in the night and found the colonel's place was vacant. Fact three: in the morning Paul and I discovered the intruder's weapon on the floor of the barn. It was the broken neck of a sake bottle.*

"*It is hard to tell one's self that a man would wish to destroy another at such a time—especially when they were both fellow-prisoners. But the facts are damning. I can read but one answer from them: Colonel Hardin, in one of the drunken rages that possessed him so often, did try to stab Paul as he slept.*

"*Here at Pyongyang the prison camp to which we are assigned is a fearful place. Each day men starve and die in the barracks, and the disease rate is appalling. Paul would have known how to cope with such conditions had he been allowed to ride with us in the truck.*

"*I reproach myself for the weakness which forced me to accept a place in the truck instead of marching with the others. Not that it would have remedied matters. Hardin would never have permitted Paul to ride.*

"*Tonight I have said a prayer for Paul and Kay —and for the others who stayed on Hill 1049 to be captured and are now following the long, cruel road to Pyongyang. May they all reach this compound in safety. It is the only hope for our survival.*"

Archbishop Steifel closed the confession book quietly,

but the sound seemed to echo from the walls of the courtroom. Once again he glanced at Hi.

"I feel that I have read enough," he said. "More than
enough, perhaps. Do you wish to question me further, Mr.
Saunders?"

"No, Your Excellency. The defense rests—and will forgo
a closing argument."

The president leaned down from the bench. "Does trial
counsel wish to question the witness?"

MacArdle rose at last, and seemed about to approach the
witness box. Then, steadying himself with one hand on the
table, he settled in his chair again.

"Trial counsel has no questions, sir."

"You may step down, Your Excellency. Thank you for
your testimony."

The prelate rose. "I pray God that the verdict of this
court will be a just and merciful one," he said. "I am sure
Father O'Fallon would want only that."

"You may be assured it will be."

The exchange came to Paul from a vast distance: the
tears that brimmed his eyelids kept him from seeing the
archbishop's exit clearly. Somewhere in a misty void he
heard a sound of cheering—and realized that the spectators
were applauding the witness as he left the room. He could
guess the court's verdict when he saw that Colonel Sellers
had made no move to check the demonstration.

On a pier in San Pedro, Father O'Fallon had snatched
him back from doom, as surely as though his hand had
closed upon his arm. Today that same gentle hand had
reached beyond the grave to repeat the service.

vi

Thirty minutes later the court had acquitted him of all
charges—but the sense of remoteness persisted.

He was aware of a babble of voices—and realized that

the reporters had descended upon him en masse. He endured their questions patiently, just as he submitted to the glare of the flash bulbs. He knew that his hand was shaken a dozen times, that Hi Saunders' fist was pummeling his ribs in a victory jubilation that seemed never-ending. . . . One voice stood out in the melee. The questioner, he saw, was Larry Kirk.

"What about Hardin? Are you bringing charges against him?"

"There'll be no charges. I'm not his judge—a higher authority will see to that."

His mind dwelt briefly on Hardin while the MPs hustled him through the crowd. What he had said to Kirk was true enough: Jasper Hardin must stand at the judgment seat eventually, and the accounting would be awesome. For the present, he could hide behind the front that had always insulated him from his fellows: there would be no persecution from his peers. But after today Hardin would never be entrusted with another command: as earthly punishments go, this one seemed appropriate.

"Well, boy?" said Hi. "Was Kay inspired when she sent for the archbishop?"

So it was Kay who had remembered the confession book in the eleventh hour. . . . Opening his eyes wide for the first time, Paul found that he was standing in the fresh air, on a side porch of the courthouse that was blessedly free of both reporters and cameras. His hair and tie, he noted absently, were both askew after the mauling inside. As he put his uniform in order, he could feel his heart swell, a burst of thanksgiving that threatened the buttons of his tunic.

"Where is she, Hi?"

"The parking lot," said the lawyer. "Maroon convertible, lane A. The end of the line."

The end of one line—but the beginning of another.